THE GIRL WHO SAVED

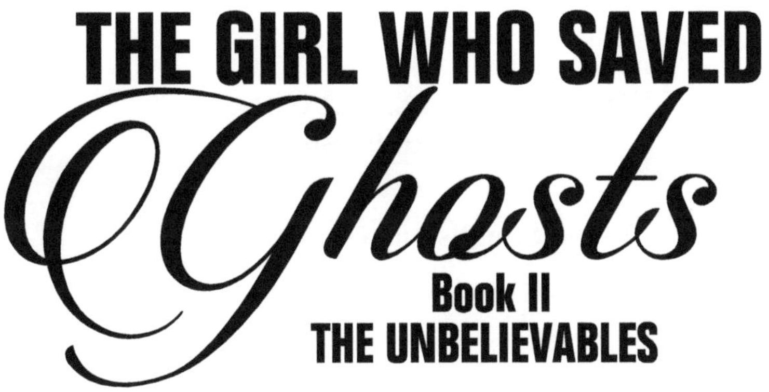

THE GIRL WHO SAVED *Ghosts*

Book II
THE UNBELIEVABLES

K.C. TANSLEY

BECKETT PUBLISHING GROUP, LLC

The Girl Who Saved Ghosts
The Unbelievables Book 2

Beckett Publishing Group, LLC

www.beckettpublishinggroupllc.com

Copyright © 2017 K.C. Tansley and Anthony Dvarskas

Written by K.C. Tansley

Created by Anthony Dvarskas and K.C. Tansley

Edited by Jessica Jernigan

Cover Art by Creative Paramita

Internal Design by Nick DeSimone

Author Photograph by Brett D. Helgren

ISBN Paperback: 978-1-943024-04-9

ISBN Ebook: 978-1-943024-05-6

To Mom,
for always being there to share every crazy
and beautiful moment of this life.

Chapter 1

"I can't help you now," I said to the ghost beside my desk. I tucked my blond hair behind my ear and pushed my tortoiseshell glasses higher on my nose.

He remained there in his high-waisted, dark gray suit and fedora hat. Definitely circa the 1920s. He folded his arms and leaned against my desk, the picture of patience. "I can wait."

I looked out the window in front of me. On the sidewalk below, parents helped my classmates lug their belongings into the dorm. Today was the start of my senior year at McTernan Academy. And a return to normal.

But this was the third ghost to visit my dorm for his reckoning, that one final piece of business they had to complete before they could move on.

Not believing in ghosts had kept them away for years until this summer, when I was forced to confront some incredible unbelievables—ghosts, spells, curses, and time travel. I couldn't pretend to not believe anymore, so, since then, ghosts kept appearing and asking for my help. I wanted to help them. I truly did.

But it was exhausting. Every time a ghost appeared, it stole energy from the living. And I was always the nearest living person. I scarfed down junk food and sugary snacks to keep my energy up. It wasn't enough. At seventeen, I had regressed to daily naps.

I'd spent most of August trying to get ahead of their reckonings before the school year started. I really thought it was possible. For a while, it even distracted me from my own issues; but senior year was starting, and the

1

ghosts were becoming a serious problem.

I took a bite of my Twix and tried to reason with the ghost. "Someone might see you in my dorm. Can you all form a line and meet me in the park on Saturdays?" I could devote my Saturdays to the ghosts, just not my every day.

He glanced back over his shoulder and smiled like he saw something I didn't. "We've been in line for years."

A dull pounding started in the base of my skull. "I can't keep up this pace." My voice thinned the way a plastic bag does when you put too much in it.

His smile flickered. "But we need your help."

"And there's no one else?" I wasn't the only person who saw ghosts. There were other believers out there. Some of them were my friends.

"No one quite like you."

Sometimes I really wished I were mediocre. Being special meant that the ghosts were going to take over my life again. I couldn't let that happen. Luckily, ghosts from his era were polite. He'd introduced himself when he arrived and that gave me the power to send him away. "Gilbert Wells, go away."

He frowned and faded into a shimmer of dust that disappeared into a shadow.

It was the best I could do.

I got up and a wave of dizziness made me stumble. I needed to rest for a bit. I sat on my bright blue comforter, laid my head on my pillow, and was asleep in seconds.

I woke up two hours later. The sun cut through the windows, warming my feet. The clock on my nightstand read 2:30 p.m.

I pressed my back against the headboard and picked up the photo on my nightstand. My best friend Morgan and I had taken it at the end of junior year. She did her sassy sideways pose where she put her hand on her hip and jutted out her butt. Her black hair hung down to her waist. I'd tilted my head and looked to the side like something interesting had caught my attention. Morgan had taught me that move when I complained about looking bad in pictures.

I wanted to go back and be the girl in that photo again. The girl I was before this summer when Seth, Morgan, Evan, and I had set off to research a century-old wedding-night murder at Castle Creighton. We were supposed to create theories about what had happened to the bride and groom based on research and evidence. Instead, Evan and I time-traveled through a mirror to 1886, possessed the bodies of our ancestors, and lived out the days leading up to the murder.

Yeah, wrap your head around that one. I dare you.

I tightened my grip on the picture as the realization came over me: There was no going back to who I had been. As much as I had dreamed of school being normal, it wasn't going to happen. The ghosts had followed me here. I put the photo back on the nightstand and played with the star sapphire ring on my finger. I could use it to summon the ghost back. And I would. Eventually.

All I had to do was twist the ring and concentrate on what I wanted. The ring would usually make it happen, but there could be serious consequences, so I only used it when I absolutely needed it.

The ring was a powerful Langley family heirloom. My ancestor, Toria Langley, had worn the same ring because, well, she came from a long line of priestesses who tapped into its power. Like them, I had magic in my blood and I was meant to wield the ring. The revelation had flipped my world upside-down, and it still hadn't righted itself.

Toria's ghost wouldn't teach me more about how to use the ring because the unbelievables lurk within shadows and could eavesdrop on everything that I did here. She didn't want any of our enemies to know what I knew. It made it easier for them to attack me.

Why hadn't I known any of this family lore until this summer? Because my father abandoned me when I was a baby. My dad's side of the family, the Langleys, had never been a part of my life. Neither my head nor my heart could make sense of it.

My chest tightened like my lungs were shrinking away from my thoughts. My father had sent me this ring. He knew I was the Langley heir, making it both my responsibility and my destiny to protect the Radcliffes from the unbelievables.

My father had let me wander blind into my destiny. It had almost cost me my life. I still didn't understand how he could do that to me—his own daughter. Thinking of him was a wildfire of emotion burning in my direction. Inevitably, it would devour me.

All of August, I had longed for answers. I'd even tried to summon my Langley relatives with the ring, but I couldn't. And I didn't know why. The Langleys and my father remained big, fat question marks in my existence.

I grabbed my phone off the desk, settled back on my bed, and called Evan in London. I'd done that a lot while he visited with his parents. He answered on the third ring.

"What's going on?" His British accent was like an ocean wave lapping at my ankles—cool, soothing, and supportive.

"I feel like I'm stuck." I sighed. "Toria says Dumbarton is protected by ancestral magic that keeps it safe from unwanted unbelievables. That's where I have to train. But the Langleys aren't bringing me to Dumbarton. So I'm stuck. It's ridiculous." A geyser of frustration welled up in my voice.

"I'll be back in a few days. We'll go see Professor Astor. If he can't help find the Langleys, then we'll go out to Castle Creighton and demand answers from Joshua." The certainty in Evan's voice washed over me.

I'd trusted him with my life this summer and he'd never let me down. Not once. "What if we still can't find them?"

"We keep looking. You're not in this alone."

"Evan…" The rest of my sentence caught in my throat. *Thank you* felt inadequate, but it was all I had. "Thanks."

"Always." He lowered his voice. "Any sign of Pastor Fitzgerald?"

"No." I shuddered. When we'd broken the Radcliffe curse, we'd angered Pastor Fitzgerald's ghost. He merged with the shadows and became something unknown. Toria couldn't find out anything with her ghost connections. There was no trace of him, and that scared me. He had held onto his hatred for centuries. It was only a matter of time before he came after all of us for destroying his revenge.

"Morgan and Joshua are okay?"

"So far." But there was one person who we hadn't heard from: Evan's best friend and Pastor Fitzgerald's descendant, Seth. "Any word from Seth?"

"No."

He'd left Castle Creighton and went to Argentina to visit his mom's parents. Since then, no calls, no emails. Nothing.

"Don't say he just needs time, Kat."

"Maybe he's having trouble dealing with what his ancestors did." I was descended from the Langleys, and Evan was from the Kingsleys. Both families were devoted to protecting the Radcliffes. Seth's ancestors had set out to destroy them. "His family was the bad guys."

"But what they did isn't on him. Seth helped break the curse."

"Maybe that's part of the problem. Not only did he have to face what his ancestors did, but he also betrayed them to help Joshua."

"Are you making excuses for Seth?" Evan's tone veered toward incredulous.

"I'm trying to explain why he's MIA."

"How could he walk away from us? We bled into a bowl together. We called on our ancestors together to break that blasted curse." His anger was an avalanche cascading over me.

"You aren't mad at him. You're worried about him." His silence only made me push onward. "It's Seth. Chances are he's doing something decadent and dangerous to forget about this summer. I bet you Seth comes back with the best tan. And a story involving a snake, a gorgeous woman, and a yacht."

"I hope you're right, Kat."

I hoped so, too.

Twenty minutes later, the door to my dorm room flew open and banged against the wall. Morgan stood there, about to lose her grip on everything in her arms. Her long black hair was trapped against her body by two lamps, a crystal vase, and a makeup mirror. A duffle bag wrapped around her back and a carry-on bag hung from her arm. Somehow, she'd managed to loop her suitcase handle over her arm and drag it along with her.

"A little help, Kitty Kat." She sounded breathless and bordering on annoyed.

I leapt off my bed, grabbed the lamps and mirror, and put them on her bed. As soon as her arms were free, she hugged me. Her freesia scent wrapped around me. I closed my eyes for a second. Morgan was back. Now, senior year could begin.

When she let me go, I looked at the lamps lying on her bed. "Did you bring this stuff all the way from Connecticut on the train?"

She threw her head back and laughed. "Nope. On my way here, Tiffany and Scarlett were fighting over their room décor. Scarlett thrust the lamps into my arms. Then Tiffany handed me Scarlett's vase. So Scarlett grabbed Tiffany's mirror and gave it to me."

"And you're keeping it all?"

"I never say no to expensive freebies. I love when those two get in a fight. Rich girls giving away each other's stuff. Everyone wins." Her turquoise eyes danced with mischief. She breezed by me and put the lamps on our desks. "Perfect for studying."

The mirror ended up in our bathroom and the vase went into the small bookcase near her desk. She gave a quick nod like that was settled and turned to her suitcase.

I sat on my bed, watching her unpack. "How are things with Adam?" When I'd left them in Wright, they were so into each other.

Her hair fell over her face. "He might come visit Columbus Day." There was something in her voice—a hint of hesitation.

It made me ask, "Everything okay there?"

She focused all her attention on lining up her shoes in her closet. "I don't know. We're so young…"

I leaned over my footboard. "What happened?"

"Joshua's paying for college. I can go to Georgetown, UCLA, or NYU. I thought I'd be at UCONN. That was all we could afford, but now I can go anywhere."

"The perk of being a long lost relative of the Radcliffes." Morgan was descended from the secret love child of Toria Langley and Sebastian Radcliffe, which made us sort of related, and linked her to Joshua, too.

"Adam doesn't want to leave Wright. He says it's because of his grandfather, but, really, it's Adam. He likes living there." Her nose wrinkled up in distaste. Morgan's sole desire since the day we met was to escape Wright.

"College is still a year away. Things can change."

"This won't." She gave me her it's-for-the-best smile.

"You didn't break up?" Despite a century old family feud between Adam's family and the Radcliffes, he'd snuck out to Castle Creighton to protect her. It was beautiful and romantic and intense.

"Not yet. But I don't want my family to be depending on Joshua for charity. I have to do things right, so we won't have to worry about money anymore. They've sacrificed so much to give me a chance at something better."

"But what about love?" I asked quietly.

"Love is something I can't afford. Not yet." She sounded like this was all settled, but her eyes glistened. She sat across from me on her bed. "Enough about me. I don't know how you managed to stay with your grandparents a month without them finding out about the ghosts."

"When you've lived with a secret as long as I have, keeping it is easier than sharing it."

"Did you tell your mom?"

She was supposed to be home by August, but August was almost over and we were still video chatting because of exciting discoveries at the archaeological site where she was working. Unexpected finds. Something truly remarkable, she promised. "She's still in Africa."

I couldn't bring up the topic of my dad's family, the Langleys, over Skype. With the video freezing and voices garbling and the calls dropping, it would be a nightmare. I pictured myself screaming, "I see ghosts and it's because I'm a Langley," over and over again. I winced. Nope. That was a conversation we had to have in person. She promised she'd be back in September, for at least a week.

I was nervous. We never talked about my dad, and now I was going to have to tell her that I was the Langley heir. It was a weight I didn't want to share with her because, in my bones, I knew I had more to face. Like a gathering storm on a sunny day, it wasn't here yet, but it was coming.

I think Joshua felt it, too. He called to check in on me every week. After I saved his life, he suddenly felt responsible for mine. It was a weird twist of fate. My ring made me responsible for his safety, but the ties between our families made him worry about me, too.

"Kat?" Morgan asked in a way that sounded like it wasn't the first time. "Where'd you go?"

"Just thinking about stuff."

"How's Evan doing?" She gave me a sly look.

"Happy he got to see his parents, but wishing he'd had time to go to Hong Kong and see his grandfather." His dad is British and his mom is Chinese. She'd left her family behind to be with Evan's father. Sometimes I think Evan wished that his dad had chosen to stay in Hong Kong instead.

"You miss him." Morgan tilted her head and studied me.

"Of course. I missed you, too."

Morgan smiled like she knew something I didn't. "Yeah, it's exactly the same thing."

"No. I've known you longer. And you're my best friend."

She burst out laughing. "I'm not jealous. I just think you and Evan have a different kind of bond, Kat."

"The kind that is forged in life and death scenarios."

"The most intense kind of bond."

"Definitely."

I got the feeling she was laughing at me, but I let it go. It felt good to be back with Morgan. We'd been planning our senior year since we'd met at freshman orientation. Maybe I could find a way to balance the ghosts and my family inheritance and senior year. And maybe, just maybe, I might make it to graduation without having to save someone's life or travel through time.

A girl can hope.

Chapter 2

While everyone else rushed off to lunch after class, too many Mountain Dews forced me to duck into the ladies' room. No matter how quick I was, I was still alone in an old building—a ghost's paradise. I was washing my hands at the sink when an artic coldness brushed against my neck. The shadow beside the sink darkened. A ghost was on its way.

Not now. Not here. I grabbed for a paper towel and tried to leave, but it was too late. The shadow began to shimmer and white smoke unfurled from it.

A ghost took form in the middle of the ladies' room. She was young. Maybe eleven. Fear lurked in her round, moss-green eyes. Two curtains of long, light brown hair hung around her face. Lacy pantalettes peeked out from under a periwinkle dress that was trimmed with white ribbon at the waist and hem. When she had completely materialized, I couldn't stop staring at the blood smeared across her dress. It stained her cheek and her neck too. Crimson. Like it was fresh.

My heart lurched and I pressed my hand to my chest to stop my heart from leaping out.

In death, ghosts usually held onto the good moments of their existence, choosing to appear to me at the peak of health and happiness. But this one hadn't. What I was seeing had to be from the worst moment of her life, and she was clinging to it in death. What had happened to her?

I stepped back and bumped into the sink.

"Help me," she pleaded with a lilting Scottish accent.

I gripped the lip of the porcelain sink, letting its coolness seep into my palms. *Calm down. You can handle this.* I took a deep breath and quickly checked under the stalls.

At least, I was alone in here. "What do you need?"

"I need you to tell the Kingsleys something for me."

A message. I could pass along a message. Especially to the Kingsleys—they were Evan's family. But I had to get the ghost out of here before a classmate walked in and caught me talking to myself in the bathroom. Or worse, if she was a believer, she'd see me talking to a ghost and I'd become the campus freak.

"What's the message?" My words ran together in their rush to be spoken.

"I didn't kill Percy. I wouldn't do that." Her fingers curled into fists. It seemed like her entire body vibrated at a higher frequency. Her ghost form blurred.

"I'll tell them. What's your name?"

She came back into focus. "Ellie. Ellie Harding."

"Who killed him, Ellie?"

Her face scrunched up. "I can't remember. But I didn't."

The lights flickered.

"Is this your reckoning?"

She shook her head. "You have to find out who killed Percy."

"Percy who? When did he die?"

"Percy Kingsley. In 1831." She cocked her head to the side, like she was hearing something I couldn't. Her ghostly form faded in and out. "It's coming after you."

"What are you talking about?"

She looked around like it could hear us. "The Dark One," she whispered. "It's coming for you."

"What's the Dark One?"

"It's ancient. Pure Darkness." She shuddered and blurred again.

"Why is it coming after me?"

"You upset the balance for the unbelievables this summer when you changed the past."

"Is that why the ghosts are rushing to get their reckonings from me?"

She looked too solemn for a child. "They don't think you will survive the Dark One."

"What do I do?" My pulse fluttered in my wrist like a captured moth.

Her lips parted in surprise. Fear. "I have to go."

As she faded away, I lost my balance and slid to the floor. Leaning my head back against the wall tiles, I looked up at the fluorescent lights.

Senior year was not going to be anything like Morgan and I had imagined.

Chapter 3

After classes ended, I went back to my dorm room. I slammed the door and leaned against it, glancing longingly at my bed. My body needed a nap, but my brain needed answers. I was always reluctant to call on Toria at school, because I swore I'd keep the magic to a minimum until I understood it better, but this seemed like an emergency. I turned my ring three times and summoned her with my thoughts.

Within moments, her ghost appeared before me in a bright blue Victorian dress. She wore a long jacket, trimmed in blue velvet, that skimmed halfway down her dress. Her skirt was gathered up a few inches in several spots to expose the darker blue underskirt. Her curly red hair was piled high atop her head. The sunlight streamed through my window, making her semi-transparent.

"What's wrong, Kat?"

"What do you know about Percy Kingsley and Ellie Harding?"

A look of distaste crossed her face. "Why do you ask?"

"Ellie's ghost came to me today."

Toria adjusted her skirts. "What did she want?"

"She wants me to tell the Kingsleys that she didn't kill Percy. And she wants me to figure out who did." I dropped down on my bed. Exhaustion crept over me. I wasn't sure I could take on Ellie's reckoning right now.

Toria's eyes flashed with indignation. "I don't know what Ellie's game is, but she did it. She's the one who murdered Percy."

"How can you be so sure?"

"Percy was Alistair's second cousin twice removed. Ellie was the sister of the Langley heir. When her sister died, Ellie lost her mind and killed Percy."

"Wait. Ellie was a Langley?" An ancestor of mine.

"On her mother's side." She made Ellie sound like something the Langleys hid in the basement and spoke of in hushed tones.

Over the summer, Toria had lectured me so much about the bonds of family and friendship, about my responsibilities as the Langley heir. She'd begged me to save Joshua Radcliffe for her after we realized her spell accidentally caused the Radcliffe curse. And I'd done it, because Toria was family. "Ellie's family, Toria."

Toria sighed and sat down beside me on the bed. "She was found with the knife and blood all over her dress in their hotel room. No one else was there. She even admitted that she'd done it. It was her, Kat." Toria's voice flattened under the weight of all that evidence.

"She appeared to me in the bloody dress." I trusted Toria. She wasn't just the ghost of another Langley heir. We had a connection that went beyond family. Her ghost was a shard that broke away from her soul in death. My soul was the latest reincarnation of what remained of hers. She was the only Langley I trusted—the only Langley that had trusted me.

Still, something about Ellie wouldn't let me be. "She seemed so sad and so scared, Toria. And she was just a little girl. How could she have killed Percy?"

"If not her, who?" Toria raised an eyebrow. "Did she tell you?"

"She didn't remember."

"That's because she doesn't want to. Some ghosts can't face what they did in life. But she can't escape the dress because she can't escape that moment, even in the afterlife." Her vehemence made me doubt myself.

"Why?" I asked.

"When we die, the ghost faces the punishment or reaps the rewards for the lifetime she just lived. Each time our soul moves on, that new existence is a reflection of the cumulative choices we've made across lifetimes—all our good deeds and our bad deeds."

I didn't know the details of Toria's many lifetimes, but I knew enough to know that she had endured some tough consequences.

So maybe Ellie deserved her fate. And maybe I was being naïve to think that a little girl couldn't commit a heinous act. But I'd helped a lot of ghosts find their reckonings, and I believed Ellie. My gut feeling wasn't going to convince Toria, though, and there was more I needed to know from her. I let the subject drop and told her what Ellie had said about the Dark One.

Toria seemed hesitant to speak, which terrified me. Finally, she said, "There have been rumblings among the ghosts."

"What is the Dark One?"

"I've asked the ancestors, but they just give me vague answers about a great evil that has always existed. I don't think they know for sure. I don't think anyone knows for sure."

She stared pointedly at the shadows cast by my bookcase, beside my desk, and across my bed. There were shadows everywhere. And that was how the unbelievables moved. They could lurk inside a shadow and overhear everything.

I didn't care. I had to know. "Can I beat it?"

I saw the truth in her eyes before she said the words. "Not without training. You need to go to Dumbarton."

Dumbarton was her answer to every question I asked—about my destiny, my ring, my powers, my family. She'd promised that the Langleys would find me, that they'd claim me and help me understand my birthright. But it hadn't happened, and I had given up hope that it ever would. "The Langleys aren't coming for me." Rejection edged my words. "My father left me, and his family doesn't want me."

"Kat, that's not true."

"Which part, Toria?" She flushed, because of course there was no denying that my father had abandoned me to a fate I couldn't possibly understand without his help. "Joshua said that the Langleys would contact me. You told me that the Langleys would contact me. But they haven't contacted me. They don't want me, not even if they need me." Acid burned the back of my throat. The ache of being unwanted.

Toria's emerald-green eyes reflected the frustration I felt in my soul. "The Langleys will find you. Soon."

I wanted to scream at her. I wanted to throw a chair. I wanted to smash my fist into the wall. Instead, I sat there. "I can't take this waiting."

My phone rang. It was Professor Astor.

Toria gave me a confident smile and faded away.

"Kat, could you come by my office on Friday?" he asked.

It was three days away. Professor Astor was planning ahead. How unlike him. "Sure. Is this about Castle Creighton?"

"No. Well, yes. Sort of. Joshua will be paying us a visit." He paused. "And the Langleys are going to video conference with us."

The Langleys. My family. I froze. Time slowed. My heartbeat echoed in my ears.

"Kat?"

I barely got the words out. "My father?"

"I'm afraid not, dear. We should expect a call from, well, I suppose they'd be your great aunts."

Suddenly time sped up. Dozens of questions bounced around in my brain. The most logical one popped out. "What time?"

I barely heard the professor say, "Come by at 3."

Chapter 4

In my dream, someone brushed the hair off my forehead like my mom used to do when I was a kid.

"My little Katarina." Mom's voice was soft and warm. Reassuring.

I woke up in my dorm room bed, but she was sitting beside me. Her long blond hair was pulled back. Her skin was tan from working outside all summer. Her dark gray-blue eyes always reminded me of kyanite, and they were watching me with concern.

She was here. Really here.

I sat up and threw my arms around her. "What? How?"

"Barry said you needed me." She'd known Professor Astor for a long time, but it was always weird to think of him as *Barry*. "And Mr. Radcliffe loaned me his plane."

Joshua wanted to make up for risking my life. As I hugged my mom, I figured Joshua and I were just about even.

I buried my face in her shoulder and breathed in her cherry blossom scent. "I missed you."

She squeezed me tighter. "I missed you too, baby girl."

When she released me, I kept touching her, reassuring myself that this wasn't a dream.

She took my hand in hers. "Tell me everything that happened."

I glanced at Morgan's bed, worried about waking her, but her sheets were rumpled and she was gone. Probably an early morning class. I wasn't sure where to begin. "Did Professor Astor—"

She interrupted me. "Barry told me that I should talk to you." Worry lines scrawled across her forehead.

I'd rehearsed the explanation a hundred times in my head. Trying to figure out the best way to lay out my relationship with ghosts, my connection to the Radcliffe curse, and what I'd done to save Joshua from the unbelievables.

Now that my mom was actually here, though, I wanted to tell her absolutely everything, so I started at the very beginning. Way back when I was a kid and the ghosts first started coming for their reckonings. Shock and surprise and fear moved across her face.

"I'd hear you talking to the ghosts when you were little. I thought they were imaginary friends," she confessed. "I should have done more."

"You were my normal." I squeezed her hand, willing her to understand how grateful I was for that.

I fast-forwarded to the time travel and she gasped. The hardest part was telling her how I'd witnessed a murder. I knew I'd never get that out of my head, and I hated burdening my mom with that knowledge. But I needed for her to understand. I described the curse-breaking and the spell casting. Finally, I told her that I was the Langley heir, without knowing whether or not she would have any idea what that meant.

Her eyes widened—whether in shock or in horror, I couldn't say. "Your father never wanted this for you."

"Did he tell you about what could happen to me? Did you know?"

"No." She cupped my face in her hand. "He wouldn't tell me much. All I knew was that his family had a terrible legacy that he hoped you could escape."

She looked so overwhelmed—and so guilty. There was no way I could tell her about the Dark One. I couldn't let her know how much danger I was really in. She'd try to protect me, and she couldn't protect me. And I couldn't let her get hurt trying. But, still, she knew more about my father's family than I had suspected. I needed to know what she knew. I chose my words carefully. "This legacy, do you think he was talking about protecting the Radcliffes?"

"He never told me the details." She plucked at a loose thread in my comforter. "I pushed, but he always said it was safer for me not to know." Her frustration spilled over into her voice. "And I believed him."

I was relieved that my mom hadn't had any idea what being a Langley meant, and she had trusted that I was safe. I was grateful for that. But I was also disappointed that she had nothing new to tell me.

We were both silent for a few moments. I had never asked my mom why my father had abandoned us—abandoned me—and I had to gather my courage to ask now. "Is that why he left us? To protect me?"

"Yes, Kat, I think so. I think he wanted to protect us from the unbelievables, as you call them."

I choked back a laugh. "Well, it didn't work." I held up my hand and showed her my ring. "He sent me the Langley family ring without any explanation. How could he do that to me?"

"Honey, I don't know. But he had to have a reason. Your father"—pain slashed across her face—"is a good man. And a very smart man. He wouldn't do anything without a reason."

"How can you defend him? He left us."

"He hurt me, too." She held onto my hand like it was the most precious thing in the world. "He made a choice that we all had to live with. And it didn't spare you anything. So, it looks like it was a bad choice."

"But I'm the reason he left?" This is what I had always feared. What I'd always assumed. Now it seemed like it was actually true.

"Oh, sweetie, there were a lot of reasons we couldn't be together." Sadness saturated her voice. "He was a wanderer. School anchored him for a few years, but every summer he was on a different continent. That's just who he was."

It was who she was, too. Mom loved her digs. She might say she did them for me, working to earn money for us, but she did them for herself, too.

"But he always came back to you until I was born?" The question scraped against the back of my throat, leaving a terrible ache in its wake.

"Things changed. We graduated. School wasn't holding him here anymore. He was never going to stay. I always knew that."

She had so many excuses, but deep down I knew the real reason was me. "Did he see me? Was he even there when I was born?" My voice sounded so small and fragile, like her answer would break me.

"He said you were beautiful and then..." Her voice trailed off like she couldn't bear to hurt me.

"...he saw my green eyes."

She nodded and gave me the most sorrowful look.

All the Langley heirs had green eyes. So, I was the reason my dad left. I was the reason Mom was alone. Me and my cursed green eyes. The air fled my lungs. I tried to hold onto it, but I couldn't. "Did he have green eyes, too?"

"Yes."

"Do you have a picture of him?" I needed to put a face to my father. Even a father who didn't want me.

She shook her head. "He destroyed them all before he left."

"Oh."

Mom must have heard the disappointment in my voice. She pushed herself to keep talking about him, despite how much it hurt her. "His eyes had more gray to them. He had dark, straight black hair. And he was tall, like you."

That explained my height. "I have to meet his family."

"I'd rather you didn't. They aren't like us…" She seemed to scramble for a reason to override all my reasons for reaching out. "You don't need them. You never did."

"I've got these abilities that I don't understand. And they do."

"Come back to Africa with me instead." She sounded desperate, like she wanted to take me away from all that my life had become.

If only it could be that easy, but the Langley legacy would follow me. The ghosts would follow me, too. The best thing I could do was get her as far away from me and the unbelievables as I could. I wanted my mother safe, even if I was beginning to believe that I never would be again. Especially because I was beginning to believe that I never would be again. "I'll be okay, Mom. You can get back to your dig."

But she knew that I wouldn't be okay. I could see it in her eyes. "If this is what you truly want, I'll help you find the Langleys."

When I told her Professor Astor had already scheduled a video chat with them, something flickered in her eyes. It might have been resignation. It might have been fear.

"I'll be there." She squeezed my hand one more time. Tight.

After my last class of the day, AP Psychology, I stepped outside the stone building and the sun blinded me. The din of overlapping conversations surrounded me. So many voices at once. Then Evan shouted my name. He was sitting on a stone bench, surrounded by a group of adoring girls. With his British accent and his striking looks, almost every girl at McTernan Academy had a crush on him. They found excuses to talk to him. His TA office hours usually had a long line of girls snaking around the hallway.

His labradorite-colored eyes looked more green than brown in the sunlight. His golden-bronze skin glowed. His straight, dark brown hair swept across his forehead. His features were a mix of his English father and Chinese mother.

I couldn't help smiling at him as he excused his way through his fan club to get to me. I didn't mind the dirty looks coming my way because he was here and I had a warm, this-might-all-work-out feeling in my stomach.

"Kat." He held out his arms for a hug and I fell right into them. "How's today?"

"Almost okay," I mumbled into his shoulder.

When I stepped back, he offered me his arm and said, "Let's go somewhere we can talk."

I slid my hand into the crook of his elbow, and he led me toward the brick sidewalk that wound away from the heart of campus. We followed it until it snaked around the back of an administrative building and into a stand of trees.

Once we were truly alone, I asked, "Have you heard from Seth?"

He rolled his eyes. "It was a yacht and an heiress and a desire to escape this summer. Just like you said."

"One less thing to worry about."

"So, tell me about what's on your worry list."

I caught him up on Ellie Harding's visit and her message about Percy Kingsley, my mom's arrival, and the upcoming Langley video chat.

"Look what happens when we go two days without talking," he said.

"Too much." But somehow telling him made it seem less overwhelming.

Evan stroked his chin. "I'm intrigued about Percy Kingsley. I'll try to dig up some more information on him and Ellie."

"Thanks." If anyone could find out more, it was Evan.

"I'm glad you finally got to tell your mom about the summer."

"Even if you didn't tell your parents," I teased.

"We're in different situations. I'm just a Kingsley with no prophecies written about me. You're the chosen one."

I sighed. Apparently, I was supposed to restore the peace between the four families—the Radcliffes, the Kingsleys, the Mallorys, and the Langleys. This was in addition to my ghost-related duties. "You want to swap? I'd love to just be an average Kingsley."

"Would that we could." He smiled and the corners of his eyes crinkled up.

I'd missed that smile.

"You don't seem excited about finally getting to talk to the Langleys."

"I am. It's just…Mom wants to be there. And my dad being a Langley is the reason why he left us."

Evan grimaced. "That could make for an uncomfortable family reunion."

"I know." I tried to sound calmer than I felt. "Hopefully, Professor Astor will be a buffer."

"I'm a better buffer."

"You don't have to…" I didn't bother finishing the sentence because I couldn't make my voice sound convincing. I wanted him to be there.

"Stop. I'll be there."

"Thanks."

"So, you've brought me up to speed on everything?"

"Almost." I told him how the Dark One was coming after me and the ghosts were rushing for their reckonings because they didn't think I'd survive.

When I finished, he said, "Way to bury the lede."

I laughed, and was surprised that I was still capable of it. Then we walked without talking for a few moments.

Just when it was getting weird, he broke the silence. "Toria told you that Pastor Fitzgerald merged with the shadows and became a new unbelievable when we were at Castle Creighton. He disappears just as an ancient evil rises to take you on." Evan squinted like he was doing long division in his head. "Seems too coincidental to me. I think the Dark One may be part of Pastor Fitzgerald's revenge."

"So, my two enemies may be working together." Which would make everything seven times as bad as I thought it was. Hopelessness made my shoulders slump forward.

Evan patted my arm. "We'll get through this."

I wanted to believe him. But something told me that this time we might not be strong enough to face what was coming.

Chapter 5

Mom and I were the first to arrive at Professor Astor's office, which had somehow gotten more cluttered since my last visit. Three new two-feet-tall piles of papers stood beside his chair. The wall of bookcases had books triple-stacked and looked ready to collapse. His desk was entirely hidden beneath layers of papers. I had no idea how we'd all get in here for the video chat.

Professor Astor gave Mom a quick greeting and returned to his desk, trying to get the Skype connection to work. Mom teased him about his sweater vest collection, but his light blue eyes remained focused behind his spectacles. His salt and pepper hair was especially Einstein-like today.

He kept swiveling his monitor to face us and then back to face him to make sure it was set up correctly. At one point, he accidentally swept several layers of papers off his desk and onto the floor. I stared at them, wondering how he'd ever get things back in order—if there had been any order in the first place.

When Evan arrived, I introduced him to Mom.

"Since you're here, could I ask you a few questions about your paper on the burial practices at Ahafa?" Evan asked.

Mom looked stunned.

I burst out laughing. Evan couldn't let an opportunity to do academic research pass him by, even in the middle of my family drama.

Mom answered his questions until Joshua came in. His deep blue-violet eyes no longer looked haunted. His tanned skin had a healthy glow. He smiled and I felt how grateful he was for each new day. Days that Toria, Evan, and I had made possible. It was an amazing feeling to save a life.

I'd barely finished the introductions when Mom launched into a lecture about how he had no right to risk my life. I tried to stop her, but there was no stopping Mom when she was fighting for me. Joshua took her hand and apologized. Mom's face shifted from furious to understanding. I couldn't believe how easily he'd won her over. She was smiling at him as we took our seats.

The Radcliffes had that effect on people. It made me wonder if his charisma had a supernatural component. Something that allowed him to sway anyone. For me, it felt absolutely right to be around him. I might not understand how our family connections worked, but I felt them tugging us together. When I stared into his dark eyes, I just knew that everything was going to be okay. It was ridiculous, and yet I clung to that feeling.

Once Professor Astor was certain everything was working, he bustled around the desk to stand beside Mom. Evan and Joshua stood next to me. Both were careful not to make any sudden moves that might topple Professor Astor's books and papers.

I couldn't believe this moment was finally here. I was going to see my Langley relatives. I wanted it to go well. I wanted them to like me. It felt like vampire butterflies were gnawing at my belly. Mom reached over and squeezed my hand. Suddenly, the butterflies calmed down. I gave her a quick smile and faced the screen.

Two older women appeared there. My great-aunts looked to be in their 60s. Vivian wore lavender cat-eye glasses and had warm brown eyes. When she smiled at me, it radiated out of the computer screen. Her curly, auburn hair refused to be confined by hairpins.

Jacqueline had her hair pulled back severely. It was jet black and streaked with white. Not gray, but pure white. She just stared at me with her dark eyes. They were so close to black. I wasn't sure if they were brown or blue.

The Langleys seemed surprised to see my mother. Vivian said a polite hello and Jacqueline nodded. That was it. A nod. An acknowledgment of her existence. What did I expect from the family that had ignored me for seventeen years?

After a few rounds of pleasantries, Jacqueline said, "We think it would be best for the girl to come out to Dumbarton next weekend."

"School just started. It's her senior year. *The girl* is not taking any road trips." My mother used her never-going-to-happen tone.

Vivian rested her hand on Jacqueline's arm. "We understand that Kat's schoolwork is very important. But there are things we cannot discuss over the phone or on the computer. Surely, a weekend away will be acceptable?"

Professor Astor jumped in. "Labor Day is a long weekend. There are no papers due this early in the term. A trip won't interfere with her school work."

"I'm not sending her off to who knows what again." The accusation in Mom's voice whipped around the room.

Joshua had the grace to wince. So did Professor Astor.

"Valerie, please. These women want to help," Professor Astor said.

"Dr. Preston, I've known Jacqueline and Vivian all my life. After everything Kat's done to help me, I wouldn't put her at risk again." Joshua's eyes were as sincere as I'd ever seen them, but Mom gave him her death stare. I guess even the Radcliffe charm had its limits. He pressed onward. "I give you my word. She is safe with them at Dumbarton."

"Why can't you come here and meet with her?" Mom asked the Langleys.

Vivian and Jacqueline exchanged a glance. Something unspoken passed between them.

"We don't travel much. Health issues at our age," Jacqueline said.

Vivian picked that moment to cough delicately into her handkerchief.

They wanted me to go to Dumbarton. Toria wanted me to go to Dumbarton. She said it was the only place they could train me. It all meant that I needed to go to Dumbarton. "I am going to Dumbarton."

"Not alone. I'm going with you," Mom announced.

"Valerie, this is Langley family business." Jacqueline's tone could ice over a bridge and send a driver plummeting to her death.

"Then my *Preston* daughter won't be going there." Mom clipped the ends of her words the way she did when she was furious.

"Mom, it's not your decision."

"You aren't going out there alone."

Evan gently squeezed my shoulder to stop me from speaking. "I'd be happy to go with her. As a Kingsley, I'm embroiled in these age-old family connections."

"Kingsleys, Radcliffes, and Mallorys are always welcome here." Jacqueline stared right at my mom when she said it.

Mom's spine grew two inches. Her eyes narrowed like she was about to say something awful.

Joshua stepped in front of my mom and added, "Evan is very trustworthy."

"He's taken excellent care of Kat in the past." Professor Astor's expression turned apologetic like he caught his accidental pun. "Sorry, was that too soon?"

I couldn't help smiling at him. "No. And you're right." I turned to Mom, willing her to understand. "Whatever they know, it could help me. I have to go to Dumbarton."

"I don't understand why we can't talk about everything right now." Mom sounded exasperated.

"It's not safe." Vivian's tone was more serious than a final thesis paper.

"And I can't come there because I'm not family." Mom gripped my hand. "Then Kat can't go there."

All the happiness and relief I'd felt when I'd first seen my mom began to curdle into frustration. I had done my best to help her understand, but, ultimately, she wasn't a Langley, and this wasn't her problem. "Mom I'm seventeen, not seven. This is not your decision."

Mom dropped my hand like it burned to touch me.

Professor Astor rushed to smooth things over. "You've raised a great girl. She's smart and capable. And independent. She's everything you wanted her to be. Trust her."

Mom refused to look at me.

I looked up at Evan and he nodded.

"She won't be there alone, Dr. Preston," Evan said.

Mom didn't say anything.

I had one more question, and I knew that she wasn't going to like it. "Will my father be at Dumbarton? Can I meet him?"

Sure enough, Mom tensed.

Vivian gave me a sympathetic smile. "We'll help you get in touch with him. At the very least, we can show you family photos of him."

It was what I'd wanted all my life. To know the other side of my family. To see my father's face and know if I looked anything like him. I looked past my mom and spoke to Evan. "Can we leave next Thursday?"

"I'll make it work," he said.

The great aunts nodded. "That will give us enough time to prepare."

"Prepare for what?" I asked.

"Everything," Jacqueline replied right before she ended the call.

Mom tugged me off the brick walkway and into the grass. She stopped in the shade of a four-hundred-year-old oak tree and looked around, making sure we were alone. "You don't understand what you are getting into. Once you get involved with them, you can't get out."

"What happened with them, Mom?" There was something she hadn't told me.

"They took your father away from us."

"This morning, you said he left to protect us. Now his family stole him away. Which is it?"

Mom rubbed her forehead. "If you are going to spend time with them you need to know what they can do. Their disapproval drove a wedge between your father and me. They never thought I was good enough. I'm trying to spare you from the hurt. You will never be good enough for them." Her voice was stripped bare. Gone was my powerful parent. In her place was a broken woman who'd lost the man she loved.

"I'm not you."

"You are half mine. They'll never accept you fully."

"I'm not going there for acceptance. I'm going there for answers." The first part was a lie, but she didn't need to know it.

Her face crumbled. "I can't lose you, too."

"You will never lose me."

"Your father said the same thing. And then he was gone." Tears filled her eyes. "You don't need them. You have me and Grandma and Grandpa." She clutched at my arms, like she felt me slipping away.

"You will always be my mom, but those two old women are the only people who can help me understand what it means to be a Langley." I held up my hand and wiggled the ring.

"Give them back the ring. Forget about being a Langley and be a Preston." She looked like she wanted to tear the ring off my finger and erase the past few months of my life.

"It doesn't work that way." Before we left Castle Creighton, Toria had made it clear that the ring picks one wearer. If I chose not to wear it, no one else could wield its power until I died. I wouldn't be saving myself; I would be leaving myself totally unprotected. It would be a death sentence. "I'll always be a Preston. But I'm also a Langley. I don't have any choice."

"I don't want this for you." Desperation filled her voice.

I hugged her. "I've waited my whole life to meet them, not just to see if I looked like them, but to know my other half. I need to go to Dumbarton. It's just one weekend."

"One weekend can change everything."

Chapter 6

The next day, Mom packed her bag and headed for the airport. She didn't ask me to leave with her. I didn't ask her to stay. I needed her to be as far from all my supernatural drama as she could be. There wasn't much time to dwell on her absence because the ghosts were coming for their reckonings at an everincreasing pace.

They grew cleverer, refusing to tell me their names—the one piece of information I needed to send them away. Napping wasn't enough. Six meals a day didn't help. The ghosts were exhausting me. I had to find ways to delay their visits, so I resorted to my old tactics.

When I wasn't in class, I hung out at the student center. Lots of people who didn't believe in ghosts plus a brand-new building made it harder for the ghosts to appear. I layered on jewelry—stones and precious metals were still a deterrent. But I knew that none of these moves was a permanent solution.

Eventually, I had to go to AP English Lit in Garthwait Hall, the oldest building on campus. There was no escaping being alone in the bathroom. And that was when they came for me, three at a time. At least they waited outside the stall for me instead of joining me inside.

They were in such a rush for reckonings. For two, I just had to do a little research. But the other one wanted me to find something. I tried to explain that I'd get to it when I could.

I told her I wasn't planning to die soon, but she looked at me with such despair, like she knew something I didn't and said, "It's too bad about the Langley legacy."

"It's a burden, protecting the Radcliffe heir and everything." I didn't mention that it might be easier to handle without ghosts stalking me.

She cocked her head to one side, as if I'd confused her. "But…"

I clutched the edge of the sink and stared at my reflection in the mirror. The dark circles under my eyes looked like bruises. My skin was dull and even paler than usual. "I'll be okay."

She hovered behind me. "For now."

I made eye contact with her in the mirror. "What do you mean?"

She turned as if she heard someone else. I didn't see anyone there, but it might have been another ghost or unbelievable that didn't want to be seen.

"It's not for me to say." She faded away.

I was tired of all the secrets. I was just days away from Dumbarton, but I needed answers now.

I marched back to my dorm, stopping only to buy a couple of Twix bars from a vending machine—after my encounter with the ghost, I needed to do some carbo-loading. As soon as I was inside my room, I summoned Toria.

And there she was, in a Kelly-green ball gown, perched on the end of my bed. The bustle and crinoline made sitting difficult. Emeralds dripped from her neck and her ears. Her red hair was intricately arranged on top of her head.

"Going somewhere?" I still didn't understand how things worked in the afterlife.

"Yes."

"A party?"

She shrugged. "Ghosts are stuck here on earth. Sometimes we entertain ourselves by watching the living. Sometimes we try to remember what it was like when we were living ourselves."

It seemed sort of sad. "Does that help?"

"Well, we're still dead." She sounded resigned, but I swore I heard a note of bitterness, too.

I leaned toward her. "A ghost just mentioned 'the Langley legacy.' She seemed to think that there was more to it than protecting the Radcliffe heir. And that it's bad."

Her face tightened. "Vivian and Jacqueline should explain it."

"Don't tell me to wait until I'm at Dumbarton." My voice was serrated, ready to slice through her excuses. "I understand why my training has to happen there. I can do it in secret, without the Dark One or anyone—or anything else—knowing about it. But if random ghosts know about this 'Langley legacy,' the Dark One does, too. There's no reason for you not to tell me. Here. Now."

Toria looked out the window as if something fascinating was just beyond it.

Her refusal to make eye contact frightened me. "Toria, look at me. Am I going to die?"

Her gaze finally met mine. "We all die. But you will get to live first. A lot of people can't say that."

Goosebumps rippled over my arms. "When we were at Castle Creighton, you made it clear you didn't want me to be the next heir. Is it because of the Langley legacy?"

"Yes." Her voice was softer than footsteps in fresh snow. "The heirs' lives are fraught with pain and sorrow and danger." She traced a design into my comforter. "And they die young."

"How young?" My throat went dry. The kind of dry that swallowing couldn't help.

"I've never heard of any who lived beyond forty."

I felt like all the air had been sucked from the room. I wanted to cry and scream and hit the pillows, but I couldn't. I couldn't breathe. Couldn't move. Couldn't speak. And then logic seized control of me. I still had twenty-three years ahead of me. Two and a half decades—almost. That was something. I could cram a lot of living into those years. Suddenly, there was air. I gasped, and regained control of myself. "So why do all the ghosts think I am going to die soon?"

"Forty is what we can hope for, but not many of us reach it." She bit her lip. "And the Dark One has just made a declaration of your death."

She made it sound more fatal than a bullet to my heart. All I could do was echo her words. "A declaration of my death?"

"The Dark One will stop at nothing to make your death a reality and he has proclaimed it to all the unbelievables."

"Why do I matter so much to such an ancient evil?" My voice rose like a wave about to break on shore.

"Because you freed the souls of Cassie and Sebastian from the mirror, saved Joshua's life, and gave him back his family's heirloom. You changed the past and, in doing so, altered the balance of dark and light."

I pressed my palm to my forehead, trying to make sense of what she was saying. Thinking about Cassie and Sebastian brought up Pastor Fitzgerald too. I suppressed a shudder. "Evan has a theory. Do you think—I mean—could the Dark One be connected to Pastor Fitzgerald? Or—I guess—is it possible that Pastor Fitzgerald joined the Dark One? Is that where he went when I ruined his revenge?"

"It's possible." She got up and paced the room. "Kat, being dead doesn't make me all-knowing. I wish it did. But I'm scrambling to figure things out on my side too. The ancestors say the Dark One is amassing power. It could be weeks or months before the Dark One strikes."

"But not years."

Her face was a mosaic of sympathy, regret, and something I couldn't name.

I could be dead before the end of my senior year. My stomach clenched up and flipped over. I felt like I was going to throw up and pass out at the same time. There were so many things I'd never get to do and see. I couldn't die this young. I wouldn't. Sweat burst across my scalp. A question crawled out of my mouth. "How old were you when you died?"

"Twenty."

Three years older than I was right now. "What happened?"

"Sebastian's death drove me mad."

"Did they put you in a sanitarium?"

"I was a skilled priestess who'd lost her mind, a danger to others. They used magic to lock me in the attic." Her voice came out hushed, like she was ashamed of what she had become.

I didn't want to know, but I had to ask. "How did you die?"

"My neck broke."

She'd answered my question, but not really. Whether it was suicide, murder, or an accident—I was afraid to ask.

The truth burned in her eyes. "We die saving the Radcliffes from their enemies or we die from our own madness and grief when we fail. That's the Langley legacy."

"So, if Joshua had died this summer..." I couldn't finish that sentence.

"You would have lost your mind." She said it as if it was simply the way of the world.

"Why didn't you tell me?" I scrambled off the bed and faced her. She was much shorter than I was, so I had to look down into her eyes.

"Would it have helped you to know?" Fierce affection filled her features. "Could you have done what you did knowing that your sanity—your life—not just Joshua's survival hung in the balance?"

Probably not. But I was tired of being lied to. "Still, you should have told me."

"Kat, I did what I had to do to help you survive, and that meant helping you do your duty as the Langley heir." She sounded as frustrated as I felt.

In a flash, I realized that I had never known much about Toria's life after the wedding-night murder. I had imagined that she and Alistair had married, had a family, grown old together. I knew how much they had loved each other. After I'd traveled through the mirror, I had *been* Toria. And Evan had *been* Alistair. Alistair had wanted to propose. At Cassie and Sebastian's wedding, Alistair had been so close to asking Toria to marry him.

But nothing had come of their love. Sebastian's death had ruined it.

Tears pricked my eyes. I blinked them back, wanting to be strong for Toria. "What happened to Alistair?"

"Eventually, he died, too." Her voice was devoid of emotion, but her hands clenched at her sides.

"Do you see him? Now, I mean?"

"No."

I hated to think of her unhappy in the afterlife. If anyone deserved some happiness, it was Toria. My words came out tentatively. "Is there anything I can do?"

She gave me a quick smile that disappeared before it could reach her eyes. "Here I am, telling you the worst news about your future, and you're worried about me."

"If I can help you, I will."

"Thank you." She reached for my pale hand with her translucent one. Her touch was cold, but I didn't care.

We stood there for a while. Neither of us saying anything. I considered the possible futures I faced: dying at the hands of the Dark One, sacrificing myself to save Joshua, going insane if I failed to do that, or finding a way to defy the Langley legacy.

Chapter 7

A few hours later, I sat at my desk, gazing out the window at the sidewalk down below. Students gathered and dispersed in an infinite dance of hello and goodbye. The sky darkened and the stars awakened.

The door to my room flew open and Morgan stomped into our room. "You won't believe what some sophomore tried to pull today at the library." Her bag thumped on the floor. "Hey, did you hear me?"

I couldn't get my lips to form words or my body to move.

"Kitty Kat?" Morgan rested her hand on my shoulder and used her gentlest voice—the one that made me feel like a precious antique being rolled in bubble wrap.

When my mom had left, Morgan had been there for me. She'd listened to all my fears about going to Dumbarton vs. not going to Dumbarton. Now, I no longer had any secrets from her and I wasn't about to start again.

I closed my eyes and thought about Jesse Starr, my best friend in middle school. When he got sick, he told me. I got to make the most of our time together, letting him know how much I loved him and saying goodbye. It was a small comfort when I lost him.

I couldn't deny her the same comfort. I wouldn't.

I opened my eyes and looked up at her. Concern and confusion swirled across her features "What is it?"

I told her everything I'd just learned about the Langley legacy, including my looming death.

She crouched beside my chair and hugged me. "We'll figure this out."

"How? Toria didn't know how to fight it. She still doesn't know how to fight it." My voice sounded scratched up like every emotion I held inside was clawing its way out.

Morgan paced around the room. "Can't Evan protect you? He's a Kingsley. That's, like, his job."

"Look what happened to Toria. She had Alistair and he couldn't save her. Evan knows even less than I do. I'm the one protecting him." I grabbed a tissue to blow my nose.

Morgan made a few more turns around the room and bumped into the end of my bed. "What about your Langley ancestors. Can't Toria ask them for help?"

"The ancestors didn't intervene to save Sebastian or Toria. Why would they do it for me?"

"Hold on. Let me think." Morgan rubbed her temples and walked in tiny circles near the door. She stopped and looked directly at me. "As long as Joshua is alive, your sanity is safe."

I had been so busy thinking about me, I had forgotten to warn him. If the Dark One wanted me dead, killing Joshua would be an easy shortcut.

I grabbed my phone and called him. He answered on the third ring.

"Kat, what's going on?" There was so much background noise, I could barely hear him. "I'm about to get on a helicopter to the mainland."

The *whuff whuff whuff* of the helicopter blades matched the accelerating beat of my heart. "DON'T."

"Why?" he shouted back.

"You're in danger. If you die, I will lose my mind." As I said the words, I realized how crazy they sounded.

"What?" He must have walked away from the helicopter because I could hear him much more clearly. "Slow down. Tell me what's going on."

I dropped my voice back to normal volume and spoke more slowly. "I know about the Langley legacy."

"Yes, the ring and all its responsibilities." His tone brushed off my concerns.

I was relieved. Some part of me had been hurt by the idea that Joshua had known what was in store for me—what it would likely cost me to protect him.

As quickly as I could, I explained about the Langley legacy, how the Dark One wanted me dead, and that killing Joshua would make that easier to accomplish.

"What can I do?" The steadiness in his voice made me feel stronger.

I bit my lip, trying to remember what Toria had said about the Radcliffe rubies. Reuniting Joshua with his family's most precious heirloom had restored his family's power and made the Isle of Acacia safe again. Anyone who wished to harm Joshua—human or otherwise—could not set foot on the isle.

"Stay on the isle. Don't leave."

"This is a really important meeting…" Now, he sounded uncertain.

"More important than our lives?" My tone was harsher than a Siberian winter.

He sighed. "All right. I'll reschedule."

After I hung up with Joshua, I dropped down onto my bed.

Joshua was safe for now, which meant I was safe—at least from insanity for the moment. I wasn't safe from death, of course, but the question remained: How fast was it coming for me?

I looked at Morgan. "I don't want to die." The emotional dam inside me burst and I fell apart.

Morgan held me and stroked my hair. "I won't let you die. Or go crazy. Or go crazy and then die."

I almost laughed, and then I gasped, trying to get the words out. "You can't stop it. No one can. It's my fate."

"Forget fate, Kat. We make our own destiny."

She sounded so sure. I wished that I could believe her. But Morgan wasn't wrapped up in the fate of the four families like I was. For her, being a Radcliffe descendant meant choices she'd never imagined. It meant she could go to whatever college she wanted. But, for me…

Toria hadn't been able to save herself, because she hadn't been able to save Sebastian. She had died an early death because that was the Langley legacy. That was what my father had tried to protect me from, and he had failed.

Thinking about my father filled me with panic all over again.

"What if I never get to meet my dad?" My voice shattered like a crystal vase dropped from a skyscraper. Too many pieces to ever come back together again.

"We won't let that happen."

"It's been seventeen years without him. I might not have more to wait." Horror swirled through my words.

Morgan patted my back. "I remember reading about a rare plant in the Amazon that cured a disease. I don't remember the plant, or the disease. I just remember that this rare plant only grew deep in the jungle and it was the only cure. Maybe there's something you and I don't know about, something that can fix this situation. We just have to search for it."

"Do you think?" Hope stirred within me.

"Anything is possible. As long as we don't give up."

"But sometimes death wins." I twisted my ring and asked for calm. Soothing feelings washed over me. And there it was: calm. Eerie, inexplicable calm.

"Are you going to tell Evan?" she asked.

He kept saying we'd get through everything. He'd probably do something stupid to try to save my life. I couldn't risk it. "No."

"You have to." I heard the underlying threat in her tone: *or I will.*

I raked my teeth over my bottom lip and scrambled for the words to sway her. "Just give me a little time to figure things out first."

"How much time?" Her eyes narrowed, x-raying my soul for lies.

"A few days."

"A few days." She didn't sound satisfied.

"Promise me."

She pinky swore. "Now you owe me a promise."

I didn't like the way she said it. "What?"

"Tonight, we are going to go out and live like there is no tomorrow." She gave me a blinding smile.

"Morgan..." The last thing I wanted to do was go out.

"Come on. Just shut your brain off for a bit and cut loose." She stood up and held out her hand to me.

"I shouldn't." My hand crept toward hers.

"What's the worst that could happen?" She tilted her head like a curious puppy and fluttered her eyelashes.

"Death or insanity." I slid my hand into hers and let her drag me toward our closets.

"Let's make sure you live before either of those happens. Come on,

Kat. Aren't you tired of playing it safe? Of always being good?"

She had a point. I'd been careful and cautious. So practical and sensible all my life. If I was going to die soon, I needed to get some living in. Now.

Chapter 8

From my closet, Morgan dug out a sheer, flesh-toned top with a black velvet tribal symbol on the chest. She'd convinced me to buy it junior year, but I had hidden it in the back of my closet and sworn I'd never wear it outside our dorm room.

Never became our theme for the night.

"It will look so cool with your pale skin." She tossed it on my bed.

"What am I wearing under it?"

"A bra?" She winked at me.

"A bra *and....*"

"Fine." She rummaged through my dresser and tossed a flesh-colored spandex tank top on the bed. She went through her closet and found a black velvet mini-skirt.

"I can't fit into that." Morgan was as petite and toned as I was tall and curvy.

She held it up and tugged at the seams. "It stretches."

Before I could voice my concerns about my thighs, she added black tights to the outfit.

She picked up her black platform Mary Janes and put them on the floor next to the outfit. Her studded wrist cuff and velvet choker were the final pieces that she laid out on the bed so I could see how it would look.

I was definitely going goth tonight. "Morgan..." I eyed the kohl eyeliner and black lipstick.

"Come on, Kat. The black makeup will make your blond hair pop."

The platform shoes would make me 5'11". I looked down at my carb-filled belly. It wasn't nearly as bloated as I expected. Probably because I was burning through so much energy during the ghost visits.

I must have had a dubious expression on my face because Morgan said, "You never let me dress you like this."

And there it was again. *Never.* All the things I'd never done. That I might never do. I could feel the weight of *never* pressing down on me, making it harder to breathe. "Okay." The pressure in my chest eased.

She smiled and danced over to her closet. "Wait until you see what I'm wearing."

She ended up in a black sleeveless dress with a hood. It was so short it barely covered her behind. The material was sheer, requiring a black slip underneath. Her garter belt and black striped stockings peeked out between where the dress ended and the top of her over-the-knee, black pirate boots began. Her blue butterfly-wing necklace set off her warm, tawny-brown skin and complemented her turquoise eyes, which she lined with perfect cat eyes. Then she painted her lips a metallic purple-blue.

She twisted her long black hair into a bunch of mini-buns. She pulled my hair up in a tight ponytail and clipped blue and purple extensions in it.

When we were finished getting ready, I gazed at myself in the mirror. I'd put my contacts in, and she'd painted my lips black and drawn a tribal tattoo on my cheek with her black eyeliner. My cheeks seemed more defined and my green eyes looked sexy. I barely recognized myself. And I liked it. "How are we sneaking out?"

She looked pointedly at the star sapphire ring I wore on my right hand. "I figured you could take care of that." Her voice was more sugarcoated than Fruity Pebbles.

"I'm not supposed to use the ring's powers for stuff like this."

"And tonight we are breaking the rules. Come on, Kat." Her eyes dared me.

I might not have another chance to be bad. Besides this was such a tiny request. How many consequences could it really have? I twisted my ring and asked that no one would catch us sneaking out of the dorm or back into it.

When we went into the hallway, no one was around. We didn't encounter a single person as we snuck out of the dorm or walked across campus. It was kind of eerie. And then we were at the campus gate, hailing a cab. We slid inside and were on our way.

"That was so cool," Morgan whispered.

I felt such a rush doing things I'd never done before. Things I wasn't supposed to do. I wanted to do something else I would never do. The words were out of my mouth before I realized it. "I'm going to kiss the hottest guy at the club tonight."

She grinned. "Really?"

"Yeah."

"I like Never Kat."

"I do, too."

By the time the taxi pulled up in front of Tracks, an 18-and-over club in Southeast D.C., the line snaked around the building. Guys stood there in leather pants or shredded black jeans with wrist cuffs, piercings, and chains. Some wore long leather duster coats despite the warm September night. A few had painted their faces to resemble skulls. The girls were a sea of corsets, razored T-shirts, fishnet dresses, lacy miniskirts, leather shorts, and shredded leggings. Their outfits were inspired by vampires, ghosts, and demons. I wondered how they would react if they knew that a girl who talked to ghosts was in their midst.

I started for the end of the line, but Morgan pulled me aside. "We don't have to wait."

"Are we on the list?"

"We don't need the list. Not when we've got your ring."

"I shouldn't..."

"I bet your ancestors never had this much fun."

She was probably right. "How old do you want to be?"

She beamed at me. "Twenty-one, of course."

I twisted my ring and asked for what we wanted. We walked up to the front of the line and the bouncer gave us our 21-and-over bracelets. We stepped into the club, where a dim reddish hue hung over everything. My eyes needed a moment to adjust to the lack of light. Pounding music enveloped us. So did the crowd. I grabbed Morgan's hand so I wouldn't lose her.

She weaved through the throngs of people and over to the bar. "Let's get a round of shots."

"Morgan..."

"Just one or two won't kill you."

There were so many other things that would. "Okay."

We ended up doing three shots of tequila. They tasted awful even with the salt and lime, but when they hit me, I was so warm inside. Alive. I wanted to dance. I pulled Morgan out on the crowded dance floor. The music felt amazing, like every song was meant for me and me alone. I moved to it without any of my normal hesitation, like I was dancing with the music itself.

I'd never felt so alive. This was what she wanted me to do: to stop thinking and worrying. To stay in the moment and live.

An hour later, I was drenched in sweat and overwhelmed by thirst. We made our way off the dance floor to get some water.

"So, who are you going to kiss?" She eyed the boys near us at the bar.

I'd almost forgotten about that decision I'd made in the cab. I tried to sound cool and shrugged. "Whoever's the hottest guy here."

"Let's find him." She took my hand and led me around the club, past the pool table, onto the patio, and back toward the dance floor. I got a little nervous. Could I really kiss a stranger?

I wanted to. I really wanted to.

Morgan pointed out a couple of potentials. The dimness and the strobe light made it hard to tell who was truly good looking vs. benefiting from the lighting. I was starting to think this was a crazy idea when we saw Seth. *GQ*-cover gorgeous Seth. He wore black leather pants and a black T-shirt and black Doc Martens. I never pictured Seth goth, but he'd never looked sexier. His silver eyes stood out against his tan skin. His chiseled jaw could break a heart.

"He's the hottest guy here." Morgan grinned and gave me a candy. "Go. I'll be right here."

I clutched her arm. "I can't kiss him. It's Seth." Evan's best friend and the biggest flirt at Georgetown University. "He parties with heiresses and models."

"Kat, it's just a kiss."

She pushed me in his direction. I got halfway to him and faltered. *Come on, Kat. You've faced so much worse. This is no big deal. So he's hot. Lava hot.* I took a deep breath and walked up to him.

"I thought this was an 18-and-over club." He leaned close and his warm breath tickled my ear.

"It is."

His eyes swept over me. "Loving the new look."

"I'm experimenting. I didn't know you were into goth."

He touched my cheek. "There's a lot you don't know about me."

"I'd like to do something, but I don't want it to be weird."

"Now, I'm intrigued." He flashed a grin.

My insides went all Jelloey. I blurted out, "I told Morgan I'd kiss the hottest guy here tonight. And well, um, that's you."

His eyebrows rose. "Kat, are you asking if you can kiss me?"

Heat rushed to my cheeks. My heartbeat throbbed in my neck. "No. I mean, I guess. It's just a kiss."

"Dance with me first." Before I could reply, he pulled me out on the dance floor. I glanced back through the crowd at Morgan and she winked at me.

For just a few moments, I got to be that girl. The one dancing with the hottest guy in the club. His eyes were so silver. I'd never noticed how beautiful they were because I spent so much time not making eye contact. Trying not to be noticed. Tonight, though, I wanted to be seen.

"Do you want some water?" he shouted over the pounding bass.

I shook my head. What I wanted was to not be facing a death sentence. I wanted to be a normal teenage girl. I wanted to escape the Langley legacy and my fate for a few moments.

"Kat?" For once, Seth sounded uncertain.

I wanted to kiss him. To know what it was like to kiss someone that gorgeous. I danced closer, wrapped my arms around his neck, and gently brushed my lips against his. And I kissed him like this was the last kiss I'd ever have. It just might be.

The music, the club, the people, everything around us faded away. It was just Seth and me. I never wanted it to end.

And then someone pulled us apart. I opened my eyes and Evan was standing between us in dark jeans and a black T-shirt. People shifted away from us as if they sensed an argument's arrival.

"What are you doing?" Evan looked like he might punch Seth. "You don't snog high school girls."

I grabbed his arm. "It was my fault."

"What?" Evan asked.

"I kissed Seth," I shouted.

Evan let go of Seth. "Don't be daft. Why would you? With him?"

"I wanted to," I yelled.

"Are you into him?" Evan's expression twisted up.

"It wasn't like that." I didn't want to explain why I needed a Never Night. Not yet.

But I didn't have to because Seth said, "She wanted to kiss the hottest guy here. Don't be offended, Evan. She might not have seen you." There was a mischievous glint in his eye. "Your loss. It was a great kiss. Thanks, Kat." Seth made a mock bow.

Evan shot him a look that silenced him. Then he turned toward me with such disappointment on his face. "What were you thinking?"

"I'm not a child. I can do whatever I want."

Morgan suddenly appeared by my side. "Calm down, Evan. It's just a kiss."

"What are you doing here? You're both underage," Evan said through gritted teeth.

"Sometimes Kat needs a night to just be a normal teenager." Morgan put her hands on her hips like she was daring him to disagree.

"Not with this wanker." He jerked his thumb toward Seth.

"It's just a kiss, Evan." To prove her point, she grabbed Evan's face and kissed him.

He immediately pushed her away. "I don't kiss underage girls."

"That's probably why you're so frustrated." She glanced at me and then said to him, "But I turned 18 a few weeks ago, so don't worry."

"Have you been drinking?" Evan sounded positively parental.

"We're a little tipsy," I said.

"I'm taking you home." He reached for my arm.

But I stepped out of his grasp. "No. Tonight is Never Night and I'm having fun."

Morgan grabbed my hand. "We've got more dancing to do."
We left Seth and Evan behind to argue about what they'd done.

45

Chapter 9

I sat on a wooden bench behind my favorite brick building on campus, gazing at the stone fountain. The sound of trickling water always soothed me. I closed my eyes and lifted my face to the sun. Normally, I hated sunlight because it stung my pale skin, but today it reminded me that I was still here. Everything felt more real. Maybe it was the threat of death. Maybe it was doing things that scared me. Maybe it was realizing how precious each moment was.

I could have stayed there forever, but the bench vibrated beneath me signaling a new arrival. I jerked and opened my eyes. Morgan sat with one leg folded under her and the other swinging back and forth. She held out a bag of gummy worms to me.

I grabbed one. "You startled me."

"Sorry." She lowered her chin and peeked up at me through her lashes. "So, last night was interesting."

"It was pretty awesome until Evan went all parental on me." My voice wavered between surprised and indignant.

"He's not parental; he's protective." She tapped her foot against mine. "Come on, Kat. Think about it. You guys went through so much this summer. It's clear that he cares about you."

"I know. We're good friends."

"Friends, huh?" Morgan sounded skeptical. "I think he has feelings for you. Feelings he would never act on because you're 17 and he's 20. Feelings he probably can't even admit to himself."

46

"Stop teasing me."

"How else would you explain his reaction to you kissing Seth?" She held her hand up. "And don't say parental."

"Fine. He's protecting me because Seth's a player."

"Your obstinacy is adorable."

White puffy clouds scattered across the bright blue sky. The air was warm, but not humid, like fall was starting to take hold. After ten minutes of waiting for Evan at the gates to McTernan Academy, I called his phone, but it went straight to voicemail. It wasn't like him to be late, especially when we had a train to catch to meet my Langley relatives.

I swayed back and forth in place, debating if I should go alone or wait for him. As soon as I decided to leave, he stalked toward me, dragging his suitcase. Seth was a few paces behind him. Great. The kiss had been two nights ago, but my cheeks still kindled when I saw him. So much for us all being adults.

"Apologies for being late. Seth will explain." Evan brushed past me and moved quickly into the street to search for a cab.

Amusement lurked in Seth's eyes. Before he could tease me about the kiss, I asked, "What happened?"

He slid his hands in his jean pockets and looked sheepish. "I thought I had my keys when I shut the door."

"I told you I didn't have mine," Evan shouted from a few feet away.

"Everything worked out fine." Seth sounded like he wished it were otherwise. "You and Kat will be on your way."

"What about your keys?" They couldn't have had time to call a locksmith.

"I always hide a spare set in my office," Evan said.

Seth looked like he would rather Evan stayed here. He stepped closer to me and said, "How about a goodbye kiss?"

"That was a one-time thing."

He reached up and pushed a few stray hairs back behind my ear. "Are you sure about that? Not even for luck?"

My ear tingled where he'd touched me. "Yeah." My voice came out wobblier than I wanted.

"If we don't get a cab soon, we'll miss our train." Evan's voice was like a hand shoving me away from Seth.

I stepped back and glanced down at the pavement.

"But you'll get to come to a killer party tonight," Seth said.

"We'd just catch a later train." I raised my voice to ask Evan, "Can we make this one?"

"If we get a taxi soon and traffic isn't bad." Evan stood in the middle of the street, half a block away, looking for any sign of a taxi.

I looked at my ring. What was one more time? I twisted it and wished that a taxi would appear.

A taxi immediately pulled up and Evan and I jumped in. Seth blew me a kiss. Evan gave him a thunderous look.

Once we were on our way, I asked, "So what killer party are you missing?"

"Seth's throwing a huge bash at our place. I'm sure you and Morgan would have loved to sneak in." The disapproval in his tone made me squirm.

"I bet there will be a ton to clean up. Luckily, you'll be in Connecticut."

"He'll just leave it for when I get back."

The taxi sped along in silence.

Finally, Evan said, "You know Seth's too old and too experienced for you."

"I'll be eighteen in two months." As soon as the words were out of my mouth, the reality of it hit me. *If I make it that long.*

"Why do you look like you just saw a ghost?" He dropped his voice low so only I could hear him. "Is there one in the cab?"

I forced a smile. "No. I was just thinking about how Cassie died young."

He nudged me with his shoulder. "Are you worried about dying?"

"We all die." I glanced out the window at the passing buildings to avoid his gaze.

"Kat, is there something you're not telling me?"

Before I could answer, the taxi pulled up in front of Union Station.

"If we run, we can make our train." I leapt out of the taxi and sprinted away from his question.

We found two seats together on the train and settled in for our six-hour ride to Connecticut.

I was reaching inside my backpack for my homework, when Evan said, "I did some digging into Percy Kingsley and Ellie Harding."

I dropped the books back inside the backpack. I'd almost forgotten about her. My impending destruction was making it hard to focus on the ghosts' reckonings. I leaned closer. "And?"

"It wasn't easy to get my hands on the Austrian newspapers from that era. *Wiener Zeitung*, the oldest newspaper in Austria, said she was eleven years old when she killed Percy. They hypothesized that he kidnapped her and she was trying to escape the hotel room. The defunct *Das Veritas* was a bit more salacious. It said that she was unstable after Percy caused her sister's death."

The second theory fit with what Toria told me. "What do you think happened?"

"I don't have enough information yet. But something seems off. Ellie's family was living in Glasgow at the time. Percy's family was from Wales, but he was living in America." He rubbed his fingers across his lips. "I can't figure out how Ellie and Percy ended up in Vienna together. He was thirty and she was eleven. They weren't related. The only family connection is he's a Kingsley and she's a Langley."

"Could she have become the Langley heir when her sister died?" If she was, the madness argument had more merit than he knew. I clutched at his shirt. "Who was the Radcliffe heir back then? Was he alive when all this was happening?"

"What difference does it make?"

I blurted out, "If Ellie was the Langley heir and the Radcliffe heir died on her watch, she'd have gone insane."

"Kat, what are you talking about?" He pried my fingers loose from his shirt.

There was no going back. I had to tell him about the Langley legacy— what Sebastian's death had done to Toria and how my sanity was tied to Joshua's life.

"When did you find out about this?" His eyes burned mine.

"Two nights ago."

He settled back in his seat. "It all makes sense now."

"What?"

"Kissing Seth." He rested his hand on mine. It was warm and reassuring. "We'll make sure Joshua is safe and your sanity remains intact. I promise."

My throat clogged with emotion. He'd keep that promise, even if it put him in jeopardy. And I couldn't let that happen. Morgan was right about how much I cared about him. I forced a smile and prodded him back on topic. "So, Ellie?"

"I'll look into the heir situation, but keep in mind regular people can go insane, too."

"Did you find out what happened to Ellie after Percy was killed?" His hand remained on mine. I liked it there.

"No. It's like she disappeared. At least in the papers from that time."

"People don't just disappear."

"No, but the records from back then do. Kat, it was the early 1800s in the Austro-Hungarian Empire." He moved his thumb back and forth across my hand. It was soothing.

"What about family journals and records?"

"I have my uncle Tobias searching through them. He's into all that stuff. I'm hoping he can find more on Percy and possibly Ellie."

A few hours later, I closed my calculus book, leaned my head against the train window, and stared out at the blur of scenery. Houses gave way to trees—long stretches of green and brown blurs.

Evan tapped my hand with his pen. "How are you doing with knowing we'll see the Langleys in a few hours?"

"I have to do it." Inside my stomach, vampire butterflies sank their fangs into me.

"I didn't ask about what you have to do. I asked how you feel, Kat." When I didn't answer, he dropped his voice to a confidential quiet. "It would be normal to be scared."

"I am."

"But you seem remarkably calm." He made serenity sound like a bad thing.

"Compared to insanity or death? This isn't so bad."

"Maybe. But there's something else. What aren't you telling me?" He studied my face.

A part of me knew I should tell Evan about the Dark One's death declaration, but I was really worried about what Evan might do to protect me. I wanted to protect him, too. Deep down, I knew we were always better as a team. I had just about decided to tell him when our train pulled into the station. It was one of those shorter platforms that required you to move up a few cars to exit the train. We grabbed our bags and rushed up three cars and barely made it off the train in time.

It was dark out, but the platform was well-lit. Only a few other passengers got off. The Langleys said they'd send their driver, but no one was there to greet us. I tried to act like it didn't matter, but it did. We waited a few minutes to be sure. Then we made our way to the front of the station. The place looked deserted. Still I stood under the spotlight, hoping our ride would see us and pull up. But no one did.

It was too dark to see if there was a driver inside any of the cars that were parked in the gravel lot. The parking lot could have used a few more lights. I stepped off the sidewalk to get a closer look. Evan was a few steps behind me.

I was so focused on searching the parking lot for our ride that I didn't see the car barreling toward me until it was almost too late. Everything happened so quickly. Bright headlights bore down on me. Evan screamed my name and shoved me out of the way. I hit the ground and heard the sickening thud of the car slamming into him. Tires tore across the gravel and the driver sped away. I tried to catch a glimpse of the car, but it was too dark to see the model or the license plate.

I pushed myself up. My palms were scraped and I ached all over, but nothing felt broken. I turned to check on Evan.

He was face down on the pavement. I rushed to him.

"Evan!" I rolled him over.

Blood poured out of his nose. He was gagging on blood.

"Evan, stay calm. You're going to be okay." He had to be okay. He just had to be.

I fumbled for my phone. There were no bars. No reception. I screamed for help, but no one came. This couldn't be happening.

I cradled Evan's battered body in my arms. His hazel eyes dimmed with pain. He tried to talk, but blood bubbled up from his lips. My heart thundered in my ears. I had to do something fast. I twisted my ring and called out to Toria.

She materialized instantly. "What happened?"

"A car almost hit me. Evan shoved me out of the way. It just kept going." I couldn't stop shaking.

Toria knelt beside us. She touched his forehead and frowned. "He's dying."

"No. No. No. We'll get an ambulance. He'll be okay." Terror surged through my veins, making my hands shake. I couldn't lose him.

"There's no time for panic, Kat." Toria rested her palm on my shoulder. It was ghost-cold. I couldn't bear to think of Evan being that cold.

"We have to save him." I choked on fear. "I'll do anything, please. Help me save him."

Toria's expression turned grave. "There is a way. But it's dangerous for both of you."

"I don't care." Evan was dying because of me.

"You have to tear a piece of your soul away and give it to him. It's excruciating for you and it might not work."

"But it might save him?" My breath came in little gasps.

She nodded.

"How?"

"You need a blood bond. Cut your hand and his hand and hold them tightly together."

His hand was already cut and bleeding. I looked around for something to cut my hand on. Anything. I grabbed a shard of a broken beer bottle and sliced my hand. Then I slid my fingers through Evan's and held on tight.

"Call on the ring's power. Command it to tear your soul. Envision your soul ripping. The pain will be agonizing, but don't stop, no matter what. Then tell Evan to take what he needs to be healthy," she said.

Evan tried to pull away from me, but I held on tight. "I can't face any of what's coming without you. Please, Evan, for me."

As he stared up into my eyes, I could see the life fading from him.

I swallowed and did what Toria told me to do.

The ring's star sapphire glowed. Its power ignited. Heat wrapped around me. It spread out to Evan. I would do anything to keep life in his eyes.

"You're going to be okay," I promised.

Suddenly, I felt my core ripping. A shredding of me. Sharp and cruel. An agony beyond any I'd ever known. I screamed, but it barely scraped the surface of this pain. It went on for what felt like an eternity. I knew my mind would break–that I would break–but I held on tight to Evan's hand and locked my gaze on his hazel eyes.

And then everything went white.

Chapter 10

I woke up as waves of awareness lapped over my mind. I didn't know where I was or what had happened. My memories blurred together. *Wait.* Something came into focus. I had been on the train with Evan, and then, blinding pain. My mind recoiled from the memory as if remembering would bring it all back.

And I couldn't get my eyes to open.

In the distance, I heard hushed voices. Voices I couldn't identify. I tried to tell them—whoever they were—that I was awake, but my mouth wouldn't work. My hands couldn't move, either. My entire body felt like it was still asleep, and, no matter how hard I tried, it refused to awaken. Just like when I time-traveled. *Not again, please not again.* I couldn't wake up in another body in another time. Not now. Not without Evan. Not before I got to Dumbarton. Not while the Dark One was stalking me and I had no idea how to fight it.

The voices grew closer and more distinct. They spoke softly, as if they feared waking me. Female voices, voices I began to recognize. My great aunts.

"Stupid girl, she took such a risk for that boy." This had to be Jacqueline.

"She needs him. Without him, she's more vulnerable." Vivian's voice was gentle, but insistent.

"In his current state, he can't protect himself, let alone Kat. Not without the dagger. Look what happened when he tried to save her life."

"She's doing the best she can. At least Joshua is safe."

"For now." Gloom hovered over Jacqueline's words.

Evan was still in danger. I had to get up and protect him, but I couldn't. *Come on eyelids. Open.*

Finally, I managed to open my eyes, but everything was blurry.

An awful and intense awareness rushed over me. Every sensation was worse than the last. Aching, throbbing, burning. And then an unbearable coldness. My teeth chattered. My skin was goose-bumped beneath the layer of blankets on me. I couldn't stop shivering.

I tried to sit up, but I couldn't even lift my head off the pillow. "What's wrong with me?" My voice was so raw, I barely recognized it.

Vivian rushed over. "It's all right, dear. You're safe." She pressed her palm to my forehead. "Her temperature is still too low." She was speaking to her sister now, not to me.

She slid my glasses onto my face, and everything finally came into focus. I lay on a four-poster bed. The furniture around me was antique. The lights were a comforting dim. Definitely not in a hospital.

"Where am I?" I asked.

"Dumbarton, dear." Vivian put another blanket over me.

Across the room, I saw Jacqueline's perfectly straight back. She turned sideways, giving me a glimpse of the herbs and oils littering the desk in front of her. To the glass in her hand, she added a few pinches of something. "Almost there." She murmured a few words. I couldn't understand them, but they sounded ancient, rusty. Like they hadn't been spoken aloud in a long time. A spell.

I cleared my throat. "What happened?"

"You don't remember?" Vivian's eyebrows knit together.

I searched my memories. "We got off the train. It was dark. No one was around. We couldn't find your driver. And then a car hit Evan." I whispered, "He was dying." I tried to sit up, but I couldn't. My muscles spasmed and burned. "I had to save him. I cast a spell and tore my soul."

"Our driver found you collapsed on top of him. Lying out in the road. Protecting him." Jacqueline wrapped disapproval around each word.

"You haven't had enough training for that level of spellwork. You nearly died." Vivian shook her head. "All spells have a price. This one was too high."

"Toria said it was the only way."

Jacqueline barked a laugh. "Toria. She's taking Toria's advice. We're doomed."

"You know Toria?" I asked.

"She's a troublesome ghost." Jacqueline didn't look at me. She stirred her concoction until it turned purple.

Vivian sat beside me on the bed and smoothed my hair back from my face. "What you did was very dangerous."

"Evan saved my life. I couldn't let him die." I looked around and realized it was just the three of us in here. My pulse got fluttery and I felt like I might float out of my body. "Where is he?" *Not dead, please not dead.* I struggled to sit up.

Vivian stopped me from getting out of bed. "He's resting in the room next door. He needs to sleep now. He'll be better tomorrow. So will you."

"After a few more of my tonics." Jacqueline tapped the stirrer against the top of the glass.

"Can I see him?" My teeth chattered so loudly I could barely get the words out.

"In the morning," Vivian said.

Jacqueline harrumphed and handed the cup of purple liquid to Vivian.

"You need to drink this." Vivian put the glass on my nightstand and helped me sit up.

"What is it?" I eyed the purple liquid.

"A tonic to restore your energy and help your soul mend." Her tone was firm, but kind, as she handed me the glass. "It's a Langley recipe. Trust me, it will help."

I drank the tonic. It was sweet and hot and sour like a very tart apple cider. When I was done, the shivers eased. My teeth stopped chattering. The aches receded into tingles. The bed felt so soft beneath me, like I was sinking into a marshmallow.

Warmth flared in my core. It flickered and slowly ignited, trickling out to my extremities. "I heard you before talking about Evan. What dagger does he need to survive?"

"We'll talk about it tomorrow, when you're better," Vivian said.

Tomorrow sounded good. Tonight, I'd just slip back into sleep. My mind started to let go. *No.* Evan was in danger. I had to stay awake. I bit the inside of my cheek until I tasted blood. "Please tell me now."

Vivian hesitated.

Jacqueline didn't. "The Dark One isn't just coming after you. He will come after Evan now that he's seen how weak Evan is. Without the Kingsley dagger, Evan isn't strong enough to protect himself or you."

My eyes felt heavy, but I fought to keep them open. "How do we get the dagger?"

"That is the complicated part, dear." Vivian stroked my forehead.

It felt wonderful. I couldn't stop my eyes from sliding shut.

"We'll tell you everything in the morning," Vivian said.

The great aunts faded away and sleep claimed me.

Chapter 11

My dreams were deeper and darker than they had ever been. I wasn't me in them. Instead, I fell into strange bodies, inhabited strange lives.

First, I was a man sitting in an old pub. The floors were dark and stained from a lifetime of ale and dirt. The chipped wooden chairs told stories of alcohol-fueled fights. The smell of fire and sweat filled the air. The low hanging beams in the ceiling made it feel small and cramped—less room to maneuver with no easy escape route. I sat with my back to the wall like I always did. No one would be able to sneak up behind me again. I had to compensate for the left eye I'd lost that way.

I drank my pint of Stiegl and leaned back. Did my best to appear like any other man seeking a pint and some shelter, but this wasn't just any other night for me. Everything depended on this meeting. I promised I'd save Ellie. If he didn't show up, she was doomed.

It wasn't safe out in the open, so I kept to the shadows even though I knew what lingered in the darkness. I stared down at the dagger that hung from my belt. The sheath was decorated with a diamond and a ruby and a star sapphire in an intricate triple spiral design. The large emerald embedded in the end of the hilt glinted back at me, letting me know it was ready for whatever we would face.

The dagger was all that stood between me and death.

A dagger like that in a place like this would make most men a target for thieves. But Sarah had put a cloaking spell on it years ago. I could wear it anywhere and no one outside our four families could see it.

I shifted and my gaze went to the door. I saw him before he saw me. He took his time, ordering a pint and then meandering over. At least Jonas had sent a better messenger this time. One that wouldn't get us killed tonight.

Suddenly, the room blurred and everything shifted. I left the pub behind. Now, I was in a hotel room, lying in bed. Not my bed. And not my body. This one was smaller. A child's. My brow was drenched. Every time I wiped my hand against it, fresh sweat sprang up.

I was so cold. It didn't matter that three blankets were piled on me; I couldn't get warm. Percy and I had had to travel fast. We hadn't had time for boats and carriages. It had taken all the strength I had to open the portal and pull Percy here with me. And now I was paying for it. The fever wouldn't let me be. I'd fought it all week, and the days were tolerable, but the fever was still winning at night.

My magic wasn't powerful like Sarah's. She'd promised that, in time, I would grow into mine. But we didn't have time. Sarah had said that I had to run and Percy was the only one who could keep me safe. I begged him to stay with her, but there was nothing anyone could do—not even him. She was dying.

I'd always wanted her ring, but not like this. Never like this.

Bright sunlight snuck through the curtains. I rolled away from it and buried my face in the pillow. It smelled of roses. I dozed for a while. Eventually, I woke up to flu-like aches throughout my body.

I sat up in bed and groped for my glasses on the nightstand. I slid them on to see where I was. The walls were the palest mint green. There were four sets of windows, all with forest green velvet curtains. I looked down at the intricate pattern of dragons and phoenixes that twisted over the duvet cover. Throw pillows were scattered on the floor, clearly victims of my tossing and turning.

A vanity sat in the corner of the room, but I wasn't quite ready to see how I looked. A chaise lounge hugged the wall to my right. Next to it stood a tall antique bronze lamp. Perfect for reading.

Across from the end of my bed, my bag stood neatly beside the armoire. There was a desk beside it. It seemed important, but I couldn't remember why. And then I got distracted by my need for the bathroom. Luckily, there was one attached to my room. I could see part of the giant white tub from my bed.

When I stood up, I felt like I wasn't anchored inside my body. A wave of nausea followed. After I used the toilet, I pressed a wet washcloth to my neck. Then I sat on the cold tile floor and waited for my stomach to settle.

As soon as I was sure I wouldn't throw up, I got my toothbrush from my bag and brushed my teeth. Glancing in the mirror, I almost spit toothpaste all over it. My hair looked like pixies had spent the night tying it into knots. I wasn't sure a brush would make its way through that mess, but I went back to the bag to grab mine.

I pulled the brush from the bottom of my bag, but, instead of going to the vanity, I found myself drawn to the desk. Something tugged at the back of my mind—a memory of this room from last night. Jacqueline had stood where I was standing now, mixing some concoction.

Last night. It all came flooding back. I dropped my brush and froze in place. In my mind, I saw blinding headlights bearing down on me. That car had meant to hit me. If Evan hadn't pushed me out of the way, I'd be dead right now. And Evan wouldn't be a new target.

Evan. My stomach tightened with fear and another wave of dizziness passed over me. I held onto the desk to stay upright. I twisted my ring and called for strength. A dull pain hit me in the belly. I sank back onto the chair and waited for it to stop.

When it did, I felt colder, like a chill had taken hold of my bones. All I had on was a long nightgown. It wasn't mine. The great aunts must have put me in it. I needed something warmer, but I had to find Evan. I looked for something, anything, to keep me warm. I saw a blanket balled up at the end of the bed and grabbed it.

I flung open the door of my room, and a long hallway stretched in front of me. Just beyond my room, there were two doors on either side of the hallway. At the end of the hallway, there was so much light that I was disoriented.

Focus, Kat. Last night Vivian had said Evan was next door. I tried the door to my left and peeked inside. The bed was perfectly made. No one was in here. I tugged the door shut and tried the one to my right.

It swung open.

Jacqueline was leaning over Evan, whispering words and rubbing his forehead.

I clutched the blanket around my shoulders and padded into the room. "What are you doing?"

"Making sure he gets better." She continued her work as though I wasn't there.

The cuts on Evan's face were almost healed. I hoped everything inside him was healing at the same speed.

Jacqueline's eyes looked pinched. Tired. In daylight, they were the darkest brown I'd ever seen. Almost black. A few strands of hair had escaped her bun. I'd swear there were new streaks of white, too.

"Can I help?"

"No." She whipped around and her gaze was so intense I took a step back. "Every spell has a cost. You're lucky you survived. You need to let your body rest and recover. No spells for a few days." She pointed to the new white streaks in her hair, as if she had read my mind. "This is the cost of healing for me. I lose some of my vitality. My life flows into you and Evan."

"But Evan—"

"—is recovering. Because I'm healing him." Her tone slammed the door on this discussion.

I waited until she seemed to be finished to ask, "Are you a priestess like Toria?"

"No. We aren't all priestesses."

I bit my lip. "Am I?"

"You're on your way to becoming one."

"You're casting spells. Are you a witch?"

She gave me a look of disgust. "I'm far more advanced than a witch. A witch is the most basic magic worker."

I hadn't meant to insult her. "This is all really new to me."

"Well, I suppose you'll have to learn quickly then." Her words came out cold.

I tried to connect with her. "Spells can be draining."

"Doing so many healing spells in a day certainly has been."

"I'm sorry we came here needing your help."

She just nodded.

Everything I said to her was the wrong thing. "Thank you for saving him, and me."

"You're welcome." She gathered her stuff. "When you're done in here, make yourself presentable and ring for Vivian and me. We have a great deal to discuss."

She shut the door behind her.

Alone with Evan, I pulled a chair close to his bed and sat down. To look at him now, you'd never know how near to death he'd been. My throat constricted. I'd never forgive myself if he died because of me. I took his hand in mine and felt his blood beating in his veins. Relief trickled over me. "Thank God, you're okay."

"Thank Kat, actually," he murmured with his eyes closed.

"How long have you been awake?"

"A while. But it's bloody difficult to get my eyelids open. Like when we time-traveled at Castle Creighton."

I squeezed his hand. "Don't worry. I had the same reaction. Must have something to do with being near death."

"Were we?" His eyes finally opened.

I gripped his hand tighter. "You were dying."

"But you were okay." He said it like that made the rest acceptable.

I leaned closer. "My life isn't worth yours. Trust me."

"Kat, you matter."

"So do you."

He studied my face. Whatever he saw there must have worried him because his brow tightened. "What you did to save me—are you okay?"

"A bit tired, but I'm in much better shape than you are."

He raised an eyebrow. "Have you seen your hair?"

I reached up self-consciously. "I'd have bedhead every day if it meant you were okay."

He gave me a lopsided smile. It faded away as he said, "The car didn't slow down."

"The driver meant to hit me."

"You don't sound surprised."

"I'm not." I told him about the Dark One coming for me. How I was so busy protecting Joshua, I forgot about Evan. That this was my fault.

"Kat, none of this is your doing. You saved me."

"But your life was at risk because of me."

"Because of who we are. I'm a Kingsley. It sounds like saving Joshua this summer made us a lot of enemies amongst the unbelievables."

I stared out the window next to Evan's bed. A bright blue sky waited for us. Everything looked fine. I should have come to Dumbarton alone. If I had, Evan would be safe. "I should have kept you out of this."

"I wouldn't let you." He squeezed my hand. "We're in this together."

"Maybe we shouldn't be." I tried to pull my hand away, but he wouldn't let me.

"It's too late for that now." He held my gaze until I nodded.

His eyes slipped shut. He struggled to keep them open, but eventually they stayed closed. I waited until his breathing slowed. Once I was certain that he was asleep, I ignored Jacqueline's warning against working magic and asked my ring to heal him.

It glowed. Bright light radiated out of it and over Evan. Pain stabbed me in the stomach. I gasped and doubled over.

Toria's ghost appeared beside me. "You need to listen to Jacqueline. You're weak right now, and that makes you vulnerable."

I held my stomach, waiting for the ache to become bearable. When it did, my skin felt clammy-cold beneath the blanket. "I broke the curse on the rubies and removed the retribution spell in a single day at Castle Creighton. Jacqueline doesn't know what I can do."

"A soul-sharing spell is different, Kat. A lot of people don't survive it. If they do, they need a week of bedrest afterwards. You shouldn't do any spells for a few days."

"I don't have time to rest."

"If you keep pushing yourself, we won't have to worry about the Dark One because you'll do yourself in." She put her hands on her hips and glowered at me.

"Wouldn't that be the best ending for me?" At least it wouldn't be insanity or a gruesome death at the Dark One's hands.

"You're too important. You must listen to your great aunts. They know so much about magic, and about our family. They can teach you things I can't. They can train you properly."

"All right." I held up my hands in defeat. "Do you have any idea who hit Evan?"

"I don't. And that worries me." Her lips compressed.

"Do you think it was the Dark One?"

Her expression was soaked in uncertainty. "Driving that car? I don't think so, but it could have taken control of a human to do its dirty work, to test how strong you are."

"So, there will be more attempts on my life?"

"You're safe here." She sounded so certain that I almost believed her. "Dumbarton is protected with the strongest wards. Anyone who wishes to harm a Langley cannot break through our protective barriers."

"What about Evan? Is he safe here?"

"All our allies are granted protection at our family homes."

So maybe we really were safe. For now. "What happens when we leave Dumbarton?"

"The Langleys can help you with that." As suddenly as she had arrived, Toria faded away.

Chapter 12

I took a shower, got dressed, and sat down on my bed, feeling more tired than I did after a dozen ghost visits. If I let myself lay down, I'd be asleep in minutes. But I wouldn't have the answers I needed, so I pushed myself to my feet and left my room.

I ignored my aching muscles and headed down the hall toward the center of the house. Ornate wall sconces lit my way. The quiet surprised me. Castle Creighton had had servants moving around, but this place felt like it was in a slumber. The hallway spilled out into a larger hallway that split in two to go around walls of French doors. So much natural light streamed in through the windows. It was the closest you could be to outside while still inside.

I peeked out the window to see what was below: a courtyard big enough to fit a small house inside. White pebbles formed a meandering walkway that snaked through the grass and flowerbeds. A koi pond nestled in one corner and Greek statues were scattered about. In the distance, beneath a lilac tree, there was a wrought iron bench. Toria's ghost sat there with her shoulders slumped in despair.

A man with brown, wavy hair walked the gravel path. He tilted his head up, and I recognized that face: Alistair. I waved to her and signaled where he was, but she didn't move. I banged on the window to get his attention, but he didn't notice me. I opened the French door and leaned over the railing to shout down to them, but both ghosts disappeared without acknowledging me.

Then I remembered that Toria had said she never saw Alistair's ghost. I hadn't realized that they could be this close to each other without knowing it. I wondered if Jacqueline and Vivian could help me reunite Toria and Alistair.

But first, I had to figure out how to stay alive. And I wasn't going to be able to do much of anything without finding my great aunts.

To my right, an ornate chandelier hung in the vaulted ceiling of the main entryway, and a white marble staircase wound downstairs. I rested my hand on the banister. It was cool, soothing. It made me feel like I belonged there. Then something tugged at the corner of my mind: a vague memory of coming down these stairs. Not from my own life, but from Toria's. I tried to grasp it, but the more I concentrated, the more elusive it became.

I made my way downstairs, but didn't know where to go next. French doors enclosed the courtyard on the lower floor, creating a burst of life in the quiet center of the house. I glanced into the room to my right and found an empty parlor. The main hallway stretched to my right and left with shut doors on both sides. I hesitated until my instincts pushed me to turn right. As I rounded the corner, Vivian walked toward me in a pink sweater set and gray wool pants. A strand of white pearls hung around her neck and her auburn curls bounced around her shoulders.

"I was just coming up to check on you. You shouldn't be out of bed yet." Her forehead creased with concern. Crow's feet gathered in the corners of her eyes and smile lines hugged her lips.

"I'm okay." I tried to smile back, but my face refused to lie as easily as my voice did.

"How are you really feeling, dear?"

"Like I have the flu."

"That's your body trying to make you rest." She lowered her chin and looked at me over the top of her lavender glasses, making me feel chastened and cared for in the way that only family can.

"But I'm hungry."

She laughed and looped her arm through mine. "You're headed in the right direction. Come join me in the breakfast room."

She led me to a room with pale pink and cream-striped wallpaper and cream wainscoting. A pastel floral rug covered most of the hardwood floor, and on top of the rug sat a round table with a pink embroidered tablecloth. A delicate chandelier dangled over the table from the twelve-foot high ceiling. Sunlight flooded through the windows that were topped with crescents of glass, making the crystals in the chandelier sparkle.

"What a cheerful room." For some reason, I expected the room to be darker. I didn't know why, but I did.

"It used to be very dark. But I redid it." Vivian blushed. "I wanted it to feel like spring in here."

"It does." The table was laid out for two with fine bone china. The teacups had a yellow chrysanthemum floral design that matched the plates. "Where should I sit?"

"Here." She gestured to the place setting that was already laid out next to her.

"Are you sure? Isn't that Jacqueline's seat?" I didn't want to give her another reason to be annoyed with me.

Vivian waved away my concern. "Sit."

A maid quickly appeared and laid out a third setting on Vivian's other side for Jacqueline.

I filled a cup with coffee and cream and another with orange juice. Now that I was here, where did I begin? There was so much I wanted to know about my family and my powers. In that order.

"Jacqueline will be down in a few minutes," Vivian said to me before she conferred with her maid and sent her on her way. "Let's get some food in you and then we have much to discuss."

Moments later, the maid reappeared with a plate of bacon, sausage, scrambled eggs, French toast, and a fruit cup. The minute the bacon hit my tongue, I realized how hungry I was. I spent the next ten minutes shoveling food into my mouth and sucking down coffee.

I was almost done with breakfast by the time Jacqueline joined us. She wore a sedate navy dress with her hair in a perfect French twist. There were definitely more white streaks in her dark hair than there had been the first time I saw her, and deeper lines on her face. She took the seat beside Vivian, politely spread her napkin across her lap, and stared at me like I was a barely tolerable intrusion.

I swallowed the bit of food in my mouth and wiped my face on my napkin. "I'm sorry for any trouble we caused with the way we arrived." I peeked up at Jacqueline, hoping my words would help smooth things over. She seemed perpetually annoyed by me.

"We should have expected trouble." Vivian waved her hand like it was nothing to keep them up all night saving Evan's life and mine.

Jacqueline filled her coffee and sipped it black. "It's my duty to heal you." She made me sound like a responsibility she never wanted.

"Then I'm sorry you're stuck with me." I couldn't keep the hurt out of my voice as I pushed the eggs around on my plate.

Vivian shot her a look that screamed *be nice.* "We are happy to help you." Her voice was sweeter than the syrup on my French toast.

"Then why did you take so long to reach out to me?" I wasn't just talking about after I had become the Langley heir. I was talking about before, when I had been just their grandniece. I had spent seventeen years wanting to know about the other half of my family.

"Your father never wanted this life for you. He prayed that you wouldn't be chosen by the ring. He thought that if he stayed far away from you—and kept you away from us—the ring might not even recognize you as a Langley." Vivian sighed with seventeen years of regret. "He thought the ring would be drawn to someone it knew, someone in closer proximity. He thought that he could trick the ring into forgetting about you. He made us promise to let you have a normal life, so we watched and we waited." Her eyes pleaded with me to understand.

My father wanted me to have a normal life. The life I wanted for myself was the one he'd wanted for me. My heartstrings tangled together. "Why didn't he tell me any of this himself? When it was clear that the ring had chosen me, why did he send it to me instead of bringing it to me?"

"Green-eyed Langleys are all potential heirs. They have tremendous power, which makes them easier to track in groups. After Toria died, someone started hunting them. They had to scatter far and wide to stay alive. If they gather together, they are easily located, attacked, and killed by our enemies. The only safe place they can meet is at Dumbarton." Jacqueline sounded as if she were reciting facts, not a monstrous fate for me and my father.

"So, if he had come to see me—"

"—both of you would have been targeted by our enemies and killed." Vivian's eyes were haunted by the losses she had endured.

"Why isn't he here now? Doesn't he want to meet me?" My eyes darted from Vivian's face to Jacqueline's, daring them to explain.

"Of course he does. But we don't know where he is. It's safer for him, but it makes it harder to get a message to him." Jacqueline gave me a look that made me feel like a silly little girl with ridiculous expectations.

"He will come to see you, I promise." Vivian laid her hand on mine, warming my fingers and my heart.

The maid came in with Jacqueline's breakfast, and Vivian asked her to fetch a couple scrapbooks and albums.

Through the windows, I saw a sprawling estate in the middle of nowhere. No neighbors, no roads, nothing. And since I had been unconscious when their driver had brought me here, I had no memory of the journey from the train station. "Where are we, exactly?"

"In Starling, Connecticut—about an hour by car from the train station. We have thirty acres, land that has been in our family for generations. The boundaries are heavily warded, as is the house itself. To outsiders, it looks like a private farm, but only Langleys and our allies can come here. If anyone else steps foot on the property, they will feel ill and immediately want to leave. If they wish to do us harm, it will be particularly painful for them." Jacqueline's smile turned feral.

"If it's so safe here, why don't all the green-eyed Langleys just live here?"

"We wish they would, but this place begins to feel like a prison to them. They'd rather take their chances out there." Vivian gestured out the window. "And as long as they stay separate and keep moving, it's hard to track them—for our enemies, but also for us."

I twisted my ring, trying to take in everything they were telling me about my family. My inheritance. I held up my hand and the star sapphire flashed in the morning sun. "Did you know that the ring would choose me?"

"The ring decides on the next wearer when the current one dies. We can't predict who the heir will be." Vivian sipped her tea. "However, the ring always selects a green-eyed Langley because they are priestesses or warlocks."

"Do all Langleys have powers?" I asked.

Vivian nodded. "Our powers develop in childhood and are always rooted in the past, the present, or the future. Each of us can do something different. There are teleporters, psychics, and healers, just to name a few. Every Langley can also cast spells, to varying degrees. But the green-eyed

Langleys work the most powerful magic."

"I went back in time and I talk to ghosts, so are my powers rooted in the past?" I asked.

"Indeed," Vivian said.

"What's your power?"

Vivian sat forward, like she was eager to share. "I can read tea leaves and palms. I get occasional visions of the future, too." Jacqueline sliced into her French toast and took a bite, so Vivian went on, "Jacqueline's powers are grounded in the present. She can heal almost anything."

"What about," I hesitated, "my dad?"

Jacqueline's face tightened. I wasn't sure if it was talking about my dad or talking to me that bothered her. "He can move objects with his mind. His powers are related to the present, too."

"When was the last time you saw him?" I tucked my hair behind my ear.

"At his sister's funeral last year." Jacqueline's voice hardened around the word funeral, like it had to build a wall between that day and her.

I tried to figure out the best way to ask my next question, but there wasn't one, so I asked it as softly as I could to cushion the awfulness. "How did she die?"

"It was a fire." Vivian looked away, like it was too painful to speak of.

"A brutal and unnatural ending." Jacqueline clenched her fork in her hand. "She was burned from the inside out."

My hand shook so much that when I tried to put my coffee cup down, it clattered in its saucer. "What?"

"Her apartment was fine. Her skin was untouched. It looked as if a fire had started inside her and burned its way to the surface through her eyes and mouth." Jacqueline's explanation made my knees weaken. I was grateful I was already sitting.

"Poor Shannon. If only she'd listened to my prediction." Vivian gazed into her tea cup. Emotions I couldn't name flickered across her face.

My aunt had died a terrible death. A fate that awaited me. My heart sped up, trying to escape an awful future. "Do you think the Dark One came after her?"

"We don't know. Though I suspect Shannon was murdered for the ring." Vivian lowered her voice to a quiet reserved for churches and cemeteries. "It was the last heirloom in the hands of its family. When it was forged, the ring was bound to the Langley family, but in our lifetime, I've seen how our enemies have focused on the ring. They are determined to break that bond. The ring, however, disappears when its current owner dies and only reappears in the hands of another Langley. Unfortunately, the bond between the ring and the heir has led to the hunting of green-eyed Langleys."

And that included me. I was next on the list of the hunted. A shiver rattled my spine. "How many green-eyed Langleys are left?"

"There are six alive right now," Vivian said.

"If we all die, what happens to the ring?" My voice wobbled.

"We don't know." Fear flickered in Jacqueline's eyes and sent a chill through my soul. "We hope we never find out."

My appetite disappeared, and I pushed my plate away.

"You need to eat, Kat. You have to get your strength back." The way Vivian said it made me sip my coffee. She nudged a cinnamon roll toward me. I tore off a piece and ate it.

"Toria mentioned the Dark One, but you keep talking about 'our enemies'—plural. Who are they and why are they after us?"

"No one knows precisely what the Dark One is, or when it came into existence. Our enemies have varied over time, but many have allied themselves with the Dark One. When it consumes someone—or something—it gains the power of that entity. In exchange, the Dark One will make the enemies of the consumed its own."

On his own, Pastor Fitzgerald scared me and he had tortured my ancestors. I had destroyed his revenge, but I hadn't destroyed him. "And Pastor Fitzgerald's ghost is now part of the Dark One?"

"I'm afraid so." Concern splashed across Vivian's face.

My heart sank, sank, sank past my knees. "But why do we have enemies at all? Why does anyone want to hurt us?"

"Powerful families make powerful enemies. We don't know what the earliest generations did. We assume that our enemies wanted power or revenge. Supernatural beings that felt wronged by us could continue to come after us for centuries, long after the people who wronged them died." Decades of frustration flooded Jacqueline's voice. "From what we've been able to piece together, the Kingsleys, Langleys, and Mallorys swore an oath to the Radcliffes, and that oath has bound our families for many centuries. The Radcliffes were nobles who cared about their people's safety. The Langleys were trusted counsel who protected the Radcliffes from supernatural threats. The Kingsleys were honorable warriors who fought for the Radcliffes. The Mallorys were recordkeepers of all the families' history."

"It's a lot to ask that I give my life for the Radcliffes without knowing why." I thought coming here would give me that answer: the why behind all that I was expected to risk—whether I chose to or not.

Vivian patted my hand. "I wish we knew more. It's frustrating for us too. I've spent decades trying to figure this out. But the only person who knows all the details is the Mallory heir."

"Can we ask him or her?" I had no idea who the Mallory heir was.

She glanced at Jacqueline, who nodded like she granted permission for Vivian to go on. "No one knows who the Mallory heir is. It's too risky. If our enemies got him, they would have access to all the information ever recorded about our families. They would be able to annihilate all of us."

"Wait. So, let me get this straight. The Kingsley and Langley heirs just blindly save the Radcliffes, with no idea why we are risking our lives? But the Mallorys know." My voice rose an octave with my annoyance. "And the Mallorys get to sit on the sidelines, writing it all down and never risking anything?"

"The heirs always honor the oaths that our families made, it's their duty." Jacqueline made it sound so simple.

My face must have screamed disbelief because Vivian took my hand in hers. "Kat, it isn't fair. None of this is fair. And, from a modern perspective, none of this makes much sense. The oaths and spells that bind our families—and bind each of us to our own task—are relics of another age. But that doesn't mean that we can ignore them or escape them. The fact that the ring chose you, despite your father's precautions, is proof of that. The fact that the Dark One has already tried to kill is proof of that. I hate that you are being sucked into an ancient conflict that none of us can completely understand. And I hate that we can't protect you." I felt her frustration grow with each word.

"Thank you." It helped to know that I wasn't the only one upset by this situation. My mind tried to come up with another solution. "What if I summon our earliest ancestors' ghosts here? Then we can ask them whatever we want." I'd never tried to summon anything that old, but I was willing to try.

Vivian gave me a wistful smile. "That's not a bad idea, Kat. Your gift might help us learn what we need to know, and I'll do what I can to help you. But you'll have to get stronger—"

"The earliest ancestors aren't like other ghosts. They don't often come when called or answer questions." Jacqueline's words were sharp enough to cut to the truth.

I flashed back to when Toria tried to ask our ancestors about Sebastian's fate. She'd been brought to them in a cave and I'd been dragged along with her. None of them had answered her question and when they sensed me they sent her away. "It's still worth a try, isn't it?"

I was still waiting for an answer when the maid returned with a stack of photo albums. She placed them beside Vivian and then she cleared our plates.

Vivian scooted her chair closer to mine, pulled an album toward us, and started flipping through the pages. "I believe we promised you some photos."

"We have other things to discuss," Jacqueline reminded her.

"This first. Kat should know that being a Langley isn't all gloom and doom." For once, Vivian's voice was implacable.

Jacqueline made a noise in her throat. "I'll leave you to it then." She got up and left the room.

"She's always rather cranky after major healings," Vivian said. "She needs more rest."

Sure. Rest. That would make her less difficult.

Vivian continued flipping pages, like she was trying to find a specific photo.

While she searched, I studied her face. Up close, she looked to be in her sixties, maybe early seventies. It was hard to tell. "How long have you lived here?"

"All my life."

"You never moved away?"

"We can't."

"Why not?"

She stopped searching the album and looked up at me. "Jacqueline and I are the guardians of Dumbarton. We cannot leave the property. As long as we live, we will remain here, ensuring that Langleys always have a safe place. When we die, we will be buried here."

"Does Castle Creighton have a guardian?" Maybe that ornery old groundskeeper Perkins?

She shook her head. "Just Dumbarton."

"Why?"

She tapped the photo album. "Photos first, then I'll show you why."

"Can't you tell me?"

"It will make more sense if I show you. Trust me." She patted my arm.

I trusted Vivian, so I let it drop.

She made a pleased sound when she found the page she wanted. She smoothed it with her hand. In the center, there was a baby picture. A shock of black hair above a smushed baby face with light-green eyes. Vivian's finger stroked the picture like it was something precious. "This is your father, Maximillian."

My father. *Maximillian.* Finally, I knew his name. My mom had never even told me that. It was weird to have my first glimpse of my dad be a baby photo.

"We called him Max." She turned the page and chuckled. "Oh, I'd forgotten about this one."

Now he was a sturdy kid—four or five, maybe?—nestled in the lap of a gorgeous young woman with raven hair. Her smile lit up her whole face.

"Is that my dad with his mom?"

"No. Take another look. Don't you recognize her?"

How was I supposed to know who she was? I shook my head.

Vivian's face fell. "That's Jacqueline. She's his godmother. Your grandmother, Max's mother, died when he was three. So did his father."

This was a lot to take in all at once. I was trying to imagine what it must have been like for my father to lose his parents when he was so little while I was struggling to accept that the radiant, happy young woman in the photo was my great-aunt Jacqueline.

"Maribel was our youngest sister." Vivian's voice quivered with emotion. "She had green eyes, and so did Max and Shannon. We warned her that she and her children would only be safe together at Dumbarton, but she thought her magic was strong enough to cloak them all. She wanted her children to have a normal life, like your father wanted for you."

Vivian paused, then she continued. "But once Maribel, Max and Shannon—three green-eyed-Langleys—left Dumbarton together… Well, you can understand why your father was so afraid to be near you. It wasn't just about protecting you from the ring."

"But if we'd lived here, if my father had brought my mom and me to Dumbarton, we would have been safe from our enemies."

"But you wouldn't have been safe from the ring." Vivian's eyes made a silent promise. "Max really thought he was protecting you, Kat."

"But he didn't. I wasn't safe from the ring, and I've spent my whole life without a father. Maybe if I had grown up with him, it might be a little easier to face these threats now."

Vivian sighed. "You know, Jacqueline and I raised your father and his sister after their parents died."

I could tell she wanted to change the subject, and I let her. Talking about what might have been wasn't going to change anything, and there was still so much I wanted to know. "What was my dad like?"

"Mischievous. Smart. Exceptionally kind." Vivian's eyes softened and her voice bathed me in sunshine. "He had a knack for sensing what went unsaid. He could tell when Jacqueline was upset and he'd give her a hug or pick flowers for her. She loved him more than any of the other kids in the family."

"Does she miss him?"

"So much more than anyone understands." Vivian leaned closer and her arm brushed against mine. "She doesn't mean to be unfriendly, but it hurts her to see you. You remind her of how much she misses him."

Vivian flipped through the pages, and I saw pictures of my great uncles and great aunts. Cousins I never knew I had. Family. So much family. I saw my father as a teenager. The same dark hair he'd had as a baby and a little kid. A strong nose. Chiseled cheekbones. I reached out to trace his face. He was always hanging out with a dark-haired girl. "Is that his sister?"

Vivian nodded.

My aunt Shannon. The last heir. I looked into her eyes and wondered how she felt when she found out she was the heir. "They look so much alike."

"They should. They were twins."

I couldn't believe I hadn't even known that.

She flipped a few more pages. "I still remember the day your father brought your mom to visit." She tapped a photo.

It took me a second to realize that the woman in the photo was my mom. She'd changed a lot in eighteen years. She had on a bright turquoise slip dress. Her wavy blond hair hung loose around her shoulders. She sat next to a strikingly handsome guy. My dad. That was how he had looked when she fell in love with him.

In the picture, he was teasing her with a deviled egg and she had tossed her head back in laughter. I had never seen her look this happy.

Vivian took the picture out of the album. "You can keep this one."

It was the first picture I had of both my parents. My voice clotted with emotion. "Thanks."

Vivian didn't act like she disliked my mom, but Mom had been adamant that Vivian and Jacqueline disapproved of her. I wanted to hear Vivian's side. "Did you like my mom?"

"She was a smart and lovely person." Vivian's face became a battleground for her emotions. "I wanted your father to be happy, but I foresaw that loving her would split him in two."

"Did it?" I asked softly.

"Losing his mother, leaving you and your mother, and Shannon's death were the three things that shattered your father's heart. He went from being a wanderer to a daredevil, like being close to death was the only thing that made him feel alive anymore." She raked her teeth over her bottom lip and her eyes grew hazy, like she was lost in thought.

"Is he okay?"

"He will be."

She turned the page and I saw a woman who looked like Vivian but with darker hair, a rounder face, and bright green eyes.

I pointed at the photo. "Who's that?"

"Your grandmother." She touched the photo with such reverence, as if it was her last link to her sister.

"I wonder if she would have liked me."

"She would have loved you."

"Do you think my dad will like me?" It was silly to hope, but inside me that little girl remained. The one waiting for her father's affection. "It's not like he's ever been interested in knowing me."

"That's not true." Vivian grabbed a scrapbook.

She flipped it open. There were baby pictures of me in the hospital. Pictures of me winning the tug of war in third grade. The fifth-grade math award. Eighth grade graduation. A newspaper clipping about my scholarship to McTernan Academy. "He started this scrapbook because he always wanted to know what you were doing. Jacqueline keeps adding to it, so every time he visits, he can see everything you've been up to."

My throat constricted. "He cares. He wants to know me."

Vivian put her arm around me and pulled me closer, offering comfort. "He does and he will."

I wanted a dad. I had always wanted a dad.

Chapter 13

After we finished looking at photos, Vivian took me to the living room. The armchairs were a dark blue velvet that matched the couch. Dark wooden shelves lined the wall across from me and were filled with books and photo albums and knickknacks.

Even though this was my first visit to this room, it felt familiar—not to me, but to Toria, to the part of me that remained connected to her. This had been Toria's childhood home. It could have been a part of my childhood, too, if my father had made different choices. It stung my heart to think about all I'd missed out on.

I sat on the couch and melted into the cushions. Vivian slid off my shoes and put my legs up on the couch.

"You should rest, dear."

I laid my head on a pillow. Vivian tucked a furry blanket around me. It was soft and warm. I snuggled into it. My eyes drifted shut—I don't know for how long.

When I opened them, Vivian stood over me with another vial of that purple concoction from Jacqueline. "This should help."

I tossed it back as quickly as I could. The taste was odd, but the effects were amazing. The vinegar burned. The honey soothed.

"Let the medicine do its job." She rubbed my forehead. "Get some sleep."

I yawned. A delicious warmth spread to my fingers and toes. My body stopped aching. My eyes were heavy. So heavy. And then I slipped into a dream.

I sat alone in the courtyard at Dumbarton. The coldness of the wrought iron bench seeped through my dress. I didn't care. None of it mattered anymore. I didn't matter anymore. My long red hair hung in front of my eyes. A tangle of curls. I didn't want anyone to see me. Not after I'd let Sebastian die. It was all my fault. If only I had paid more attention, been faster. I could have saved him.

Something laughed. It was hidden in shadow.

Ever since Sebastian had died, I'd been inviting the darkness in. I couldn't help it. I let the shadows slip through our wards. A tiny part of me whispered, *Don't look.* It might have been the last of my sanity, trying to protect me. My eyes didn't listen and shifted to the shadow that the lilac tree cast beside me. The shadow darkened and shimmered.

"Sebastian died because of you. You don't deserve Alistair. You don't deserve to live." From the shadow came a rich and compelling male voice.

I felt it in my bones: The shadow was right.

The words slipped from my lips. "I don't deserve Alistair. I don't deserve to live."

"They are going to have to lock you away. You'd better end it quickly."

"End it quickly. Yes." It made sense. This world without Sebastian—I couldn't stay here. "But how?"

The wind chimes echoed over my head.

"One deep cut is all it would take," the shadow voice said.

"I heal too quickly. The ring won't let me bleed to death."

"Take the ring off. It can't help you if you don't let it." The voice sounded so reasonable, I barely noticed the excitement echoing in each word.

I tried to slide the ring off, but I couldn't. The star sapphire glowed at me. "It's stuck."

The shadow swirled and writhed. "You selfish girl. You think you can keep living after you let him die?" The anger in his tone sliced through what remained of my heart.

"I don't want to live. I can't." I had failed Sebastian. The pain was too much. I hurt every minute of every day. And it was getting worse. My mind…my mind was shattering. I could feel myself slipping away. There was nothing I could do to stop it: I was going insane.

"Soon all that will remain is a screaming, drooling remnant of what you were. You won't be able to help anyone. You'll be everything you fear."

I couldn't let that happen to me. I wouldn't.

"When they put you away tonight, you know what you have to do." His certainty clung to me.

I nodded. It all made sense.

Tonight, I'd end the madness. Tonight, I had to die.

And then everything dissipated.

Now, I stood in the woods huddled together with Evan and Morgan. Their faces were dirty and bloodied. Bruised and beaten. A battle had been lost. Worry carved lines across Morgan's forehead. Doubt snuck into Evan's eyes. They promised to keep me safe. Their words were tinged with desperation and hope. They would do anything for me, but it wouldn't be enough.

And then the scene shifted again.

I stood alone in front of a grave.

The gray stone was inscribed: To the Valiant One, Katarina Langley.

I was dead. I had failed everyone.

I heard someone weeping. Morgan materialized in front of my grave. Evan stood beside her. They lived. I tried to tell them it would be okay, but they couldn't see me.

In the distance, I saw Toria. I ran to her. I begged her to tell me what happened. Toria didn't say a word. She just reached out and tore the ring from my hand.

I sat up, gasping. Coughing and sputtering as if hundreds of pounds of dirt had been piled onto my chest.

"What happened?" Vivian was right there beside me on the couch.

I buried my face in her shoulder. "I was Toria. I saw...I heard...It was awful..."

That voice in the shadows had been Pastor Fitzgerald's ghost. He had convinced Toria to end her life.

Vivian rubbed my back. "It's all right. Everything is all right."

"But it isn't. Nothing is." She needed to understand. "No matter what I do, things just get worse." The starkness of what I'd seen slipped into my voice. "I was at my own grave. Toria took back the ring."

"You can't see the future, dear." Vivian held me closer, wrapping me in reassurance. "That's just the fear and anxiety taking over. No one has been able to do what you did. You're the one we've been waiting for. The one the prophecy promised us. You went back in time and changed the past. My darling girl, you grabbed the Radcliffe rubies back from our enemies."

"What are you talking about? I just picked them off the ground in Cassie's room in 1886."

"The rubies disappeared in 1886 and we believe our enemies stole them. We spent decades trying to locate them, but we couldn't. The Radcliffes wouldn't have them back if it weren't for you."

"Why do your enemies want the Radcliffe family heirloom too?"

Vivian adjusted her glasses. "Our enemies seek to undo the good that our alliance has done. We have made things lighter and safer in the world. There are those who want to make the world a darker, less safe place. Taking our heirlooms weakens us. It's what has allowed them to win for years. You're the one who turned the tide back in our favor this summer."

I sat up on the couch and tucked the blanket around me. "I don't understand."

Jacqueline walked in the room as if she was here to dispense knowledge and no one was stopping her. "We have come up with a plan to keep building on what you did." She glanced at Vivian. "It's time we tell her."

"She needs to rest more," Vivian said.

Jacqueline folded her arms and leaned against the wall. "If last night taught us one thing, it's that we don't have the luxury of time, Vivian."

I looked from Vivian's scowl to Jacqueline's smile. "Please tell me."

"You know the Radcliffes have their ruby necklace, and you have the star sapphire ring?" Jacqueline took a seat in the nearest armchair.

I turned to face her. "Family heirlooms."

"The Mallorys and the Kingsleys also had family heirlooms, but they were separated from them ages ago. When they lost their heirloom, their power was greatly diminished, and the alliance between our four families was weakened," Jacqueline said. "You see, these heirlooms are actually amulets, powerful magical objects that protect each family. The Mallorys had a bracelet that rendered them invisible. The Kingsleys had an emerald dagger that made them much stronger than they are now. The Kingsley heir was the ultimate warrior and guardian of the Radcliffes."

"Almost unkillable," Vivian said.

"Can anyone inherit the dagger?" I asked.

"The dagger goes to the strongest person born in each generation. It's usually a combination of physical, mental, and emotional strength. A clever businessman can be picked over a burly football player," Jacqueline said. "Usually it's a man, but there were a few women who wielded the dagger over the centuries. The Kingsley ancestors choose the heir and the dagger will only work for the heir. It protects him. It strengthens him. When the heir uses the dagger, the slightest cut can sever the tie between body and soul. In any other hands, though, it's just a dagger." There was an unexpected note of awe in Jacqueline's voice.

It made me realize just how special the dagger was. "So, who has the dagger now?"

"It disappeared in 1831, and no one has seen it since. But the current heir needs it desperately." Jacqueline's gaze rose towards the ceiling.

A terrible thought crushed me. "Evan?"

"I saw it in his palm." Vivian shifted closer to me, like her nearness could help me. "He's the Kingsley heir."

All this time, I'd thought that I'd dragged him into my mess, but it had always been *our* mess. I just hadn't known it. "Does he know?"

"I've spoken to him." Jacqueline leaned forward. "With the dagger, he is strong enough to protect you and Joshua from physical harm. Without it, he can barely protect himself, let alone either of you."

Her words pinched my heart. "He's still in danger?"

"He will die saving you. That is his destiny." Vivian's lips thinned with sympathy.

I felt like I was going to float out of my body. I clutched the blanket. "Is there any way to change his destiny?"

"You did last night," Jacqueline said.

"You bought him more time," Vivian admitted.

"The future can always be changed." Jacqueline held up her palms. "How many times have the lines changed on my hands, Vivian?"

"A few." Vivian said it like she was loath to admit it.

Clearly the ability to change the future wasn't something they agreed on. But I had more important questions. "How do I save Evan?"

"You need to get that dagger back in his possession," Vivian said.

"How do I find it?"

"Percy Kingsley was the last Kingsley to have it in 1831."

"Percy?" His name was popping up way too much lately.

"Yes, Percival Kingsley was the third son." Vivian spoke quickly in her excitement to share the family lore. "Some were surprised that the dagger went to him, because his older brothers were physically much stronger than he was. But he had a way of getting out of scrapes without resorting to violence. He had the look of a pirate, too. Wore an eye patch and always had a weapon hidden in his boot."

Percy had lost an eye. My dream came back to me. The man with one eye. His dagger. My blood quickened, bouncing off my fingertips and rushing to my brain. "The Kingsley dagger, does it have an emerald in the hilt and a triple spiral design with a ruby, diamond, and star sapphire in the sheath?"

"How did you know that?" Jacqueline's perfectly controlled voice went pitchy.

"I had a dream last night. I think I was Percy. I had that dagger. Was he protecting Ellie Harding?"

They exchanged a glance. "You have dreams about the past?" Vivian asked.

"Sometimes. Last night, I was him and I think I was Ellie, too. A week ago, Ellie's ghost came to me. She said she didn't kill him and asked me to figure out who did."

"All evidence pointed to her," Jacqueline said.

"That's what Toria said..." My voice trailed off because both great aunts had guarded expressions.

"Ellie and Percy can wait. The dagger has to be your priority right now." Jacqueline's tone left no room for discussion.

So, I let it drop. For now.

"You need to go back in time and retrieve that dagger, like you did with the rubies," Vivian said.

As much as I didn't want to time-travel again, I'd do it for Evan. "Okay."

"We've been working on this plan since you brought the rubies back," Jacqueline said.

"We want to train you, too," Vivian said. "We have so many wards and spells in place here. It's one of the few places we can keep the unwanted unbelievables out. We didn't want anyone to know about our plan or your training."

"How do I get to the dagger?" I asked.

"Evan can help you find Percy when he still had the blade in 1831," Jacqueline said.

"And you want me to take it from Percy?" I would be stealing an amulet from the rightful heir. "It seems wrong."

"He's already lost it. This is your chance to reclaim it for the Kingsleys," Jacqueline said.

"But if I change the past..."

"You already did this summer when you reclaimed the Radcliffe rubies. You can't change everything, but you can make a difference. That's your special ability. The stronger you are, the more you can impact things in the past," Vivian said.

I thought about what that meant. "After you train me, can I go back and save Cassie and Sebastian?" It was my one regret from my trip into the past.

"It's possible," Jacqueline said.

Fear and hope tumbled around in my stomach. I wasn't sure which came out on top. "When do we need to retrieve the Kingsley dagger?"

Jacqueline's dark brown eyes met mine. "You have to do it this weekend."

"Evan can't time-travel. He almost died last night." And if I was being honest, I wasn't sure I was ready to time-travel, either.

"Why do you think I've been healing him all night and day? He'll be fine by dinner," Jacqueline said. "After last night's attack, you can't leave Dumbarton without the dagger. It's too dangerous for both of you."

"Why don't we stay here a week and then time-travel when we are both stronger?" I asked.

Jacqueline shook her head. "The moon and stars are in the perfect alignment for you to safely travel back in time without the Dark One catching you. If we wait, he may be able to sense what you're doing and stop you. You must time-travel this weekend."

Vivian rubbed her pointer finger and thumb together nervously. "Time traveling requires a great deal of energy."

I crossed my arms. "Energy Evan and I don't have."

"We hadn't expected you to arrive here near death," Jacqueline said.

"You're not alone in this, though. I should have enough power to open a portal. That, at least, we can spare you," Vivian said.

I wished I felt as confident as Vivian sounded.

Chapter 14

Vivian promised to explain more about the families' connections during her tour of Dumbarton. The large manor house was much older than the mansions of Newport, but it still reminded me of Rosecliff—my grandmother's favorite. Here, on the main floor, the windows were slender pairs of doors with a crescent of glass at the top. According to Jacqueline, there were two floors for Vivian and her and then the servants' quarters on the upper level. Seth would approve of that design choice.

Seth. Evan and I had been so caught up in everything that happened since we'd gotten off that train last night. I bet Evan hadn't checked in with Seth because I had completely forgotten to check in with Morgan.

In the middle of the house tour, I pulled out my phone. "Can I text my friends that I arrived okay?"

"Certainly," Vivian said.

"Just don't mention anything we've talked about here," Jacqueline said.

"I won't."

On my phone, I had seven texts from Morgan and three voicemails. I skimmed the texts. She was worried and mad and frustrated and wanted a response ASAP. I fired off a text to her apologizing and saying Evan and I were fine and had terrible cell reception. I promised we'd talk when we got back. I sent a quick *we're fine* text to Seth too. Then I turned my phone off and got to know my family home.

The main section of the house was built around the enclosed courtyard. The living room where I'd napped looked out on the front yard and so did the parlor across the foyer.

We walked by the central courtyard to the back of the house, where the kitchen and dining room were. The dining room had dark green wallpaper with an intricate, repeating pattern and a table that stretched the entire length of the room. "This table could easily seat thirty people."

"One evening, it seated fifty." Vivian sounded like she longed for that time. "My parents threw lavish dinner parties here. The house was so full of life back then."

"When did the house become so quiet?"

"It happened slowly. And then it felt like it had always been this way. Only photos remain to remind us otherwise." She brushed her fingertip across the corner of her eye.

Jacqueline herded us back to the central corridor and walked quickly into the east wing, like she was trying to usher Vivian away from the memories.

Vivian saw me peeking in the library and said, "This is our next stop."

I stepped inside. Floor-to-ceiling glass cabinets were built into all four walls. Several large leather chairs with footstools were scattered around the room for hours of uninterrupted reading. I couldn't help checking out the titles. While I moved around the room, Jacqueline and Vivian hovered in the corner in front of another bookcase. Curious, I made my way over to them. As I got closer, the bookcase behind them faded into the wall, and a rounded metal door appeared in its place. It looked like it belonged in a dungeon in the Middle Ages.

"Where did this come from?" I reached out to touch the door and hesitated, unsure what it might do to me.

"It only becomes visible when we need to open it," Jacqueline said.

I snatched my hand back from the magical door. "Where does it lead?"

"To the heart of the house. A place where our greatest magic resides. We've been guarding it for decades." Vivian gave me a reassuring smile. "It will help you understand your powers better and shed more light on the ties between all our families."

Vivian touched the door and whispered words I couldn't place. The locks slid back and the door popped open.

My mouth formed a silent O. I shouldn't be surprised by magic, but I still was.

When we stepped inside, the nearest wall torch flared to life to light our way. The stone stairwell spiraled down into the depths of the manor house. There was no railing, so I slid my palm along the rough stone wall for balance as I followed them.

After we'd gone down a dozen or so stairs, I heard the door slam shut with a resounding finality. I jerked and looked behind me. The way back was bathed in darkness because the first torches had extinguished themselves. My only choice was to continue my descent. The stairs went deeper and deeper and deeper. I felt like we were several stories below ground by the time we finally reached the bottom. It was dark and dank and disorienting. The air clutched at my skin like a frightened child.

Jacqueline led us down a long stone corridor. Every few minutes, another corridor intercepted ours and led off to who knew where. Jacqueline turned and wove a twisted path through the underground maze. Vivian followed her, with me trailing close behind. They obviously knew this house as well as they knew themselves.

Finally, we came to another door. This time Jacqueline stepped aside. So did Vivian. They gestured for me to step forward.

I stood there, staring at the door. It was a greenish-blue metal and had an hourglass sculpted on it. Carved above the hourglass was a crescent moon and below the hourglass was a sun.

I looked from Vivian to Jacqueline, bewildered. "What am I supposed to do?"

"Open this door. It protects the family's power," Jacqueline said.

There wasn't a knob or a handle. No keyhole. Nothing. "How?"

"Touch the door. Let it know who you are and why you are here," Vivian said.

Nothing like major existential questions. I pressed my palm against the cold metal door. Who was I? Katarina Preston. Now Katarina Langley. I was a girl who spoke to ghosts and helped them with their reckonings. I was the Langley heir. A time traveler who changed the past. The one who protected the Radcliffes from supernatural harm.

Why I was here? That was complicated. I wanted to find out who my family was. I was supposed to help Evan by returning the Kingsley dagger to him. And I needed training to use my powers to protect Joshua, Evan, and everyone else I cared about. I chewed on my lip and stared at the door. Was that enough? Was there more I had to tell it?

Suddenly, the hourglass came to life. The sand began flowing in reverse from bottom to top. When it was full, the door sprang open.

Inside was a round stone room with three mirrors mounted on the wall, evenly spaced. Each mirror sat in a unique rectangular frame with a coat of arms above it. On the floor, another coat of arms had been laid out in the stones.

I was trying to guess which coat of arms belonged to which family when Jacqueline spoke. "The mirrors are portals to the homes of the Radcliffes, the Mallorys, and the Kingsleys. Each mirror faces in the direction of that family's home. And, at each family home, there is a mirror facing toward the mirror here."

"So, every family can travel to each others' homes?"

"Not exactly," Jacqueline corrected me. "They can only come here. But, from here, they can travel to the other homes."

Vivian must have seen the confusion on my face because she added, "We are the hub for the portals. The other families' homes are spokes."

"These mirrors connect to the family homes in Connecticut," Jacqueline said.

"But Evan's family is originally from Wales," I said. "Why is everything based here in Connecticut?"

"The Mallorys are the only ones who can answer that question." Jacqueline sounded dissatisfied with her own answer.

"Evan's family home is Ravenhurst," Vivian said. "It's hidden in the hills of eastern Connecticut, in Ashbury."

I stared at the mirrors, trying to process all this new information. "Is that why Toria's mirror had to stay in Cassie's room at Castle Creighton?" Toria had not liked that Cassie had been given her room, her mirror, and her Sebastian.

"It was magically anchored to that wall for the Radcliffes so that it would always be a portal back here," Jacqueline said.

"It's like an escape hatch for the families in times of danger or trouble." Vivian had a way of simplifying things.

I flashed back to Sebastian and Cassie's wedding night. "Sebastian and Cassie went into the mirror after they had been poisoned. But it didn't transport them here. It trapped them."

"The curse must have twisted the mirror's magic." Vivian's fingers curled into fists.

"But Toria told me that she didn't know how Sebastian used the portal. Wouldn't she know about these mirrors?" I tried to make sense of the conflicting information I had on the mirrors.

Jacqueline cleared her throat. "She did. We asked her to let us explain in person about the mirrors."

Another lie. I was drowning in well-intentioned lies from the Langleys. I stuffed down my outrage and decided to get as many answers as I could.

My eyes drifted to the mirror in front of me. On closer inspection, I could see that the frame had the same compass-rose design as the mirror in Cassie's room at Castle Creighton. "Does that mirror lead to Castle Creighton?"

"Indeed. That's the Radcliffe coat of arms above it," Vivian said.

While I stared at the coat of arms, Vivian explained what it all meant. The shield was divided into four quadrants. The upper left quadrant contained gold and purple fur for royalty and dignity. The upper right had a purple background to indicate leaders of noble birth. The fox in the forefront was for cunning in battle, but its silver coloring meant it was tempered by wisdom. The lower left section had a ruby for supremacy encased in a solid gold background showing generosity. A symbol indicating that the first-born son was the family's heir sat on a gold field in the lower right area.

Below the shield lay a stag, a loyal follower—the Mallory family. The unicorn and the griffin held the shield aloft. The griffin was a great warrior—the Kingleys; the unicorn, a gifted priestess—the Langleys. A mantle of acacia surrounded the shield. Atop the shield rested a king's helmet for royalty. Above that was the earth line signaling land accumulation. Upon that line sat a dragon for leadership and courage, which supported a king's crown.

I glanced at the other coats of arms and saw the same animals in different positions. Then my eyes came to rest on the mosaic below my feet. The stag and the dragon stood with their backs to the shield illustrating their reliance on the Langley family. The griffin, however, stood beneath the shield carrying it, which meant that the Kingsleys always supported the Langleys.

"What do the green bat and the peacock mean?" I asked.

"Green represents hope and loyalty in love, while the bat means having insight into darkness and chaos. The peacock represents beauty and knowledge." Vivian stared at the floor with reverence.

"And there's the star sapphire ring," I said.

"That star shape represents celestial powers, as well as the stone itself. Blue stands for truth and loyalty."

Staring at my family shield, a heaviness weighed on my chest—an anchor to who I was and a responsibility I couldn't escape. "Is that a lighthouse in that other quadrant?"

"It's more of a beacon. The Langleys are watchful and can foretell times of danger. Do you know what the harp stands for?" Vivian asked.

"Musically inclined?"

She laughed. "Not quite, it's for the link between this life and the next one. According to legend, the Langleys were great healers. They were reputed to bring people back from the brink of death. They also had the ability to understand events and see things that weren't obvious to others. This is why the Radcliffes have always relied on us for counsel."

"So, what type of leaves are surrounding the shield?"

"Woodbine. It signifies love that doesn't injure or harm those it attaches to."

Unless you were Alistair or Sebastian. I couldn't help thinking of poor Toria and what being the Langley heir had cost her: her child, her first love, her true love, her sanity, and, finally, her life. I kept these thoughts to myself.

"The wavy line below the helmet indicates water," Vivian said.

I glanced up at the wall. "The Radcliffe coat of arms had the land line."

"Each family is associated with an element. Water is ours."

I pointed over at the Kingsley coat of arms. "What's theirs?"

"Fire," she said.

Which left air for the Mallorys. I didn't want to think about them, so I asked, "Do you plan to use one of these mirrors to send Evan and me to find the dagger?"

"A Langley can activate any of these mirrors and turn it into a portal. Because your powers are grounded in the past, you can travel back in time with any of them. But you alone can change the past."

I ran my hand over the Radcliffe mirror's frame. "How old are these?"

"We believe the frames were made at the same time as the mirrors. We don't know precisely how old they are, but, because we know who made them, we know that they're at least four hundred years old."

"Who made them?" I asked.

"Lorelei. Do you know who she is?"

I nodded. I'd met her ghost when I time-traveled to 1886. She said the mirrors were made for me. I didn't understand her words then, but I did now.

"Legend has it that she used her tears to create these mirrors as portals through time and space. The Langleys can do more with these mirrors than anyone else because the mirrors are made from our ancestor's tears. We have a special link to all the mirrors. But we also have a mirror that's just for us. It's the most powerful one," Vivian said.

Jacqueline gestured for me to step back. I'd almost forgotten she was there. Once Vivian and I had stepped off the Langley coat of arms, Jacqueline spoke words that I'd never heard before. Then she pulled a blade from the pocket of her navy dress and sliced the index finger of her right hand. When a drop of her blood hit the stones, there was a shudder and a groan and the Langley coat of arms split in two.

A glimmer of light soon revealed itself as a fourth mirror. It was huge and round and surrounded by an ornate silver frame. I saw a compass rose, which reminded me of the Radcliffe rubies, in each of the four cardinal directions. There were triple spirals like I'd seen on the Kingsley dagger, and a many-pointed star that reminded me of my ring. I even recognized the knot pattern from the Mallory mirror.

"This is the Langley mirror. It is only for us to use. Your magic is strong enough to create a portal into the past from any of these mirrors, but this one is much easier to control because it is ours," Vivian explained. "I can use it to send you and Evan on your way."

I nodded.

Jacqueline cleared her throat and I sensed a lecture coming. "Time travel is not an exact science. We can aim for an event in time and try to get you close to it."

Vivian toyed with her pearls. "Percy was in Vienna the last week of his life. We need to send you there to take the dagger from him."

"Why go back so close to his death?" I asked. "Isn't it risky?"

"If we take the dagger from him too early, we alter all the good he did with it. We are trying to bring the dagger back to the present without having a detrimental impact on the past." Jacqueline made it sound obvious.

"But Evan…" I couldn't finish that sentence. If he was in Percy's body, he would die if Percy died. My blood pounded in my ears. I barely heard myself over the noise. "We can't risk, Evan."

"As long as you return before Percy dies, Evan will be fine," Vivian said.

"The whole thing should take less than an hour. Get there, get the dagger, and get back here." Jacqueline's tone demanded obedience. "No meddling in Percy's and Ellie's lives. No dilly dallying there, trying to uncover who killed Percy. Just get the dagger and bring the dagger back here."

Spoken like someone who had never actually tried to fix the past. But I hoped that Jacqueline was right. I hoped that our mission was that easy. I also knew that I was never going to have any peace if I didn't help Ellie. "I would never do anything to risk Evan's life." That was true. But that didn't mean that I wouldn't be looking for clues to who killed Percy while we were trying to find the dagger.

Jacqueline must have heard something she didn't like in my voice, because she threw her hands up in the air and said, "You deal with her, Vivian."

Vivian fixed me with a stare that was not unkind, just terribly serious. "This is a dangerous task, Kat. We wouldn't risk it, if we didn't think that you—and Evan—were entirely too vulnerable without the dagger. And if we didn't know that you'd already successfully completed a trip into the past."

She paused, waiting to make sure that I understood what she was saying.

I nodded.

"When you go through the mirror, you aren't just traveling back in time and staying at Dumbarton. You are crossing the ocean to another continent. There's no mirror waiting for you in Vienna. This necklace will be your portal home." She held up a silver locket.

The front was engraved with the four-headed knot that I recognized from the Radcliffe ruby necklace. On the back was a six-pointed star that looked just like my star sapphire ring.

Vivian opened the locket. Inside was a tiny mirror. "Just a few of Lorelei's tears. This is your only way back to us." She looked at me to make sure that I understood.

I nodded.

Then she put the chain around my neck. She closed the clasp and tugged twice to make sure it was securely fastened.

I fingered the locket and took a couple of pulls myself. It wasn't going anywhere. Or so I hoped. "How do I use it?"

"Just like the other mirrors. A drop of Langley blood will activate the portal. Then you have to focus on where you want to go. Think about Dumbarton. Visualize this room. Picture Jacqueline and me. Feel your desire to come back here, back to us," Vivian said.

"That's how I got back to Castle Creighton, last time."

"Exactly. You know how to do this. Do the same thing again and you'll come straight back to us without any problems." Vivian gave me a bracing smile.

Jacqueline's expression remained mired in doubt.

Chapter 15

Lunch was quiet and quick with Jacqueline excusing herself almost immediately. She said that she had magical work to do, but I suspected that she just wanted to get away from me. She'd barely touched her food before she left the dining room.

I had no appetite for much of anything, let alone poached chicken. Vivian picked at her salad. I thought that she would encourage me to build up my strength, but, instead, she dropped her fork on her plate with a clang and said, "Let's continue. There's so much that you still need to know."

She resumed our tour of Dumbarton. The first stop was the sitting room across the hall from the library. This room was more formal than the other rooms I'd seen so far. Everything was done in cream and gold. The cream-colored wallpaper had a pale peony print. The matching brocade couches and chairs were arranged around an ornate tea table set. Fine bone-china teacups with a delicate blue rose design were set out on the antique silver tray.

Thanks to my grandmother—my mother's mom, the antique dealer—I knew enough to recognize that this was the kind of room in which a lady might receive visitors. I could picture Toria here so vividly that I wondered if I was remembering being here, as Toria. And I couldn't help thinking of Cassie's room at Castle Creighton, a room that had remained locked in time. This room suddenly gave me the same unsettled feeling. A shiver rippled over me. I didn't say anything, though, and Vivian continued the tour.

Jacqueline's conservatory was filled with plants. Overfilled. I took a deep breath, and I was almost overwhelmed. I had always used plants to keep the ghosts at bay, but I had been limited to a dozen plants—mostly cacti and philodendron with the occasional orchid. I wanted to linger here. I would have loved to have learned how Jacqueline used these plants, but, as it turned out, this was where Jacqueline had retreated when she'd left the dining room, and she made it clear that our presence, or my presence, wasn't welcome. So, Vivian and I left the conservatory.

We backtracked through the main section of the house, back to the west wing. On the left, we passed a ballroom whose vaulted ceiling extended two stories. The room had a shiny hardwood floor that went on forever. Vivian paused.

"The dresses, Kat. They were so lovely. I have pictures of my grandmother and my mother at their debutante balls." Vivian's eyes took on a dreamy quality.

When we stepped back into the hallway, I realized we were right near the cheerful breakfast room. Next door to it was the billiard room.

She wandered inside and stroked the green felt table. "This room has hardly been used since my father passed on." Her voice was tinged with sadness.

"I like billiards." I'd played it for years with my grandfather.

"Perhaps it runs in the family." Her eyes brightened.

"Did my dad play?"

"Max was a pool shark." She chuckled like she was remembering one of their games.

Heading back to the main part of the house, we ascended the curved white marble staircase to the second floor. Vivian pointed out her bedroom and Jacqueline's, both doors were closed, and then she continued on.

We passed more rooms that had been unoccupied for years. And then one door snagged my attention. I brushed my fingers against the wood of the door, and I knew. This had been Toria's room.

Vivian knew, too. I could tell. "Can I go in?" I asked.

Vivian seemed uncertain. "There's more I want to show you."

I appreciated Vivian's kindness, and I understood that she was shielding me from the worst of Jacqueline. But I was frustrated. I wasn't just any guest, taking a tour of the house. I was the Langley heir. The Dark One was hunting me, and Vivian and Jacqueline expected me to travel back in time—again—to fetch a lost heirloom. Maybe I deserved to get my way at this point.

And then Vivian said, "Your father's things are stored in the attic. Would you like to see them?"

My first impulse was an enthusiastic "Yes" but then I remembered. "The attic. That's where Toria killed herself, isn't it?"

"Yes, I'm afraid it is. I suppose I could bring a few of your father's things down for you to see." Her voice softened with understanding.

I was so conflicted. I didn't want to go to the attic, but I wasn't going to be satisfied by seeing just a few of my dad's things. I wanted to see it all.

"The window was replaced, of course."

My confusion must have shown. I could see that Vivian regretted her words, but she had no choice, now, but to continue. "The window Toria jumped out of…"

The blood rushed from my head, making it suddenly weightless.

Vivian placed a gentle hand on my shoulder. "You don't have to do this now, Kat."

"Yes," I whispered. "I think I do."

I expected a dirty, dingy attic filled with spiders and mice. I mean, that's what attics usually involve. But evidently not a Langley attic. Everything up here was clean and organized by generation.

There was a beautiful stained glass window at the end of the long room. It made a rainbow on the floor. I expected to be upset, but I wasn't. Whatever had happened to Toria here didn't resonate with me. I felt nothing. I was so relieved.

It took us a few minutes to locate Max and Shannon's trunk. As we sorted through it, I pulled out a program from a Tori Amos concert, stacks of old books—from *L'Etranger* to *C is for Corpse*—and rocks and shells from unknown places. It was so weird to go through someone else's treasures.

I wondered which stuff was Shannon's and which was my dad's, and then I found a Georgetown University sweatshirt. I held it against me, and I knew.

"That was Max's."

I couldn't help myself. I sniffed it, hoping it would have a lingering scent from him, but it only smelled like attic and forgotten memories. Still, I wanted it.

Inside the pocket, I found a ticket stub from a Morcheeba show. It was dated a year before I was born. I wondered if he had taken my mom with him. I had a sudden need to listen to this band's music, like it would somehow bring me closer to him.

Beneath the sweatshirt were a couple of letters addressed to my father. "Can I read them?"

"I don't see the harm in it," Vivian said. "Your aunt Shannon wrote them."

The first envelope wasn't sealed. I pulled out the letter and unfolded it.

Dear Maxmil,

I am training so hard. I want a bright future for our Katarina. But the nightmares keep coming. The more I try, the more failure seems imminent. I feel like I have to run so fast just to stay in place. I am not you. I am losing ground faster than I can retrieve it. The ring should have chosen you. It made a mistake that will cost us everything. I'll keep trying. It's the least I can do for everyone. Please forgive me if I should fail.

Love,

Shannon

The next letter was dated a few months before the ring came to me, which meant it was written toward the end of Shannon's life. The envelope was still sealed. My father had never read this one.

Maxmil,

I only promised to write you. I never promised to mail these letters. I'm not going to cause you more pain. I will deal with things on my own. I will be strong for both of us. But here on this page, I will confess the truth to you.

I'm scared of dying.

Our enemy grows stronger—I can feel it in the pit of my stomach. It sickens me. I am so afraid I will fail and die, leaving the next heir too inexperienced to handle things.

I'm just beginning to understand things. I know it all somehow relates to the amulets. The weakening of each family is all grounded in the past. There is a trigger there. If we can find it, we might be able to save ourselves.

I catch glimpses of Toria, dancing on the edge of my field of vision. She is speaking, but I cannot make out the words. I know it is something dire and I am powerless to prevent it. Something is coming and no one can help me face it.

What is happening to me has nothing to do with me—that's the hardest part. We are mere soldiers in a battle we don't really understand. This is so much bigger than anyone realizes. I feel the approaching evil. It stalks me. I keep running and hiding. Delaying the inevitable. It will find me.

Maxmil, be careful. Be mindful of the shadows and trust your instincts. You will not be able to overcome this. We may be doomed. And my fall will be the worst because I had the time to train, but never the soul of a warrior.

Please forgive me,
Shannon

She had faced our enemy and she had lost. Poor Shannon. She hadn't wanted this for me. None of them had. All of them had tried to stop it from happening to me. But they couldn't.

It was my destiny.

"How can I do better than Shannon? She had all the training." My voice cracked under the enormity of it all.

"She made a deadly mistake. She thought she could handle things on her own. She was wrong. Trust your allies. Rely on them. It can be the difference between life and death." She took the letter in my hand and folded it back up. "I want to show this to Jacqueline."

I was almost at the bottom of the trunk when I found a small wooden box. There was a four-headed knot carved in the lid. The same knot that was on the mirror at Castle Creighton. The same compass rose shape as the Radcliffe ruby necklace.

I held it up. "Was that Shannon's?"

Vivian shook her head. "Max carved that."

"Why this design?"

"It's represents the four families united."

I lifted the lid. Inside there was a photo of my father and my mother holding a baby. Me. Us. Smiling. Happy. Together. It was what I had always wanted.

Chapter 16

When we got back to the second floor of the house, I wanted to tell Evan everything I'd learned about my family, but Vivian insisted he had to rest.

"Feel free to take a look around in Toria's room, but you need more rest, too." Vivian had a way of balancing the things I wanted with the things I needed. It made me instantly like her. She went downstairs, leaving me in front of Toria's door.

I opened the door, and time twisted in on itself. Long red curls bobbed in front of my face. The maid had just finished my hair. Ringlets. It hung in ringlets. And the room looked so much bigger. I glanced down at myself. My hands were tiny.

The walls were pale blue. A sleigh bed, a Victorian dresser, and a bookcase dominated the room. I ran around the bed, laughing. My maid chased after me, but she wasn't quick enough. I slid under the bed, just out of her reach.

"Miss Toria, please come out," she begged. "You have to get dressed."

I was in a nightgown. "I'm not wearing that dress." There was no wiggle room in my tone.

"But your mother said you have to."

I shook my head.

Suddenly, the door burst open. My father—no, Toria's father—stood there, looking stern. "Where is she?"

The maid gestured under the bed. "I'm sorry she's making such a ruckus, sir."

"That's Toria." My father crouched down so we were almost eye-to-eye. His were such a warm cinnamon brown, even when he was annoyed with me. "When will you behave yourself?"

"Tomorrow."

A slow smile spread across his face. "Tomorrow."

I scampered out from under the bed. He chased me around the room. I shrieked and giggled. He scooped me up in his arms.

I blinked and the scene stopped. Toria and her father dissipated into the past.

They must have been spirits, shards of the ghost that repeated a moment without any awareness of anything else. Somehow, they had sucked me into their moment. It had happened once before on the roof at Castle Creighton. I rubbed my forehead, trying to clear my thoughts.

Now it was just me standing in Toria's old bedroom. The walls were painted lavender. The same sleigh bed remained, but with a rather bland gray comforter. The dresser had been replaced with something more practical than pretty. The bookcase was gone and a sturdy wooden desk had taken its place. What did Toria think about the changes?

Cold air rushed across my arm.

I glanced beside me and Toria's ghost stood there in a bright purple walking-out dress with a matching hat, decorated with a bird and feathers, on her head.

She scanned the room and gave a little shrug. "I don't love what they've done with the place, but who am I to complain? The room stopped being mine the day I died."

I flashed back to the dream I had about her in the courtyard. "Pastor Fitzgerald's ghost talked you into killing yourself. How did he break through here? I thought Dumbarton was protected from our enemies?"

"I let him in. I wanted the darkness to come for me. My madness made me self-destructive." Her words came out like a confession—soft, honest, and awful.

"Why did you kill yourself?" She was so strong. I couldn't understand how she gave in to the darkness. And if she couldn't fight it, what chance did I stand?

"I was losing my mind. What he said made sense to me. I thought I had to die. That it was the only way."

"But it wasn't."

"I know that now. But it's too late."

I dropped down on the bed. There was something else I wanted to ask her about. "What's going on with you and Alistair? He was looking for you in the courtyard, but you didn't seem to see him. Didn't you hear me?"

She ran her translucent hand over the end of the sleigh bed and looked away. "You can't help us. No one can."

"But at Castle Creighton, I saw your ghosts together in the garden at night."

Her forehead wrinkled up. "Did we look younger?"

"Yes."

Her forehead smoothed out. "Those were just our spirits."

"So, you can't see his ghost now?"

"No."

"And he can't see yours?"

"No." She didn't say anything else. She didn't have to. The pain in her voice overwhelmed me.

"Can I do anything to help?"

"When a ghost breaks away from the soul, the ghost faces judgment for what we did in this lifetime. My punishment for killing myself is that whatever I loved most in life, I lose in death."

It made an awful sort of sense. The kind you hoped wasn't true, but couldn't dispute. I was pretty sure every religion had a punishment for suicide. "I don't know how, but I will find a way to fix this for you."

"If anyone could, it would be you." She gave me a wistful smile, but her eyes remained hopeless.

I filled her in on what Vivian and Jacqueline had planned for the Kingsley dagger and Evan.

"You can't cast a time travel spell right now." Her face tightened with annoyance.

"We're going to use the Langley mirror. Vivian can cast the spell. Jacqueline is helping her write it."

"Oh, *Jacqueline*. Well, that sets my mind at ease."

I didn't know a ghost could be so sarcastic. "She doesn't seem to like you much, either."

Toria crossed her arms. "She always thinks she knows better than I do. Forget that I've been the heir or been around much longer. She's the most uppity house guardian ever."

"She's the same with me." I wanted to understand the weird friction between them. "What's her problem with you?"

She adjusted her hat. "Jacqueline's powers are connected to the present and the living. I'm dead which means I take energy from the living when I appear. Jacqueline sees me as a necessary evil, but she thinks I shouldn't appear as much as I do."

"Then why don't the wards that protect Dumbarton make it harder for you to appear?"

"They were designed to prevent any who are not family or would do the family harm from coming on our property. I am family and I'm trying to help, so they can't keep me out. Though Jacqueline has tweaked them to limit the time I can appear. Vivian isn't so worried about ghosts. As long as I am not tiring her out, she doesn't mind the occasional visit."

I trusted Toria to tell me the truth. More than either of the great aunts. "Is there any way to leave Evan here where he'll be safe and have me find the dagger by myself?"

"I'm afraid not. If you want to get to Percy, you need Evan. Why?"

I gripped the comforter. "Evan's going to die trying to save me. Vivian saw it. I can't let that happen."

Toria tilted her head. "So, you need to cast a protection spell on him first."

"But I'm not supposed to cast spells for a few days." The strength of my soul was what kept me from disappearing into the past when I traveled through time. And right now, my soul wasn't that strong. A spell would only weaken it further.

Toria tapped her finger against her lips. "This might be something our ancestors could help with."

"Do you think they will, though?" I leaned closer. "They didn't help you save Sebastian, or when Pastor Fitzgerald drove you to take your life."

"They didn't help Sebastian because the threat was to Cassie. She wasn't the Mallory heir, so my ancestors felt no need to intercede. They didn't foresee how it would impact Sebastian. They can't stop the Langley legacy. But this protection spell is different. You and Joshua need Evan to save you and protect the Radcliffes. They just might help this time." She stood up and smoothed her skirt. "I'll ask and let you know."

Chapter 17

I went back to my room and the day caught up with me. Between family revelations and a ghost visit, I needed another nap. I didn't think I would be out for long, but it was dusk when I woke up. I looked at my clock. I'd been asleep for four hours. I stretched. The throbbing in my joints was almost gone. The aches in my muscles were barely there. I felt almost okay again.

Before I went to dinner, I tried to sneak into Evan's room to check on him. As I opened the door, he leapt back.

"That was a near miss," he said.

His face was completely healed. His skin glowed with health. He wore khakis and a dark green polo shirt. His eyes looked more green than brown with that shirt on. There was no sign of what had happened to him the night before.

"You're okay." Relief coursed through me. Without thinking, I threw myself into his arms and pressed my face into his shoulder. I smelled his cologne—it was woodsy with a hint of pine and amber. I'd missed that smell. "I'm sorry you got hurt."

He hugged me back. "I'm fine. I couldn't let you get killed." Something caught in his voice.

I was still hugging him. And he was still hugging me. I stepped back—awkwardly. "Don't scare me like that again."

He gave me a half-smile. "I'll do my best."

I ran my fingers up and down my thigh. "So, Jacqueline told you—"

He pushed his hair off his forehead. "I'm the Kingsley heir. So, I guess we are truly in this together."

"I guess so." My voice went husky. "Are you sure you're up for time travel? We can wait another day or two."

"I've been resting constantly." He looked me up and down, and quirked an eyebrow. "Are you up for this?"

"I'm feeling better."

"We can wait."

"No." The sooner we did it, the sooner he would be safe.

I didn't tell him about the protection spell that Toria was asking the ancestors about. He'd just take more foolish risks to save me and that spell was the last thing I could do to save him.

I moved restlessly around his room and rambled on about my dad and my aunt Shannon. He listened without interrupting, as if he knew that each word hurt.

When I was done, he said, "I'm so sorry, Kat."

"At least, I know my dad cared." I always thought I didn't matter. That I was nothing to him. Worse than nothing. I was the nuisance that he ran from.

Now, I knew he had been trying to save me. But all the years we lost out on—they were wasted. I was still the Langley heir. We could have had seventeen years of making memories together.

Evan reached for my hand. "We'll get through this."

"What if we don't?"

He slid his fingers through mine and squeezed. "We do impossible things together, remember?"

"If anything happens to me, be careful." I tried to sound brave, but my voice quivered. I didn't want my life to be over. Not for a long time.

He tightened his grip on my hand. "Nothing is going to happen to you." He said it like a vow. "You're going to do so much with your life. You've just got to get through a few more things first."

Somehow, I didn't see a happy ending in my future. The Langley heir was destined for death. The only way to get through this was to think about who I could save and who I could protect before death came for me.

Dinner in the breakfast room was weird, but I managed to make it even weirder. I kept staring at Evan, grateful to have him alive. The first few times he caught me, he nodded or smiled. Then he started tossing looks of concern and confusion my way. I dropped my gaze to my plate of steak and salad.

Evan cleared his throat. "So, the dagger will make me almost unkillable?"

"It will make you much stronger and protect you from harm," Vivian said.

"Does Joshua have a special power like us?" I asked.

"In a way. You will feel the call to defend him and follow him. He could inspire legions to do his bidding. The coat of arms shows him descending from royalty, but I couldn't confirm it," Vivian said.

Huh. So that was why he held so much sway over me. And probably why Mom was so quick to forgive him. I would have loved to talk more about all the abilities that ran through each of the families, but we had the whole time travel thing coming up. "I've been talking to Toria about stuff."

"What's she stirred up now?" Jacqueline's voice was laced with suspicion.

"You know she's a part of my soul?" I asked.

"The part that broke away lifetimes ago. The part you don't need." Jacqueline placed her fork on her plate, like she was preparing to argue.

Vivian shot her a quelling look. "She was one of the strongest of the Langleys."

"Doesn't mean I have to like her ghost," Jacqueline said.

"I get why you have an issue with ghosts. I do." I clenched my fork and knife in my hands. "But Toria's not like other ghosts. She's given me more than she's ever taken from me. She's been there for me when no one else in this family was."

Jacqueline's face froze. I wasn't sure if it was shock or anger. But it was scary. "The ancestors sent her to you. We've been the ones watching over you all these years. Us." She gestured at her and Vivian. "Us."

Vivian winced. "Her powers are grounded in the past, Jacqueline. The girl will always see ghosts differently than you do."

Jacqueline stood up and pressed her hands on the table. "Neither of you understand. The ghosts leech energy from the living. Toria's visits are preventing you from healing completely."

"I feel pretty good, actually. Another night's sleep and I should be fine to time-travel tomorrow." I made my voice more confident than I felt.

Jacqueline's eyes burned mine. "You're already weakened. If we push you, you won't be able to do what needs to be done. You will fail."

Before I could respond, Evan asked, "Do you think the Dark One sent that car to weaken her? Could he somehow know what you were trying to do?"

Jacqueline sat back down. "I think he sent it to test her. He wanted to see what she was capable of. And he learned how vulnerable you both are."

"I think we're all impressed by what she did." There was a warmth in Evan's voice that made my cheeks go hot. "And she couldn't have done it without Toria."

Jacqueline gave him a venomous look. He didn't seem to care and continued to eat his steak.

After dinner, I rushed back to my room and shut the door. Then I called out to Toria. She appeared quickly.

"What did the ancestors say?" I asked.

"A protection spell has been cast over Evan by two Langley priestesses."

I relaxed. "We are going back in time tomorrow morning."

"Be careful, Kat. We need you and Evan."

"I will. And thanks for helping."

"Just make sure both of you come back."

I reached for her ghost hand. It was cold, and my own hand went through it. But I think she knew what I was trying to do. "When I get back, I'll find a way to fix things for you and Alistair. You're family, Toria. And I love you."

"I love you too, Kat." Her eyes filled with such affection that I almost forgot she was a ghost. "But I have to go so I don't make tomorrow harder on you."

"I'll see you soon."

"Soon."

I got into bed, certain that I couldn't fall asleep. My thoughts churned. My short future. Shannon's death. Evan's safety. Toria's punishment. Lives—and afterlives—depended on me. People needed me to fix things. My head started to ache with actualities.

And then everything disappeared. I disappeared.

I was Toria, standing in the attic at Dumbarton. It was lunch time, but I ignored my growling stomach. This was too important. My red hair cascaded over my face as I stared at my shiny shoes. I couldn't be more than six. The question hung in the air, was I willing to swear my allegiance to them? I looked up into Alistair's hazel eyes and thought about why I shouldn't. Then I turned to Sebastian and sank into his blue-green eyes.

My decision was clear.

Without question, I solemnly swore to keep the Radcliffes and Kingsleys safe. Alistair had already sworn his loyalty to Sebastian and me. We sealed our pact by carving our initials into the wall along with the Ogham script for fidelity and protection. We were of one mind that day: Our only goal being to stay together forever.

We didn't realize this wasn't just a childhood moment. It was a bond our families had shared for centuries. And we were just one more turn of the cosmic wheel. We were nothing in the grand scheme of things.

We didn't know it then, but we would soon.

Suddenly, everything shifted.

I was inside a secret passageway. I could see and hear everything that was happening in the formal sitting room at Dumbarton. And I was still Toria, but older. I had snuck out of my room.

Alistair sat on the couch next to my mother and begged, "Let me take her away from here."

My father stood by the fireplace, staring into the flames with a shuttered expression. "It's too late. The insanity is already setting in."

"I'll take her to the elders back in Scotland. There has to be something they can do," Alistair said.

My mother's eyes had a spark of hope. "Do you think—"

My father cut her off. "There is no point. No one can help her. We either kill her or lock her away and watch her lose her mind."

"There has to be another way." Alistair approached my father. "I won't let you do this to her."

"We never wanted this for her. For either of you." My father rested his hand on Alistair's shoulder. "Son, I'm afraid this is for your own good."

My father started chanting in Scottish Gaelic. I knew those words. A banishment spell. *No. Not Alistair.*

Alistair fought it. He tried to stand his ground, but the spell pushed him out the door. He would never be allowed to set foot on this property again.

I cried out, "No!"

But it was done.

They had driven Alistair away, and he was all I had left. As soon as they sent him away, the shadows started coming for me. They begged me to give into the pain and end it. There was no one left to fight for.

I'd never felt such despair. The loss threatened to consume me.

And then everything went purple.

I was somewhere else, shrouded in gray mist. There was nothing to hold onto. In the distance, I saw flickers of light. They reminded me of lightning bugs. Except they seemed to be moving very fast, and in my direction. Before I could move out of the way, tiny rays of light crashed into my body and ripped through my skin. I cried out. It felt like my mind was exploding. I was dying. And I couldn't save them. Any of them. It was the worst way to die. Knowing that those I loved would be next.

Chapter 18

By noon, Evan and I stood in the chamber of mirrors hidden beneath the house. The dark stone walls smelled of earth and power. While Vivian prepared the spell's ingredients at a giant table, Jacqueline finished examining Evan and me.

"They should be fine," she told her sister.

Vivian gave a quick smile and continued grinding the herbs with a mortar and pestle.

"You still have the necklace?" Jacqueline's voice was tight.

I pulled it from beneath my T-shirt and held it up for her to see.

"Check the clasp," she told Evan.

Since it was our only way back here, he did as she asked. His fingers were warm against my skin. They lingered on the nape of my neck for a second, sending tingles across my back.

All too soon, Vivian gestured for Evan and me to step off the Langley coat of arms on the floor. She cut her finger and pressed it to the stone floor to get the stones to move aside and reveal the Langley mirror.

Jacqueline tucked my necklace under my shirt and took me by the shoulders. "You must retrieve the dagger and come back as quickly as you can." A fierce intensity flared in her eyes. "Percy's death date is September 7, 1831. Evan must be out of his body before he dies or Evan's soul will be trapped in 1831, disappearing forever."

All we had to do was get the dagger and come back. I wanted to help Ellie—and I would if I had the chance—but I wasn't going to do anything that might endanger Evan. "I understand. We'll be quick."

"Are you sure you're ready?" Vivian asked.

I nodded.

Vivian brushed a kiss across my cheek. "Be careful, my dear."

Then she stepped back and started the spell. I let her do the work. She sprinkled the herbs on the mirror and spoke ancient words.

Vivian handed me a blade.

My blood was required to activate the mirror and Evan's was needed to bring us back to Percy. I hated the sight of my own blood, but it was essential for the spell. I sliced into my palm and let my blood drip onto the mirror. Nausea rose up in me. I swayed, but Evan caught my arm.

His eyes told me he'd stop this if I needed him to.

"I'm okay," I whispered.

Evan cut his hand. His blood dripped onto the mirror, mingling with mine.

We grasped hands. Blood to blood.

The mirror began to pulse. Vivian's voice deepened, reverberating through me as she called out to Percy Kingsley, reaching across time and space so that he would respond and lead Evan and me to the right moment and the right place.

She wasn't alone. Several Langley ancestors suddenly appeared around us. Julia. Lorelei. The little girl. A man I'd never met. They came to lend their power and help Vivian.

Their voices merged. It was an ancient song. Of love and family. Of regret and sacrifice. The mirror liquefied beneath my feet. I started to sink into it. I was going back in time.

I held on to Evan's hand, praying this would work. That we would do what needed to be done and get back safely.

Chapter 19

I couldn't hear, smell, touch, or see anything. I knew from past experience that this would happen but it was still unnerving. I hated the moments spent waiting to figure out where I was and who I was. If things had gone right, I should be in Ellie's body. It would be weird to be an eleven-year-old again. I wondered what power she'd have. I kept flashing back to her ghost with those big, moss-green eyes and curtains of light brown hair. She didn't look like a killer, except for the blood smeared on her dress.

I couldn't imagine killing someone now, let alone as a small child. Taking a life was such a terrible act. I didn't understand how the Dark One could hate me so much that it had issued my death declaration. Knowing how horribly Shannon died and how Pastor Fitzgerald tormented Cassie, I assumed the Dark One would torture me. Vivid images played out in my mind. Razors slashing open my skin. A mallet to smash the tiny bones in my fingers. Me, bound to the rack and stretched until the cartilage, joints, and finally bones snapped.

Suddenly, I wish I hadn't paid so much attention in history class when we covered the Spanish Inquisition.

I couldn't take it. I had to force my thoughts elsewhere. They jumped to my fear of all the things I might never do. I hadn't had a serious boyfriend yet. I always figured there would be time for that later.

I'd pictured us meeting in college and bonding over our love of Ralph Waldo Emerson and Jane Austen. Drinking lattes and espressos, we'd debate the critical causes of the fall of the Qing dynasty before we spent a summer backpacking through Asia.

There was so much more I wanted to do, see, and understand before I died. I promised myself that I'd make more time for fun. I'd even let myself get into more trouble with Morgan. I'd do all the stuff I thought I'd do later, because later might not come. For now, though, there was one thing I was absolutely determined to do: I was going to stay alive long enough to meet my dad.

It felt like days passed before my senses started to return. They crept over me slowly, and then cascaded into my brain. I had to sort through so many sensations. It took me a while to realize that I was slumped over. Muscles cramped and ached from being in that position too long.

Finally, I got my eyes open. Something was off with my vision. It was crisp, but it felt like I was missing something. I couldn't figure out what it was. And then something even weirder distracted me.

The room was dark. A darkness no normal person could see through. But my vision wasn't normal anymore. I saw the outline of everything in the room. Toria would probably call it an aura. The furniture was blue. Cold. Inanimate. The embers in the fireplace had burned down. There was a flicker of yellow there. A tiny bit of heat remained.

This was crazy. How could I see this stuff?

I was still dizzy from the time travel. I clutched the armrests of the chair and tried to get accustomed to this new body. It was excruciatingly sensitive. Hyper-aware of everything. It wasn't just my sight that was more powerful, but my hearing, too. I heard every little sound. Every breath taken in the room. Mine grew shallow from anxiety. It echoed off the walls and then I realized that it wasn't an echo. The breaths came twice as fast as mine. I wasn't alone. I scanned the room until I saw a tiny form huddled behind a chair in the corner, giving off a bright red aura. Definitely human, and a child. Before I could figure out who it was, my senses were swamped with more sounds.

The clatter of hooves on the street below beat against my skull. The tinkling of the person in the next room relieving himself in a chamber pot was so loud, I swore he was standing right next to me. I recoiled from that image. I heard a drunk gentleman stumbling down the hallway. His walking stick slammed into the carpet at uneven intervals. It was all that kept him upright. That and the wall he kept bouncing off.

Everything was so loud. No one could ever sneak up on me with this supersonic hearing. It was too much sight and sound all at once. I closed my eyes and pressed my hands to my ears to block it all out. Then I took a few deep breaths and tried to calm down.

I needed to take it one thing at a time. First, I had to figure out whose body I was in. I lit the candle on the table beside me and got a clear look at what I was wearing. Black leather boots covered my feet. Black pantaloons hugged my thighs—which were way more muscular than they used to be.

I wore a dark gray waistcoat embroidered with silver. Beneath it was a white cotton shirt. I reached for my neck and felt a cravat. A crumbled mess of a cravat. My hands went to my chest. It was completely flat. I looked back down at my pants. There was more there than there used to be. I wasn't a girl; I was a guy. Definitely not Ellie Harding. My pulse sped up like a rollercoaster descending into the unknown. Whose body had I fallen into?

Panic swarmed. Suddenly, my cravat felt too tight. I couldn't breathe. I yanked off the cravat and unbuttoned my shirt. Now, I had enough air. *Calm down, Kat. You'll figure this out.* I pressed my palm against my chest, trying to slow my heart down.

Underneath all the fabric, I felt something hard and oval-shaped. I pulled it into my line of sight. It was a locket with a slight orange aura like it was almost alive. I examined it carefully. The Langley star sapphire was emblazoned on the back and the Radcliffe compass rose was etched into the front. It was the same silver locket Vivian had given me. At least, I could get home. But first, I had to figure out who I was, where I was, and what had happened to Evan.

This room looked a little familiar. Like I'd seen it before, but I wasn't sure when. The more I tried to remember, the harder it was. And I needed to remember.

I got up gingerly, grabbed my candle, and searched for a mirror. The bed beside me was empty, but the covers were tossed about as if someone had had a nightmare. Something tugged at the corner of my mind. My feverish dream during my first night at Dumbarton. *Ellie.* That bed was where Ellie had slept in my dream.

I was in the right place. But was it the right time?

I made my way to the washstand in the back corner of the room and searched for a mirror. There were towel rails on one side and a tile backsplash. A basin. A jug of water. Some soap. A lidded chamber pot. That was it. No mirror. Not even a tiny handheld mirror. How would anyone know if she'd washed her face clean?

I continued my search of the room by candlelight. Above the fireplace, something glinted at me. I headed toward it and found a mirror mounted on the wall. I stepped close enough to see my reflection and gasped. None of me remained. Not even my eyes.

I wore an eye patch over my left eye. That explained the weird vision. Well, the feeling like something was missing, anyway. It didn't explain the auras I saw. My remaining eye was labradorite-colored like Evan's. Dark stubble covered my jaw. I had wild brown hair that grew just past my ears. I wasn't just a guy: I was Percy Kingsley.

My fingers trembled against my lips. His lips.

I had the Langley locket, but I wasn't in a Langley body. I swallowed. My Adam's apple bobbed in my throat. Percy's throat. What on earth had happened?

I turned and my candle dimly lit the area around me. There was a couch, chairs, and a coffee table in front of me. A single-breasted black frock coat was draped over one of the chairs. It had to be Percy's. And if I was Percy, I wasn't here alone. Ellie was here, too.

The child behind the chair. I slapped myself in the forehead. That was where Evan should be appearing soon. I heard her hiccup. And then my consciousness was pushed aside.

Without thinking, Percy looked down at his dagger's sheath and hilt. The star sapphire didn't glow, so it wasn't a supernatural threat. The emerald in the hilt didn't sparkle, so it wasn't a physical threat. A quick glance around assured him that there was only one other person in the room: Ellie. Her bed was rumpled and empty. It had a green glow. She'd been out of bed for longer than she should be.

A shadow pulsed red behind the chair. He recognized the huddled form immediately.

"Ellie, what's wrong?" His deep voice had a hint of a Welsh accent.

There was a quick hiccup and then another. Ellie always got the hiccups when she had a nightmare. The little girl flew out of the shadows and into his arms. She trembled, like a terrified puppy in a storm.

He held her close. "It's going to be all right."

"No, it's not, Percy." Her voice was muffled against his chest, and her Scottish accent thickened with her fear.

"Shhh. You shouldn't be out of bed." He pressed his hand to her forehead. It was cooler than before. Maybe the fever had broken. Still, she needed to rest. "How do you feel?"

She kept shaking. "Scared."

He picked her up and carried her back to bed. He tucked the blankets around her and sat down beside her. Her eyes remained wide open, like she couldn't bear to go back to her dreams.

She was so young. Too young to be dragged into his world. Her powers hadn't had time to develop. Her sister Sarah was the Langley heir. She swore Ellie could be a good spell caster someday. Just not now. And maybe never, if the ring chose Ellie.

I kept eavesdropping on Percy's thoughts, hoping to learn more about their relationship so I could help Ellie's ghost in my time.

Ellie had drawn on all her power and used Sarah's necklace to get them here. She'd done it. But it had taken everything she had. She'd been in bed with a fever this week, while he searched for the one person who might be able to save them all.

Ellie was trying to save her sister and Percy was trying to save the both of them. That's how they'd ended up in Vienna together. I puzzled over that piece of information.

He stared into Ellie's eyes. They were clearer than they had been. The trip hadn't done any lasting harm to her. He relaxed. "What happened?"

"I left my body and my soul went home." She said it with such longing. "I had to check on Sarah."

That must be Ellie's special ability: astral projection.

"It's all right." He stroked her hair.

He hated that they had to leave Sarah there, but they had no choice. This was what Sarah wanted and you didn't deny a woman's dying request. It was also why Percy had taken Ellie with him.

I could see in Ellie's eyes how much she trusted Percy. Why would she kill him? None of this made any sense.

"I was at her bedside." Ellie hesitated, fiddling with her covers.

Percy took her little hand in his. "Tell me what you saw."

"It's very hard for her to breathe. She can't speak. It's like a mountain is sitting on her chest." A tremor wove through her words. "Percy she's hurting terribly. She can't take much more."

"I know." He'd seen it in Sarah's eyes before they left. She would hold on as long as she could to give him time to save Ellie. But she would suffer. He didn't want this for Sarah. He didn't want what she foresaw for Ellie, either. It was why he'd done as Sarah had asked and taken Ellie away to search for a way to save them both.

He slid into bed beside Ellie, gathered her in his arms, and rocked her. "There's nothing you can do. It's why we had to run. To keep you safe."

"I wanted the ring, but not like this. Never like this." Ellie's tears wet his shirt. "I never wanted her to die. She's my sister."

Percy stroked her hair and tried to soothe her. "Of course you don't. Sisters fight. Sisters say things. But they are always sisters."

"Percy..." Ellie's voice trailed off. Her eyes widened and then she went limp in his arms.

"Ellie, what's happening?" Was this an aftereffect of her visiting Sarah? Or was something attacking her? He wasn't sure and he couldn't do anything unless he was certain.

If it was a supernatural attack, he'd have to figure out what Sarah would do. Except he couldn't be Sarah. No one could.

He checked his dagger's sheath again. None of the stones glowed, which meant that he and Ellie weren't in any sort of danger—physical or supernatural. He lit the lamp beside the bed to drive away some of the darkness for Ellie. She hated the dark. Most people did. What you couldn't see was scary.

He'd seen too much in the dark.

Her body lay so still. He tried to revive her, but she wouldn't wake up. He pried open one of her eyes. It was dark green and unfocused. What the devil had happened to her?

He had no clue.

But I did. Someone else was joining me here.

Chapter 20

Percy's concern trickled over me. He had no idea what to do to help Ellie right now. He'd trained for every type of battle imaginable, but taking care of an ailing child was beyond him. He stroked her forehead and said her name softly, but she didn't respond. He said her name more forcefully and shook her shoulder, but she remained unconscious.

As he stared down at her, I wished I could tell him this was normal. Time traveling was hard on the traveler and the person whose body was being borrowed. It would be okay. He just had to give it a little time. I tried to think these things at him, but he didn't hear me. It hadn't worked when I was in Toria's body, either.

Tension coiled in his stomach and propelled him to move across the room. He needed a plan. Finally, he decided that if Ellie didn't wake in fifteen minutes, he would summon a doctor.

While time ticked away on his pocket watch, I tried to make the most of every moment I was here. Despite my great aunts' warnings, I still wanted to help Ellie's ghost, so I needed to understand more about what had happened to Sarah and why she and Ellie were in so much danger. And, anyway, there wasn't much I could do until I was certain that Evan was here, too. I might as well try to help Ellie.

I did my best to nudge Percy's thoughts toward Sarah. Instead of thinking back to how he'd left her, though, he went further back, to when their alliance began.

He'd devoted five years to defending the Radcliffe heir without any help from a Langley. Under his watch, Harrison Radcliffe had grown from a gawky boy to a confident young man. At twenty-five, Percy hadn't needed the new Langley heir causing problems. Besides, how could a fourteen-year-old girl help him?

He almost smiled at the memory of their first meeting.

She had been a wisp of a girl sitting on a wrought iron bench in the courtyard at Dumbarton. Her light brown hair was done in ringlets that hung around her shoulders. She wore a bonnet to protect her pale skin from the sun, but she lifted her face up to it and smiled like she was greeting an old friend. She wore a light green dress with bright green ribbons for accents. As he approached, her eyes fluttered open. They matched the green ribbons on her dress, reminding him of spearmint leaves.

"Percival Kingsley. It's good to finally meet you." She had a warm Scottish brogue that immediately made him think of haggis and kilts.

Of course, she recognized him—the eye patch always gave him away. Everyone in the families knew him by it. *There is only one pirate in the family.* He'd heard the whispers and ribbings since he'd lost his eye at nineteen. The past six years he'd learned to live without his left eye and to pretend the pirate references didn't annoy him.

"Oh, I saw you coming long before today. And it's nothing to do with your eye patch. Your soul is so bright. No one could mistake you for anyone else." The certainty in her voice irked him.

"My soul?" Percy was used to seeing auras, the energy that people and objects gave off, but he never talked about souls. He wasn't sure he had one.

"Yours is an intense rainbow."

He snorted. The Langleys loved to talk about the supernatural. The Kingsleys, however, preferred to stay in the physical realm.

"You don't believe me?" She tilted her head to the side in a gentle challenge.

"It's not my job to believe in the supernatural. You take care of that. I'll protect you and Harrison from any physical threats."

"That sounds like a fair deal." She extended her hand.

Her fingers were so slim and delicate. Did she really expect him to shake her hand? A twenty-five-year-old man making deals with a fourteen-year-old girl?

She kept her hand out for him, like she knew it was only a matter of time before he took it. "We're going to have to work together. Best we start on the right footing."

He was accustomed to working alone. The last Langley heir had died before Percy had become the Kingsley heir. And he'd never worked with a female before. He cleared his throat. "I'm not sure how this will work."

She took his hand and slid it into hers. "Like this. You give and I give and eventually we find our way."

His palm swallowed hers. He shook her hand. "Sarah."

"Yes, Percival?"

He hated hearing his full name. Only his father called him by it. "Call me Percy."

"Percy." A tiny smile crept over her face. "I should get back to my lessons."

"Your next lesson is with me, actually."

"Spell casting?" she asked hopefully.

"Hand-to-hand combat."

She looked nervous as she followed him to the training room. He didn't expect her to last twenty minutes. He wasn't easy on her, but she refused to give up. After two hours, her hair was a mess, her dress was torn, and her body was already bruising.

"I think that's enough for today." He hadn't broken a sweat yet.

Her eyes flashed with defiance. "I need to keep practicing. If you're tired, just watch me."

"Tired?" He couldn't help chuckling at her. He had more stamina than any human being. More than even she should have. "I could do this all day."

"Then let's go again." The determined set of her jaw told him she just might be worth training.

He spent the next six months helping her learn to fight with fists and swords and daggers. When she finished her first round of training with him, she gave him a gift. She put a cloaking spell on his dagger so no one outside the four families could see it. It made it easier for him to go about his business.

"Thank you," he said.

"Thanks for giving me a chance. I know you didn't want to."

"You're just so young. And a girl."

She laughed. "I'll do my best to get older, but I can't do anything about being a girl."

"I realize that."

She dropped her voice. "I won't let you down, Percy. I'll always protect you."

"As I will protect you, Sarah."

From that day onward, she'd dedicated her life to Harrison and him. Her family remained in Glasgow while she settled into Dumbarton with distant cousins that she'd never met before. She'd studied hard, never complained, shown up every time she was needed. And she'd never asked for anything.

Over the past six years, he had grown to admire and trust her. Her focus made her one of the strongest priestesses. When they were called upon to fight side-by-side, he relied on her abilities. She saved his life a few times. He took a few deadly blows that were meant for her along the way. Theirs was a bond forged in battle—a connection that no one else could possibly understand.

So much of Sarah's life reminded me of what mine was becoming. A destiny that was thrust upon her. Having to work with the Kingsley heir to protect the Radcliffe heir. Being expected to sacrifice everything for a Radcliffe. Unlike me, Sarah didn't question any of it.

Percy checked on Ellie, but she didn't respond to his voice or his touch. Ten more minutes before he went in search of a doctor, although he wasn't hopeful that a physician could do anything about an illness that was likely supernatural in its origins. As he continued to pace the hotel room, his thoughts returned to Sarah. A wave of anger rushed over him, and me.

He remembered the day, just a few months ago, when Harrison had summoned both Percy and Sarah to the study at Castle Creighton. The Radcliffe heir sat behind his desk. With his blond hair and blue-green eyes, he looked like a fairytale prince. He had the tendency to act like one, too. He enjoyed adventure, much to the dismay of the people charged with keeping him safe.

"I want to take a grand tour." Harrison's voice made it sound like he wanted to borrow a book, not risk all their lives by taking a trip to the continent.

Sarah was sitting so close to Percy that Harrison didn't notice when she brushed her hand against Percy's, but Percy did. He glanced over and her spearmint-green eyes met his in a silent request to keep calm. They'd dealt with this request before when Harrison had turned eighteen. They'd stalled him then and they could do it again.

"Of Europe?" Six years in the Americas couldn't wipe away Sarah's Scottish brogue.

"Yes."

Percy sat forward in his chair. "Have you thought about all that this would entail?" He didn't wait for Harrison to reply before he pushed onward. "It's hard enough to guard you when you leave Castle Creighton for New York or Philadelphia, but on a ship at sea for two weeks? Think about all that could go wrong: pirates, storms, shipwrecks, mutiny. And that's not even touching on the supernatural problems. You are too vulnerable. It's too risky."

Harrison's expression hardened like the stone gargoyles that adorned Percy's home, Ravenhurst. "I have always wanted to see more of the world. You and Sarah have traveled across the Atlantic. You've been to Europe. I've been stuck here. My father may have thought it best to stay close to the castle, but I won't live my entire life within these walls. I can't." A fresh bitterness dripped from Harrison's voice.

When Harrison's mother had died six months ago, something shifted inside him. Percy hadn't realized what it was until now: Harrison's need to explore while he could. It was a force to be reckoned with. Percy gave Sarah the look that silently asked for help.

Sarah licked her lips. "It's very dangerous to leave the protection of the castle and venture out onto the ocean—"

"I'm setting sail for England in two weeks. I hope you will join me." Harrison's brusqueness surprised Percy.

Percy tensed. He should have known this wasn't a discussion. Harrison was too accustomed to being safe. Perhaps that was Percy's fault. He had protected the boy so well, he'd grown into a man who didn't grasp how dangerous the world truly was. Percy was about to say just that when Sarah put her hand on his arm, a silent request to let her try first. He nodded his agreement.

"I'm sure we can find a compromise. Harrison, you want to take a trip abroad like all men your age. And Percy, you want to keep him safe. These are both entirely reasonable desires." Sarah's smile promised a solution for both of them. "I can take us to Europe using a spell and the Langley mirror at Dumbarton. We'll just have to go a day or two into the future."

"Why the future?" Harrison interrupted her with his question.

He never listened when Sarah explained how her powers worked. "Because her powers are linked to the future, so she can only go to the future using the portals."

"We can avoid the exposure and risks of sailing that way," Sarah said.

Percy couldn't help sounding doubtful. "And how will we get back?"

"I'll use my locket," Sarah said, as if it was the most obvious thing in the world.

"And what if we're in public when danger strikes?" Percy had to consider every risk.

Her lips twitched. "The locket will work anywhere. All we need is my blood."

While her plan alleviated many of Percy's concerns, he still had his own reason for not taking this trip. When he'd left Wales, he'd sworn he would never return. He'd grown accustomed to his home here. Ravenhurst was the first place that felt truly his. He didn't care if he never saw his father or his eldest brother again. He missed his mother and his other brother, George, but the thought of going back to Wales was too painful. He was happy with the life he'd built, away from all of them, in America.

"But I wanted to experience the trip across the Atlantic," Harrison said.

Anger rushed over Percy. He fought to control his expression. Harrison was going to get them all killed, and for nothing.

"Is it more important to see Europe or to sail there? Because it's very likely we won't all survive the trip." Sarah spoke in a soft, but firm tone. "And if any of us die, you'll have to return home without seeing Europe."

"We must start with the Parthenon in Greece." Harrison sat back in his chair and crossed his arms.

"We can do that." Sarah looked to Percy. "You should see Scotland, too."

Sarah, who never asked for anything, was asking for this trip.

"All right," Percy grumbled.

"Thank you." She gave him a look of gratitude that made his heart swell. "Nothing will happen to Harrison. I will keep him safe," she promised.

He should have made her promise to protect herself.

They had been two months into the trip when Sarah touched Harrison's hand and had one of her death visions. It was both her gift and her curse to see someone's final moments. She saw him in a bed, his body ravaged by poison. In her vision, he looked decades older than he was, so Harrison thought the threat was decades away and refused to stop the trip. But Sarah felt that this threat wasn't that far in the future. She did every protection spell she knew. They were on their way to Glasgow when somehow, poison snuck into his system.

Harrison deteriorated rapidly. By the time they understood that he truly had been poisoned, he was too weak to travel home by way of the locket. Sarah hoped her family would be able to help, so they pushed on to Glasgow. While her family and Sarah tried to save him, they made Harrison as comfortable as they could. He rarely stirred from his bed. His blond hair was streaked with white and his face was creased with lines. He looked like a man of sixty, even though he was only 23. He was dying. Quickly.

There was no one Percy could punch or stab or wrestle to the ground. He had never felt more useless. This was a supernatural battle and it took all of Sarah's energy to fight it. Percy watched her cast spell after spell, but none of them worked. Her family joined her for several spells, but those, too, failed.

She stood over Harrison, checking his pulse and listening to his heart. Dark circles rimmed her eyes. Her collarbones poked through her skin. Percy stood at the foot of the bed, watching and waiting.

"There is only one way left to save his life," she said.

"What is it?"

"I have to pull the poison out of him and fight it myself." Fear stalked her words. "It's one of the hardest spells to work, and I have to do it alone. I cannot risk endangering anyone else with this poison."

"You're exhausted. You need to rest."

She swayed slightly. "We don't have any more time. If I don't do this now, Harrison dies."

"And you? What happens to you?" His voice was rough like the words had clawed their way out of his mouth and left a trail of blood behind.

"If I win, we are all safe." The slight catch in her voice made his heart skip a beat.

"And if you lose?" He sounded so calm, but inside a storm of emotions gathered.

"The poison takes me instead of Harrison." Her face looked resigned, but fear flashed in her eyes, like unexpected lightning.

"No. It's too risky." Percy crossed the room and grabbed her arm.

She looked down at Harrison. "You know what will happen if I don't save him. I cannot escape the Langley legacy. Either way my life is over."

Percy tipped her chin up. "I can't lose you." His voice was husky with all the things he hadn't said because of who they were and what was expected of them.

"You'll always have me. You have from the first moment we met."

He saw the stark truth in her eyes and his throat tightened, almost trapping his words. "And you me."

She stepped closer and kissed him softly. He crushed her against him and poured everything he felt into that kiss. When she stepped back her cheeks were flushed.

She touched his face. "These six years together—I wouldn't have changed a moment."

"I would have kissed you sooner."

"I'd have liked that."

She kissed him again. It was soft and desperate and he never wanted it to end. Then she broke away and led Percy to the door. "You have to wait outside."

He gripped her hand. He hated leaving her to face this threat alone even if there was nothing he could do to help. "I'd rather stay."

"You can't."

He stepped outside and she closed the door. He paced the stretch of hallway just outside, waiting for her, and ready to run to her if she called for him. He heard scuffling. Objects slamming into the walls and the floor.

He could wait no longer. He tried to open the door, but it wouldn't budge, not even when he threw his full weight against it. He heard her scream. It cut through his body like a broad sword—burning and cleaving him in two.

With one final, tremendous heave, he smashed through the door. Sarah was engulfed in a cloud of black smoke. It thickened around her neck like a pair of claws, lifting her off the ground, choking her. Percy tried to reach her, but an invisible force kept him from her. She had placed wards around herself and Harrison. They hadn't protected her from the darkness that was squeezing the life out of her, but they were preventing Percy from getting close enough to rescue her. Rage made his vision blur and go red.

"Sarah," he bellowed.

Her eyes slipped shut. The smoke pried her lips apart and dove inside her. She collapsed on the floor. The shield that held him back disappeared. Percy stumbled forward. He scrambled across the floor and gathered her in his arms. But he was too late. The poison that had nearly killed Harrison was in her now. He could see its dark traceries swirling beneath her delicate skin.

Within hours, Harrison's face looked young and healthy again, and his hair reverted to a golden blond. His eyes opened, and they were, once again, full of life.

At the same time, Sarah grew sicker. She developed a fever. Gray streaks appeared in her hair. She was seldom conscious, and, even when she was, she was too weak to move. Her family struggled to heal her, but there was little that they could do but try to keep her comfortable. When the adults had given up, her sister Ellie snuck into Sarah's room. It broke his heart all over again to hear that little girl begging her sister to get better. Ellie's persistence reminded him of Sarah when they had first met at Dumbarton six years ago.

But the poison was too strong. Sarah was dying.

Her family gathered together and used Sarah's locket and their blood to send Harrison back to Castle Creighton, where he would be safe from further harm. Percy's first duty was to the Radcliffe heir, but Harrison insisted that Percy stay behind. With Sarah.

Sarah's mother, Pamela, had been reluctant to leave her daughter's side, but she must have heard in Percy's voice how much he needed time alone with Sarah.

Once Sarah's mother left the room, Percy grasped Sarah's hand and whispered, his voice thick with emotion, "You *must* live."

She managed a faint smile. "If anyone could intimidate someone into living, it would be you."

He dropped to his knees beside her, keeping her hand in his. He tried not to notice the coldness that had crept into her fingertips. "Sarah, I can't do this without you. I won't do this without you."

Her hand clutched at his and he watched as she gathered her remaining strength. Her spearmint green eyes were dulled with illness, but her gaze was steady. "Percy, I need you to promise me something."

"Anything."

"You have to save Ellie."

"From what?"

"I've seen her death. She's bathed in blood and wearing the star sapphire ring."

He stroked her forehead and tried to soothe her. "Sarah, it's the poison. You can't know who will get the ring next."

"I saw her death, Percy." She shuddered.

In all the years he'd known her, she'd never been wrong about how someone would die.

"There are only four green-eyed Langleys." She gripped his hand as tightly as she could. "There's a chance the ring will pick Ellie. But she's just a child. Younger than I was when I became heir—much too young for everything that means. You have to take her away, keep her safe from the legacy, make sure that the ring finds another heir." Her breaths came in gasps and wheezes now.

He couldn't bear to see her struggling. He'd do anything to help her. "What do I do?"

"I've heard rumor of a green-eyed Langley who was never chosen, even when she was the only green-eyed Langley alive. The ring skipped her."

A chill crawled down his spine. He had a suspicion about who it might be, and he didn't like thinking about her.

"You have to find out why the ring skipped her. Jonas Mallory—he knows. He must. He knows everything."

Jonas Mallory. Percy hated the thought of depending on him. Once upon a time, a Langley heir had crafted a spell to let the Mallory heir keep hidden in times of danger—hidden even from the Radcliffes, the Langleys, and the Kingsleys. As soon as Harrison was struck ill, Jonas Mallory went into hiding and took all he knew about the families with him.

Why have a history of the four families at all if that history was hidden?

Intellectually, Percy knew the answer to that question. The wisdom that the Mallory heir possessed was vast; all four families would be in danger if their enemies gained access to that knowledge. But still, while Sarah Langley and Percy Kingsley risked their lives to protect Harrison Radcliffe, Jonas Mallory kept his distance and took notes. It was impossible for Percy not to regard him as a coward.

"But how do I find Jonas, Sarah? I can track anyone or anything, but not someone hidden by Langley magic."

"Ellie can find him by using Langley magic to counter Langley magic. She can do a locator spell on him."

"But she's a child. Her training has barely begun."

Sweat beaded along Sarah's brow. "She's strong, Percy. And we have no choice. Not if we're going to save her."

Percy was willing to trust Sarah's judgment, but he couldn't bear the thought of leaving Sarah's side. "I can't go, Sarah. Not when you're like this."

Her eyes were steeped in pain. "I'm dying. Nothing can stop it. It's my fate. But I don't want this for Ellie. I thought if I was the heir, she would be safe. But she's not safe. Please, Percy, it's the last thing I'll ever ask of you. For me, save Ellie."

He stroked her cheek. "You know I would do anything for you."

Sarah's grip relaxed, and she let her head sink into her pillow. Her expression turned serene.

A terrible fire burned in his belly. He hated to ask the next question, but he had to know. "How long do I have?"

"A week. Maybe two. I'll fight as long as I can."

She would take on all the pain to save Ellie. It was why he loved her. She would fight until her last breath.

"You need to take my locket," she said.

"But you might need it."

She gave him a gentle, but knowing smile. "No, I won't. I don't have the strength to use it anymore. But Ellie does, and she will. She will need it to open a portal to wherever Jonas is. You can both use it to get back from wherever you go. And it will take you safely to Dumbarton if you get into any trouble."

"And what about you?"

"I'll stay here. I'll be buried where I was born."

Percy held both her hands in his and held tight, as if he could pour his strength into her. Tears burned his eyes but he refused to cry in front of Sarah; it would be admitting that he was losing her and he couldn't admit it. Not yet.

"I know that what I'm asking of you goes beyond your oath to the four families."

"I don't give a damn about the four families." It was true. He'd served Harrison, but since he'd trained her, his first loyalty had been to Sarah. It was her sense of duty that had kept him true.

"Hush," she chided. "It's my hope that we can protect Ellie and keep our oath to protect the Radcliffe heir at the same time. Find Jonas and find out what happened to the Langley that the ring skipped, Percy. Find out for all of us—and for me."

Tears blurred his vision and slipped down his cheeks. Everything in him told him to stay by Sarah's side, but he nodded. He would do as she asked.

She closed her eyes. Pain twisted her face. "The necklace."

He reached around her neck, gently, and undid the clasp. He was sliding it into his pocket when she stopped him. "No, you must wear it. Keep it protected until Ellie needs it."

He fastened it around his neck and sat on her bed. "How do I get your parents to let me take Ellie?"

She gave him a slight smile. "I told them that if Ellie was far away then the ring would find someone else. Someone older, and closer."

"You lied?"

The sound that escaped her lips was the ghost of a laugh. "It was the only way they'd let you take her." She reached up and cradled his face in her hand. "That eye patch scares them."

He held her hand against his cheek. "It never scared you."

She shook her head. "Never."

Her eyes were so certain. So loving. He leaned in and kissed her. Her lips were soft and warm. Alive. He wished that they could stay that way forever.

Chapter 21

Percy paced the length of his hotel room and checked his pocket watch again. It had been ten minutes since Ellie had fallen unconscious. Soon, he'd be sending for a doctor and praying that medicine could help her.

I wondered why it was taking so long for Evan to appear. I thought back to the last time we'd traveled into the past. I had fallen into Toria's body and Evan had dropped into Alistair's. I knew from my own experience that loss of consciousness was likely, but Alistair hadn't been out for nearly as long as Ellie had been, and she still showed no signs of stirring.

But then I remembered that Alistair's quick recovery was the result of Toria's healing spell. Should I do one for Ellie? Wait. How would that even work? First, I would have to fight for control of Percy's mind, and then I would have to trust that a Kingsley body could do magic if a Langley was in the driver's seat. Nothing to do but try, I guess.

Taking control of Percy was easier than I expected. We both wanted Ellie to wake, so my thoughts meshed with his. He didn't know what he was doing, but he didn't struggle as I compelled him to find something other than the Kingsley dagger—I didn't know enough about its powers to risk using that—to prick the skin of his, our, finger. He and Ellie had been taking meals in their room, so it wasn't difficult to locate another knife. I struggled to remember the words that Toria had used to heal Alistair as I guided Percy to make a small cut. It was strange, but I didn't mind seeing my own blood when it wasn't really my own. As the Kingsley heir, Percy had shed plenty of blood without flinching. If he was giving me his strength and experience, I was giving him mine. The spell would work. I was sure of it.

I cupped my bloody finger over Ellie and recited the spell.

Usually, when I cast a spell, there was a stirring inside me. A rush of energy. A feeling of my power melding with the spell and making something happen.

Right now, I didn't feel any of it.

And Ellie didn't stir.

The spell hadn't worked. I tried it again, saying the words more loudly and with all the conviction I could muster.

I felt nothing and Ellie didn't move.

I had been so certain this would work. Why wasn't it working?

I wrapped Percy's handkerchief around my finger and squeezed it to stop the flow of blood. And then I realized what the problem was. Even though my consciousness was inside Percy, it wasn't my body, my finger, or my blood.

I was sharing the body of a Kingsley. The blood I had shed was not Langley blood. I didn't know how to work magic without my ring—which was not on Percy's finger—or my own blood—which was not in Percy's veins. Why had my ring time-traveled with me to 1886, but not to 1831? I considered the facts. The ring always remained with the Langley heir and right now I was the Kingsley heir. So why did I have the locket? I didn't know.

What I did know was that I was no longer equipped to handle supernatural threats, which was the only kind of danger I knew how to fight against. I would have to rely on Percy's physical skill and heightened senses, no matter what came at us. While I trusted in Percy's prowess, and I had firsthand knowledge of his powers of perception, I hated having to rely on physical strength. Phys. Ed. was the only thing keeping me from a perfect GPA.

As I struggled to figure out what to do next, Percy resumed control of his body. He seemed puzzled by the bloodied handkerchief wrapped around his finger, but his own well-being was not his first concern. He was about to go in search of a doctor when Ellie stirred.

Percy rushed back to her side and checked her forehead. It was cool to the touch. The fever had broken. "Ellie, can you hear me?"

Her eyelids fluttered open. "Percy? What happened?"

"You had a fit of some sort. You were insensible for quite a while. I was worried."

She struggled to sit. Percy helped her, gently easing a few pillows behind her.

"I feel dizzy." She let her head sink back, as if it was too heavy to hold up.

Percy fussed around the tea tray, filling a cup with the dregs of their afternoon service. He knew that it would be cold and bitter, but he hoped that it might fortify her. "Drink this."

She wrinkled her nose, but she drank.

Then he handed her a biscuit. "Eat this."

And she did. "I'm sorry I keep falling ill." Her lower lip quivered. "You should be out searching for Jonas, not stuck here taking care of me."

He sat down on the bed beside her and took her hand in his. "You were strong enough to do the locator spell and bring us here." Ellie wasn't able to pinpoint Jonas's exact location. She only knew he was in Vienna. Ellie had used Sarah's necklace to open a portal to the city. She had done as much as she could to help. "We're so close. It'll be no time at all before we find him."

When they had first arrived in the city, Percy employed street urchins to get word to Jonas's associates in the city. He knew that word had gotten to Jonas because Jonas had sent a messenger to meet with Percy a few nights ago. Percy, however, insisted on a face-to-face with Jonas. "We just have to be patient." He said it calmly, but he hated waiting for word from the messenger.

"I'm a burden."

"No, you most certainly are not. We wouldn't have made it this far without your magic. You found Jonas, more or less, and you transported us to Vienna. Tracking him down is my job, but I couldn't have done this without you."

Hope shone in her eyes. "Do you think we can save Sarah?"

"All we can do is try."

While Percy blinked back tears and patted Ellie's leg, I clawed my way back to the surface. "Evan?" I whispered.

I saw a spark of Evan in Ellie's eyes.

"I don't know what's happening," she said in her sweet little voice.

"Evan, are you in there?" My voice startled me. It was deep and powerful. Percy's.

Something shifted in Ellie's eyes. Annoyance and surprise. Evan.

"Kat?" It was Ellie's voice, but Evan's question.

I nodded.

He reached out and rubbed the stubble on my chin. "You're a…bloke?" Ellie's voice went high. "And you've got an eye patch. Good Lord, *you're Percy*?"

"Yup." Before he could tease me, I put up my hand. "Wait until you see what's happened to you." I helped Evan out of bed.

When he stood up, the top of his head reached just above my belt. "Kat?"

He wobbled and I picked him up and carried him over to the mirror. I held him up so he could see what happened to him.

"Bloody hell." He pushed and prodded at his little girl features with his little girl hands. "Am I Ellie?" he squeaked in her little girl voice.

"You sure are."

"Put me down." When I did, he raked his gaze over me a few times. "Looks like we're both in for quite an adjustment. How in the world did this happen?"

"How should I know?" The last time we'd traveled into the past, I'd fallen into a Langley body. I'd figured I would always fall into a Langley body, and Vivian had seemed to assume the same. How was this trip into the past different from the first one?

"The protection spell."

I didn't know that I had spoken out loud until I saw Ellie's sweet little face contort with Evan's emotions.

"Kat, what did you do?"

"You were almost killed. I wanted you to be safe." My words scrambled up the curtains.

"And you knew that Percy was about to die." It was so strange to hear Evan's weary realization in Ellie's little-girl voice.

"Toria helped. We wanted to protect you."

Ellie sighed, but it was Evan I heard.

He—she—tapped the sheath attached to my belt. "We've got the dagger. Let's go."

Before we'd come here, the only thing I'd been sure of was that I wanted to protect Evan, and that meant finding the dagger. What I hadn't counted on was what it would feel like to know what Percy knew, to feel his feelings. Percy was a Kingsley and I was a Langley, but we had so much in common. He was willing to risk everything for Sarah, which meant that he would do anything for Ellie. I was here, in the past, for Evan's sake. Maybe I couldn't escape the Langley legacy, but I wouldn't let Evan die with me. Or for me.

But we still had some time. Percy had three more days to live. Maybe we could save him, or at least help Ellie's ghost. Now that I knew them both, I couldn't believe that Ellie had killed Percy. "Evan, we can't just abandon them."

"We know how it ends, Kat."

"But it doesn't have to be that way."

I sent downstairs for some food, which we both needed, and started telling Evan everything I'd learned since I'd awakened in Percy's body.

In the middle of my explanation, there was a knock at the door.

I opened it to the savory smell of stew. One word from the maid and I disappeared and Percy asserted himself. The minute Evan and I were in a room with anyone from this era, we reverted to Percy and Ellie. That was how time travel worked for us at Castle Creighton too.

Percy slipped her some bills and she curtsied and left. I forced my way back to the surface and finished telling Evan about what I'd learned about Percy and Sarah.

It took me awhile, but I'd gotten used to Evan's words coming out of a little girl's mouth.

"None of this matters, Kat. We came here to get the dagger, and we have it. As soon as we finish this veal stew, we should head straight back to Dumbarton."

I knew that he was right, but I hesitated. I tried to find the words for what I was feeling. "This isn't just about the four families for me. My powers—my responsibilities—go beyond protecting the Radcliffe heir. Ellie asked me for help, and, now that I know Ellie, now that I know Percy, I have a duty to them, too."

Evan sighed.

"I can send you back to Dumbarton. I can send you with the dagger. I can do it now. But I'm going to stay to help Percy and Ellie as long as I can."

"Do you know how dangerous this is?" I heard Evan's frustration in Ellie's tone.

"I do."

The protection spell would see him home safely. If I got hurt, well, I had the Langley legacy looming over me and the Dark One hunting me. I figured my days were numbered, anyway.

"I'll stay, Kat. Of course I'll stay. I don't know how I can help, but I'll stay." The voice was Ellie's, but the words were Evan's.

Chapter 22

Once Evan and I had agreed that we were going to try to help Percy and Ellie, I figured that I might as well enjoy the experience. I had the Langley legacy hovering over me, and who knew if I'd ever be in early-nineteenth-century Vienna again?

I was grateful that Percy could handle his heightened sense of smell because I suspected that the mass of people and horses would be overwhelming to me if I were in charge of his body. As it was, the sights and sounds were enough. The people swishing by in their frock coats and skirts. The clatter of carriages. The call of vendors. It was hard to believe that I was really here in Vienna—the same Vienna that had given the world Beethoven, Schubert, and Strauss. This was a golden age, and I was walking through it.

I was happy to let Percy navigate the winding streets. It was clear that he knew where we were going, which left me free to take in the sights.

As Percy opened the door to a pastry shop, a whiff of something freshly baked and sugary filled his nose. I would have swooned, but Percy was made of stronger stuff. He wasn't interested in pastries. He was only here for Ellie.

His memory of the past evening was fuzzy, and he assumed that had something to do with Langley magic. But he knew that he wanted to help Ellie. Despite Sarah's wishes and his best efforts, the child was being robbed of her childhood. He hadn't found Jonas Mallory yet, but he could certainly find sweets. Vienna was full of them. Candied violets, apple strudel, and marzipan. He couldn't give Ellie much, but he could give her this much.

Percy's German was halting, but it was enough to secure a box full of sweets tied up with a pink ribbon.

He didn't go straight back to the hotel, though. He couldn't. Sitting in that room and waiting for word from Jonas was slowly driving him mad. It felt good to be doing something, even if that something was just walking the streets.

When he had met with Jonas's messenger at the pub, Percy wanted to choke the messenger, but held onto his temper and gave the messenger three days to arrange a meeting with Jonas. The messenger promised he'd send word if it could be arranged. Today was the third day.

And so far, nothing. Part of him feared that something had befallen Jonas. The rest of him worried that Jonas would flee the city before he could help Percy. He didn't know what to do if Jonas failed him. If Sarah were healthy, she could have used her powers to summon the Mallory heir to her. She had been that powerful before she became sick.

Percy couldn't help remembering his first visit to Vienna. He had been eighteen, and his brother George had taken him all over Europe. They'd stayed in the finest hotels, made the acquaintance of the most beautiful women, indulged in the best food and wine. It seemed like a lifetime ago. Before he had lost his eye. Before the dagger had chosen him. Before he'd ever known Sarah.

There was a terrible fullness in his chest, like he'd explode if he took another breath, but he'd die without that breath.

He couldn't lose Sarah.

He walked faster, trying to outrun his thoughts, and headed for the nearest park, hoping to find an open space where he might think and breathe. But the Volksgarten was packed with people. As he stalked through the French gardens, ladies glanced at him. The contrast between his expensive tailoring and roguish eyepatch never failed to intrigue. One promised a secure future; the other the romance of risk. The women who tapped their fans against their cheeks when he passed had no idea how dangerous he really was.

There was no peace to be had in the park, the street, his hotel room, or his mind. He'd never felt so powerless. He left the shade of the trees and made his way out of the park.

Back on the busy street, someone bumped against him and slid something inside his pocket. Few would have the sensitivity to notice this butterfly-like touch, but Percy did. He grabbed the man's wrist. Shock passed over the man's face. He'd probably never been caught before. He was dressed in understated clothes that let him fade into the city street. The man gave the barest shake of his head.

Percy ignored it. This man might be delivering Jonas's response. He had to keep him here. "Rupert, old boy, is that you?" Percy deftly switched his grip to a handshake.

The stranger couldn't do anything but play along. "Sir, it's good to see you again."

"How's the wife doing?" Percy asked.

"She's well. Very well." This pickpocket clearly wasn't used to being forced to converse with his marks—even if he was slipping a note into a pocket rather than pulling a purse out. Percy reached into his pocket, pulled out the note, and scanned it. *Schreiberhaus.* A winery in the woods outside the city. *Midnight.* There was a "J" scribbled at the bottom. Their meeting was set.

Percy nodded. "Well, I must be off. I can't be late for my lunch engagement."

The other man looked relieved. "Yes, good to see you, sir." After one more quick handshake, he tipped his hat and slipped back into the crowd.

Clever. Jonas was clever.

But no one was faster than a Kingsley.

When Percy got back to the hotel room, Ellie greeted him at the door in a pink and green floral-patterned dress. Pantalettes peeked out from beneath the hem. Her hair was parted in the middle and curled into ringlets.

"Ellie, you look lovely," Percy said.

Her cheeks flushed and she glanced at the floor. "I had a maid come do my hair."

He'd slipped the maid some *Gulden* to bring them their food in their room while Ellie was ill. He reminded himself to give her a few more.

Sunlight streamed through the windows, brightening the room.

"I'm glad to see you're feeling better." He sat beside her on the couch and handed her the package from the pastry shop.

She opened it. "Violet candies." She immediately popped one into her mouth. Her lips melted into a smile.

"I got you some other treats, as well."

Ellie reached for the teapot on the small coffee table in front of them and poured two cups while he cut up the apple strudel and Linzer torte.

After they had eaten, he told her about the messenger. "I'll be gone for several hours tonight."

"If I take a nap, I can come with you," she offered.

Percy shook his head. "It's too dangerous."

"Then you shouldn't go alone."

"I'll be fine."

"If it's too dangerous for me to go with you, then it's not safe for you to go by yourself." She crossed her arms and stared at him.

The child was smart, just like Sarah. "You could catch a chill and end up back in bed. You have to trust me, Ellie."

"I do trust you," she insisted. "But going to a deserted area in the middle of the night, doesn't that make you nervous?"

"I've been in situations far more dangerous." He touched her arm and softened his tone. "Truly, I appreciate your concern, but I've been taking care of myself longer than you've been alive." He patted the dagger. "And she'll let me know if there is any danger."

"I don't like being alone here at night," Ellie said quietly.

"Why don't you take a nap before I go? That way you can stay up reading until I get back. You'll avoid the nightmares."

"I've been in that bed for so long. Can't we go out? Just for a little bit?" She clasped her hands together and widened her eyes. "Please. I've never been to Vienna before."

She had spent the entire week stuck in bed. Percy checked his pocket watch. He wanted a chance to survey the meeting spot before his appointment with Jonas, but, even so, there was still plenty of time for a little sightseeing and supper. Then he would be off. "Get your coat and bonnet."

She jumped up to grab them and rushed for the door. "Ready."

Looking in her dark green eyes, I saw a flash of Evan. I pushed my way to the surface. "Evan?"

Ellie blinked. A much older expression slid across her young face. "Kat, we should leave."

"Not yet." I paced around the room. "What do you think Jonas knows?"

"No one knows what the Mallorys know, Kat. But we don't need to know. We have the dagger. All we have to do is go home, to our own time."

I was conflicted. I didn't want to put Evan in danger, but I did want to help Ellie if I could. And I was starting to wonder if the Mallory heir might have information that would help me, too. Bringing up the Langley legacy seemed unfair, though, so I decided to appeal to Evan's instincts as a historian and general know-it-all. There was no way he was going to be able to resist first-hand experience of the past.

"Come on, Evan. We have a chance to talk to the elusive Mallory heir. And I know you want to see early-nineteenth-century Vienna. You won't believe what it's like out there."

"We'll stay until tomorrow," he said.

Percy took Ellie to Stephanplatz to see St. Stephan's Cathedral. She marveled at the zigzag patterns of the roof's glazed tiles. It was an inspiring sight. If he could give her one good memory in all the bad that surrounded them, he wanted to do it.

They stopped in a few shops. He bought her green gloves and a cream-colored shawl. Anything to distract her from why they were here in Vienna. They walked near the Hofburg Palace. Guards stood vigilantly at the entry points as the palace itself loomed just beyond them.

Ellie stopped and stared, like she was trying to memorize every detail. After a few minutes, she turned back to him and asked, "Can we go to the park?"

"Of course." He hailed a carriage. It wasn't that far to the Volksgarten, but he didn't want to tire her.

As the carriage bumped along the road, Ellie held onto the door and peered out the window. "Thank you, Percy."

"For what?"

She sat back and beamed at him. "For doing all this. I know you have so much on your mind."

He tapped her on the nose. "It eases my mind to see you feeling better."

While Percy stared at Ellie, I made my way to the surface. "Evan?" I whispered.

"Stephansdom, we saw Stephansdom before the damage from World War II," Evan said excitedly.

"And the Hofburg Palace when Franz II lived there." I was actually enjoying time traveling. "We get to see things that no longer exist."

He reached over and grabbed my hand. "Thanks for pushing me to stay."

"I'm glad we got to share this." I held onto his hand. And for that moment, I let myself forget about everything that threatened us and just enjoyed being there with him.

Chapter 23

There was only a sliver of moonlight but it was more than enough for Percy's heightened vision. Still, he didn't like entering the deserted vineyard at night. Riding around the property on his mare, he made sure he wasn't being watched or followed. When he was confident that he was alone, he dismounted and tied his horse to a tree. He understood Jonas's need for privacy and safety, but this kind of quiet disturbed him. No deer. No foxes. No owls. No bats. Nothing was out tonight. The lack of living creatures put him on edge.

He wasn't sure what he'd encounter. It didn't matter, though. He did it for Sarah. He'd have done anything for Sarah.

He wanted to save Ellie from a terrible end, but there was another reason he sought the Mallory heir. Jonas knew more about the Langleys than anyone else. He'd know how to help Ellie—and he might know how to save Sarah.

Percy was mildly surprised that Jonas had agreed to meet with him. Before he had become the Kingsley heir, Percy had no idea what the Mallory heir did or why he was so important. Percy had learned when he became the Kingsley heir, but he hadn't entirely trusted that Jonas would heed his summons. While the Kingsleys ran toward danger, the Mallorys had a long history of hiding from it.

Percy had spent hours exploring the vineyard, alert for any sign of a threat. But all he'd found was row upon row of grape vines. The lack of animal life was alarming, but none of the stones in his dagger was glowing. All he could do was be watchful. And wait.

It was just past midnight when Percy saw a flicker in the distance. A lantern. Suddenly, a red aura appeared. A man. Percy checked his dagger. Still no warning signs. Nevertheless, he moved with caution, coming up behind the man.

"Greetings from the Kingsley family," Percy said.

The man whirled to face Percy. He wasn't Jonas.

"Where is he?" Now Percy's voice was a growl.

The other man stared at the dagger in Percy's hand and seemed unable to speak. Light wavered as the hand holding the lantern shook.

"Where is Jonas? Why isn't he here?"

The servant found his voice. "It's not safe. For him to be here, I mean. So he sent me. To tell you."

Jonas was Percy's only hope. If he didn't talk to the Mallory heir soon, Sarah and Ellie would both be doomed.

He didn't want to scare off Jonas's servant, so Percy tried to keep the rage out of his voice. "Does Jonas understand how important it is that I speak with him?"

The servant played with his collar. Despite the chill in the air, there was a sheen of sweat on his brow. "He understands, sir. He wishes he could help. But you know how it is. The Mallorys are just chroniclers. They don't interfere."

"So, Jonas is willing to let the Langley heir die? He's willing to risk the possibility of the ring falling into the hands of an untrained child?" Something inside Percy came dangerously close to breaking.

"Master Mallory is simply doing his duty, sir." The man's voice climbed up the vines and leapt toward the night sky.

"His duty is to the Radcliffe heir, and what the Radcliffe heir needs right now is for Jonas to help protect the Langleys." Percy closed the distance between them and pressed the tip of the dagger against the servant's throat.

The servant made the mistake of swallowing and blood beaded up around the tip of Percy's blade. But Percy didn't move.

"Together, you and I are going to pay a visit to Jonas. We'll be able to move much more quickly if I take this knife from your neck, but it's entirely up to you whether or not I feel the need to use it again."

The servant whimpered.

"Stop frightening my man, Percival." A familiar voice rumbled in the shadows.

Jonas was here. Somewhere. Percy looked around, but there was no sign of another person. Or at least nothing his senses could pick up. "Jonas?"

Jonas chuckled. He had the same deep throaty chuckle he'd had when Percy was a boy. A smile tugged at Percy's lip, but he repressed it, refusing to be that little boy again.

"Who did this cloaking spell?" Percy removed the tip of his blade from the servant's throat. "It's excellent."

"Wallace."

Sarah's uncle Wallace was the previous Langley heir. He died several years before Percy became the Kingsley heir.

A rotund, middle-aged gentleman emerged from a row of vines that he had blended into perfectly. His silver spectacles gleamed in the lantern's light. He wore a gray beaver hat. A dark cape swirled around his shoulders.

"Percy, my boy." The affection in Jonas's voice was undeniable. Jonas extended a hand.

Percy sheathed his blade and grasped Jonas's thick fingers. "You've led me on quite a chase."

"Have to be careful these days." Jonas's pale blue eyes looked sharp. "How'd you manage to get here so quickly?"

"Sarah's locket."

"Is she improved?" Jonas sounded hopeful.

"No. Ellie brought me here."

"The little one?" Jonas hesitated a moment. "And Sarah?"

"She's dying." The words scorched his throat.

"I thought as much. It's a terrible thing that the Langleys endure." Resignation rolled across Jonas's face and kicked Percy in the stomach.

"And yet you Mallorys always manage to stay alive."

"We have to capture it all for the next generation." Jonas's voice reminded Percy of the charred remains of a once great house. "That's our burden."

For the first time, it occurred to Percy that staying clear of the action and recording it for posterity, might truly be a lonely and unwelcome task.

He had always imagined the Mallorys as cowards, but perhaps—just like the Langleys and the Kingsleys—they were doing their duty as best they understood it. "Can you help us?"

Jonas sighed again, and, this time, Percy didn't hear a man resigned to letting others die. Instead, he heard a man doing his best to be of service in an impossible situation.

"There's no easy way around the ring, Percy. If it wants Ellie, it will find her. She wouldn't be the first child to become the heir before she's ready."

"Is there anything we can do to make Ellie undesirable? She's not the only green-eyed Langley."

Jonas gave Percy an appraising look. "I think of you Kingsleys as a cross between a bloodhound and a Hessian mercenary, but you're no fool." Jonas turned to his servant. "You can go back to your horse, John. I need to speak with Percy alone."

The man was clearly relieved to escape.

"Let's walk." Jonas put his arm around Percy's shoulders in a fatherly way and guided him down an alley between the grape vines. "There is one way for Ellie to make herself ineligible as heir: She must kill someone— someone very close to her."

Percy's stomach twisted and his skin turned cold. "No. I can't ask her to do that. She's a child."

"I'm sorry, Percy." Jonas's voice was soft and heavy. "I know of exactly one instance of the ring refusing to go to a green-eyed Langley when there was only one living. This was a woman whose mother had died giving birth to her. In this case, the ring waited a whole generation before choosing another heir."

Percy had lived through a time when no Langley heir existed. Before Sarah, he had been alone in protecting the Radcliffes. Even though one green-eyed Langley was alive. "Lydia," he breathed.

Jonas squeezed Percy's shoulder. "It was a difficult case to understand, certainly, and an ugly precedent to establish. Nevertheless, my analysis was based on a thorough review of our four families' lore, and you can trust that the Mallory ancestors have never had cause to revise this interpretation."

Percy's throat went completely dry. He swallowed, but it didn't help. "Ellie's eleven, Jonas. You want me to get an eleven-year-old girl to kill someone she loves?"

"I don't want any of this. I never have. But you asked, and I've answered." Jonas's eyes were weighted with centuries of knowledge. "Please don't look for me again, Percy."

With that, Jonas removed his hand from Percy's shoulder, walked away, and began to dissolve into mist.

"Wait, please." Percy's voice was so loud against the unnatural silence of the vineyard.

"I can't break the rules again. Not for you. Not even for Sarah." Jonas's voice caught in his throat when he said her name.

"Is there anything I can do to save Sarah?"

Jonas paused, half visible, half cloaked in the night.

"There are tales of swapping a life for a life. But you'd need a strong priestess. A *very* strong priestess."

Percy's heart leapt. "Sarah is strong. Very strong."

"Sarah *was* strong, Percy." Jonas's voice was graveyard quiet.

It felt like Percy's heart tripped and fell to the ground.

Jonas lingered, just visible. "Is there something else?"

Percy had done what Sarah had bidden him to do, but he still needed to find a strong priestess. "Lydia. Do you know where she is?"

"Once she was exiled from the family, it was no longer my job to keep track of her. I did try to stay abreast of her whereabouts and her doings for a while, but, after she married a Frenchman and began to travel extensively, it became difficult to keep track of her. Another Langley might have enough magic to find her, but I don't suggest you try."

"Why? I know she's been banished from the family, but, she's powerful. Powerful enough to save Sarah. Maybe Lydia can reconcile with her family then."

"Reconciliation is impossible, Percy. Believe me, my boy, I tried. After all those years watching Lydia, I thought I could help her. But what she did, no one can ever forgive that." Jonas paused, as if he was weighing his words very carefully, balancing his duty with his concern. "It wasn't her mother's death that got her banished from the family. You think you've faced danger. You've never faced anything like Lydia."

With that, Jonas disappeared completely.

Percy shivered. The vineyard seemed utterly empty. But he couldn't help wondering who—or what—might have been listening.

Chapter 24

Percy had his answers. Jonas had explained how Ellie might be spared the ring and how Sarah might survive. Both were unacceptable.

Percy stomped across the vineyard to find his horse. He untied her, mounted up, put her into a trot, and headed back into the city. As he rode, he searched for another way. He let the information Jonas had given him tumble around in his mind, examining each new configuration.

Then he saw a way. If he found Lydia and Lydia agreed to save Sarah, he would achieve both his goals. Sarah would remain the Langley heir and Ellie would be spared this burden without having to commit murder.

Sarah would live. Ellie would be safe. All Percy had to do was figure out what it might cost to have Lydia work this magic for him—and what he could possibly pay for it.

He struggled to remember what he could about Lydia, and what he could remember was chilling enough. He'd never known why she'd been banished. No one among the Kingsleys, the Langleys, the Radcliffes, or the Mallorys would speak of her after she left, but the servants whispered. They seemed to think that she was capable of anything—and they weren't just talking about magic. Now, Percy had no interest in whether or not Lydia was a proper lady. But he hoped that the rumors of her power were justified.

He had reasons of his own to think that they were.

He dug his heels into the flanks of his horse and raced back to town.

He didn't want to disturb Ellie when he returned to their hotel room, so he opened the door quietly. He needn't have bothered. She was sitting on the couch with a blanket over her and a book in her hands. The fire blazed in the fireplace.

"Percy." Ellie dropped her book and flew into his arms. "Are you okay?"

"I'm fine." He hugged her back.

"Did you talk to Jonas?" She clutched at Percy's hand.

"I did." He shrugged out of his greatcoat and sat on the couch beside her. He hadn't given any thought to how he was going to explain everything he'd learned to a little girl. In the end, he decided to simply be honest and explained how she might avoid becoming the Langley heir.

When he finished, she shook her head. "Better that the ring picks me, even if I die."

"Ellie..."

There was such determination in her eyes. "I won't kill anyone. I'd rather kill myself."

"Don't ever say such a thing. You know that suicide is an awful choice."

"So is murder."

Killing oneself was giving up: the one thing he was trained never to do. "But suicide..."

"It marks your soul." She said it like it was something she'd known her entire life. "What do you think murder does? And the murder of a loved one? Don't you think it has consequences beyond this life?"

Percy paused. Ellie might be a child, but she was also a Langley. Even at eleven years old, she knew things that would always be a mystery to him. Still, he couldn't let her consider giving up. Not yet. "I'm sure that you understand the consequences better than I ever will. But my job is to keep you alive."

Ellie rubbed her lips together, thinking. "What about Sarah? Can we help her?"

Again, he opted to tell Ellie the truth. She blanched when she heard the name "Lydia." If the situation hadn't been so dire, he might have laughed. Lydia had been banished before Ellie had been born. He wondered if nursemaids had turned her into a bogey in order to make little girls go to bed on time.

"Why would she help us?" Ellie's voice was so small, but she clearly understood the difficulty of relying on the banished Langley to save Sarah.

"She's our only hope, Ellie. Do you think you can find her?"

"I think I can, but she won't help us." Ellie sounded so certain.

"How do you know?"

She looked down at her feet and twisted her fingers together, like she knew something she shouldn't. "I overheard my grandmother talking to my mum about Lydia. Mum did the spell, you know. The one that banished Lydia. After that, Mum's powers were never the same. If she were still as strong as she used to be, she might have been able to save Sarah." Ellie shrank back into the cushions, as if Lydia was in the room. "Lydia's bad, Percy. She won't help us, and she might hurt us."

He squeezed Ellie's hand and made his voice as reassuring as he could. "But maybe there's something we can do for Lydia, something no one else can. Maybe there's something she wants that she can only get from the four families." He had no idea what he was suggesting. He just knew they wouldn't lose Sarah without a fight.

He felt her locket hanging around his neck, like his promise to her that he would protect Ellie. Now, he had found a way to save them both.

"Percy?" Ellie asked. "What are you thinking about?"

He collected himself and ruffled her hair. "I'm wondering how we might find Lydia."

Ellie was quiet for a long moment. "I could do a locator spell," she said finally.

Relief and guilt fought in his chest. He knew he was putting Ellie at risk. He could only hope that he was doing what was best for her and for Sarah. "Are you sure you have the energy for that?"

"Yes, but I'm going to need supplies." She grabbed a pencil and a piece of writing paper.

Now that she was committed to the task, Ellie clearly knew what she was doing. She finished the list and handed it to him. He scanned it.

"Salt, quartz crystal, bloodstone, sandalwood oil, a yew branch, and a crow's feather." Salt was easy. As for the rest, well, he had money. Money was something that all of the four families had in abundance.

"I'll gather these things tomorrow morning, after we've both gotten some rest. Will you feel up to working a spell?"

She bit her lip. "Yes, but my magic isn't strong enough to see exactly where she is. I should be able to get close, though."

"Just knowing what country she's in would be helpful." He tried to sound reassuring. Even if they knew Lydia's precise location, that would just be the beginning. He and Ellie would still have to travel there. Journeying by land or sea would take time—time they didn't have—while asking Ellie to open a portal so soon after casting a spell would be dangerous.

He prayed that Lydia was nearby. To whom he was praying, he had no idea.

Ellie's round green eyes searched Percy's face. They went blank for a second and then sharpened.

"Kat?" Evan whispered.

I took control of Percy's body. "I'm here."

Evan grabbed my hand. "We need to leave."

There was no way I was leaving now. "Didn't you just hear what Percy told Ellie?"

"It doesn't change anything for us."

"It changes everything. We might be able to save Ellie, Sarah, and Percy."

"They don't even know where Lydia is, or if she will help. All we know is that they must have failed, because we know what happened."

"Which is why I need to be there to help them."

He crossed his arms. "How?"

"What?"

"You don't have your ring and you don't have your Langley blood. Your powers are nil here. How exactly are you going to help them with Lydia?" His tone was a challenge to a fight I couldn't win.

"I don't know. But if I'm there, Percy will have his dagger. If we take the dagger, he'll be weakened. He can't face Lydia without it. It's not safe."

Evan closed his eyes and rubbed his forehead. "Do you know how crazy this sounds?"

"It's no crazier than us being here in the first place."

"Kat, we have to get the dagger back to our time." Frustration tumbled across his face.

He was right. But I couldn't give up on Ellie, Percy, and Sarah. "And we will. But let's do some good here if we can. Or at least, not harm them."

"What if we can't help them? What if you die here?" Evan's voice rose to a tween girl whine that hurt my ears.

I winced. "I won't. I have the necklace and the dagger. You have the Langley blood. We can go home anytime."

"Things can change. Quickly. Why risk it? Why risk *us*?" He looked at me like he was trying to decipher an ancient text.

I dropped my voice lower because what I had to say was so awful to contemplate. "Percy knows that the only way to protect Ellie is to have her kill someone she loves before the ring chooses a new heir. He knows Sarah is fading fast. If they can't get Lydia to help them, I think he may get Ellie to kill him to protect her from the ring."

Evan rubbed his pointer finger across his lips like he wanted to find another explanation, but couldn't. "It makes a horrible sort of sense."

"We can't let that happen. Not to Ellie. Not to Percy." I knew what it was like to have someone almost die for me. The guilt was crushing. I couldn't let Percy actually die for Ellie. I wouldn't let that little girl carry that with her for life—and beyond.

"How can we stop it?"

"I'm not sure. But if we leave and we take his dagger from him, I know bad stuff will happen."

Evan sighed. It sounded a little ridiculous coming from an eleven-year-old. "Do whatever you can, but the second things get dicey, we are leaving. No more arguments."

"Okay." But as long as he wasn't in danger, I couldn't leave Ellie and Percy unprotected. Not yet.

Chapter 25

The next morning, it took Percy a few hours combing the streets of Vienna and quite a few *Gulden*, but he returned to their hotel room with every item that was on Ellie's list. They weren't the same ones that she used for the locator spell to find Jonas.

Percy set them on the coffee table in front of her. "Why are the ingredients different this time?"

She checked each one to make sure it was what she needed. "You have to tailor the spell to the person you're looking for."

"The quartz, you used both times."

"It just focuses the energy. It's like flour in a cake recipe—just one of the basic things you need. That's what Sarah said." Her voice tightened like violin strings on the verge of breaking.

"She'd be proud of you, you know."

Ellie's lower lip trembled and her eyes glistened. "I hope so."

"I know it's so."

She blinked back tears and pressed her lips together. "I need you to stay outside the circle while I work the spell."

Sarah had made the same request when she cast spells. She claimed it was distracting to have him inside the circle because his soul had too much energy and made it harder to focus hers.

"I promised your sister I'd keep you safe." He wasn't sure how he could keep that promise if he wasn't inside the circle.

Ellie wrinkled her nose up. "That's what the salt is for, silly." She looked around the room and frowned. "I need space to work. Could you move the furniture back, so I can set up in front of the fireplace?"

She put the items for the spell on the floor by the fireplace. He shoved the couch and the coffee table across the room. While he moved the chairs and side table out of her way, she tied back the curtains to let in more of the late-morning light.

After he cleared a spot for her to work, Ellie poured a circle of salt around herself. She put a candle in each of the four cardinal directions. Barefoot, she walked the circle carefully, lighting the candles and murmuring words in Scottish Gaelic. In her pink dress with her light brown hair flowing down her back, she reminded him of a young Sarah. His throat tightened.

He hated asking her to do a locator spell, but there was no other way. Lydia was his last hope. God help him, Lydia was his last hope.

Ellie sat quietly in the center of the circle. She took a knife and cut her hand. She smeared her blood on the bloodstone and quartz and the yew branch. She held the crow's feather to her heart and chanted.

He'd seen Sarah work her magic before, but Ellie was so different: tense and afraid of making a mistake. Suddenly, a bright light encircled Ellie. Her voice rose. Ancient words spilled from her lips. Her eyes widened and went fever-bright.

She collapsed.

Percy clenched his fists and fought the urge to help her. He had to let her find Lydia. When she had used this spell to find Jonas, it had taken half an hour. He pulled his pocket watch from his waistcoat. It was almost noon. He didn't know how he could stand by and wait that long. He walked to the window and stared down at the street below. A few gentlemen milled about in front of the hotel, waiting for their carriages. A girl hawking flowers made a sale.

A long-buried memory rose up in his mind. He hadn't meant to summon it, but it came back as though it had happened yesterday. He remembered Lydia as a ten-year-old boy would. Long, honey blond hair piled atop her head. She always let a few curls slip through to brush against her neck and her cheek. He wanted to wrap the curls around his finger.

Her eyes were a startling silver-green. The kind you couldn't look away from. She had a dolllike face: perfect pink lips and ivory skin with a hint of rose in her cheeks. At twenty years old, she was only a few inches taller than he'd been at ten.

A storm was keeping everyone indoors at the Langleys' manor house in Glasgow. Somehow, he'd ended up alone with Lydia in the drawing room. The room was done in brown and green, which gave it a masculine feel and accentuated how feminine she was. The rain pounded against the window, isolating him from the rest of the world. The lamps and candles cast a warm glow over Lydia.

She lounged on the dark green brocade sofa, flipping through a book. He sat across from her in a rather uncomfortable chair, sneaking glances at her. He couldn't help it. She was so beautiful. Even her fingers were beautiful—delicate and soft. He wondered what it would be like to hold her hand. To touch something so beautiful.

"Percival, dear, would you put your hand in the flame for me?" Her voice was so melodious that he had almost missed the repulsiveness in her request.

Startled, he dropped his book. "Why?"

"Because I want you to."

She made it sound so reasonable that he couldn't help considering it. "It will hurt."

"Definitely."

"I'll get burned." His heart beat faster, like he was a rabbit cornered by a hunter.

"You'll heal."

"Why would I do that?" His voice weakened with his will.

"Because it will make me happy," she said softly.

He stared at her. Golden blond eyelashes framed her seafoam green eyes. The need to please her overwhelmed him. He didn't want to do it, yet he couldn't stop himself. He rolled up his shirtsleeve and lifted his bare arm toward the candle's flame.

Her eyes sparkled. Deep inside him, something screamed, *Look away.* Something primordial. Something powerful. His Kingsley blood rebelled against her Langley powers.

He snatched his arm away from the flame and stuttered, "I can't do it."

Her eyes widened in surprise. "You can't?"

He yanked his sleeve down and studied the coffee table, refusing to look at her. "I'm sorry, Lydia. I won't do that for anyone. Even you."

"Oh Percival, you might just be the one I've waited for." Her voice teetered between hope and disappointment.

"What do you mean?" He glanced up. Her eyes were back to normal.

"None of the other Kingsleys can resist me. Only the heir. And he's getting on in years. Nearly thirty-five now."

His uncle Stephen was the heir. He tried not to let his fear leak into his voice. "Is he going to die?"

"We all die. Kingsley and Langley heirs happen to die young. That's why you have to live before you die."

"But I'm not the heir."

"Not yet." She beckoned him.

He hesitated, worried it might be another trick.

She patted the cushion next to her. "I won't hurt you."

He edged closer and sat gingerly beside her.

"Someday you will be the Kingsley heir. And the Langley sapphire will choose me. It has to—there's no one else. And then we will rule them all."

He shook his head. "The Radcliffes rule us all."

"For now." Her smile was like sunshine in a field of daffodils.

He couldn't help feeling happy when she smiled.

She leaned in. "This must stay between us."

He nodded. Who would believe him? He was the third-born son, the one his father didn't need or want. Percy doubted he would get to go on a grand tour like his eldest brother Richard had. How much would his father hate it if *he* was the next one to wield the family dagger?

Lydia seemed to sense where his thoughts went. "Your father won't be able to ignore you then. You will have surpassed both your brothers."

"When will it happen?"

"When you are nineteen. But you mustn't tell anyone." She dropped her voice to a conspiratorial quiet.

Lydia could see the future, but she never made a prediction that didn't come with a price. "What will it cost me?"

She stroked his cheek. "You'll learn to live without it. The strength you lose will be nothing compared to the strength you'll gain when the dagger is yours."

Her fingers were like silk against his skin. He couldn't help leaning into her touch.

"Let's seal our secret with a kiss." She closed the distance between them. Her lips were warm and tasted of strawberries.

Then she pulled back. "Percival, you will do great things for me one day."

He knew she was right and it scared him.

It felt like an hour had passed, but when Percy emerged from that memory and glanced out the window, the same gentlemen still were waiting for their carriages. According to his pocket watch, mere minutes had passed. He'd forgotten their pact. He wondered if Lydia still remembered. He adjusted his eye patch. That was the thing he had lost. His left eye had been the price.

He paced the length of the hotel room several times. He hated waiting. With Sarah it had been different. It was her job to be the Langley heir. She was older. Stronger. She was prepared. She knew what she was doing. But Ellie, she had been tossed into their world with no training.

She still lay on the floor inside the circle of salt. Her little chest rose slightly with each breath. She just remained in a dream-like trance, trying to find Lydia. He lost count of how many laps he did around the room or how many times he went to that window.

Finally, Ellie's eyelids fluttered and she sat up. Percy rushed to the edge of the circle. "Are you all right?"

Ellie didn't say anything. She looked around like she was trying to remember who she was and where she was.

Percy waited a moment before he asked, "Ellie?" She blinked a few more times. Maybe she wasn't completely back here yet. "Ellie, can you hear me?"

Finally, her eyes focused on him. "Percy?"

"Can you come out of the circle?"

"She's here," Ellie whispered.

"In the circle?" Percy checked his dagger's sheath but the star sapphire wasn't glowing.

Ellie shook her head. "Vienna. She's in Vienna."

"That's too much of a coincidence."

"She knows about Sarah. She knew we would come here." Ellie's eyes darted around the room like a skittish squirrel. "She's been here waiting for us."

"Does she know what we want?"

"I don't know, but she's really, really strong, Percy." She wrapped her arms around herself like she needed to be held. "She's worse than they said. She's got a darkness. A shadow around her soul. It's scary."

Percy crouched beside the circle. "Can you open the circle and come out?"

"I don't want to." Ellie started rocking.

"Ellie..."

"As soon as I step out, I'm not safe." Fear raised her voice and rattled her words.

"Do you think she's going to hurt you?"

Ellie trembled. "I don't know."

This was too much for her. Percy had to pull her back. He deepened his voice to a command. "Ellie, look at me."

She met his gaze, but her teeth chattered.

"Open the circle and let me in with you."

"I don't know how."

"Then release the circle and trust me." If he tried to cross the circle, it would hurt both of them.

She closed her eyes. Her hand traced over the circle and she murmured something. He didn't recognize her words, but he felt the power that held him back dissolve. He crossed the circle and scooped her up in his arms.

She couldn't stop shaking. Had the fever returned? He pressed his cheek to her forehead, but it wasn't hot. Cold emanated from her entire body.

"Did she hurt you?" He held her close, trying to warm her up.

She clutched at his frock coat. "No, but she wants to hurt everyone. We can't let her, Percy."

"Don't worry." He pried her fingers loose and tucked her under the covers of her bed.

He was going to get some tea for her, but she grabbed his hand with both of hers. "Don't go. Please. Stay here."

"I'm not going anywhere." He sat down on the bed and held her hand in his. It was so small. "Rest, okay? I'll figure out where Lydia is."

She wasn't shaking quite as much now. "You don't have to."

"It's all right. You've done enough. I'll find her and talk to her."

"No. She told me how to find her." Her eyelids drooped.

"Did she see you when you did the locator spell?" He hadn't realized the extent of Lydia's powers.

"She was waiting for me. She's expecting both of us."

"Tell me where she is."

"Nooo. I go too." Ellie slurred her words.

"Are you sure you're up for this?"

"I have to help Sarah." Despite her exhaustion, her words were an implacable vow.

Chapter 26

"Kat, I'm not going anywhere near this Lydia." Evan stood beside the couch in the hotel room. His entire four-foot-tall body vibrated with tension. "She's too dangerous."

"If we take the dagger and leave, Percy's dead. Ellie's dead." They wouldn't be able to fight Lydia.

"And if we stay, we're dead. Lydia is powerful enough to kill us all." He marched over to me and gripped my arms with surprising strength for a child. "If we take the dagger, Percy might not go to Lydia. He will realize he can't take her on without it."

"Percy will do anything to save Sarah." The blood rushed to my hands and feet. My frustration flowed through Percy's veins. "He's a Kingsley. Of course he's going to charge into a dangerous situation, especially one he's not equipped to deal with."

"I don't," Evan said quietly.

"You don't have your amulet yet." He didn't understand the pull of the amulet. The weight of duty. The responsibility that rested on Percy's shoulders. He hadn't felt what it was like to hold so many lives in his hands, but I did. "Taking the dagger away would be like stabbing Percy and Ellie."

"They'd still have a chance." The slightest quiver in Evan's voice betrayed his inner uncertainty.

I hated having to do this to him, but it was the only way. "*I've* got the dagger and the locket."

"What are you saying?" His forehead wrinkled up.

"We're not in danger yet. We've got time."

"Are you refusing to let me open the portal?" His voice went dangerously calm for a child.

"I'm saying it's not just your decision. It's my magic that brought us here. It's my magic that saved your life. Maybe you need to trust me and my magic."

He pinched the bridge of his nose like I was giving him a serious headache. "Do you want to die?"

"I don't want to live because I'm a coward who let my ancestors die without trying to help them."

"You are needed in the present. We've got a supernatural storm brewing there. That's where you can do real good." His eyes pleaded with me.

"Didn't you learn anything from what happened to Cassie and Sebastian?" Before he could reply, I rushed to add, "The dangers we end up facing are usually rooted in the past. I wouldn't have this ability to change the past if I wasn't meant to use it. If we can help Ellie and Percy, it might help us too."

"We didn't help Cassie and Sebastian."

His words stung like a slap. I didn't realize I'd taken a step back until I bumped into the fireplace mantle. "I tried my best."

"Kat, no, I didn't mean," he fumbled for the right words, "I know you did all you could for them."

Tears burned my eyes. The guilt of not doing enough in time. I turned away from him and went to the window, staring down at the street below while I got control of myself.

"You aren't going to change your mind, are you?"

"If you want, I'll send you back. I'll stay on by myself." I only needed a drop of Ellie's blood to get home.

"I'm not leaving you here alone. But I need you to do something." When I refused to answer, he came over and tugged on my sleeve until I looked down. "Promise me we will return before Percy's death date."

It was the next night. We still had a day. I nodded.

Evan stared up at me with a suspicious expression. "I want you to say the words this time."

"I promise we'll return before Percy's death date."

Evan wrapped his arms around my waist and hugged me. His face pressed against my stomach. I resisted the urge to pick him up because I knew what he was really after.

"You're not getting the necklace," I said.

"Not yet" was his muffled reply.

It was late afternoon by the time Percy woke up. He'd spent hours dozing beside Ellie. Oddly, he didn't feel rested.

As soon as Ellie was out of bed, he asked, "What's Lydia's address?"

She crossed her arm and gave him a stubborn look. "I'm going with you."

"It's best for me to go alone." He didn't trust Lydia, especially with Ellie.

"Lydia told me to bring you to her. We have to go together."

"We don't have to do what she says. Just give me the address."

"I can't."

"Why not?"

"I only know how to start. Once I get going, I'll know where to go next."

Blast it. Lydia was forcing his hand. Maneuvering them around Vienna like chess pieces.

He could play games, too.

Before they headed out, Ellie and he stopped in the hotel restaurant for some food. After Ellie devoured her roasted pork, the color came back in her cheeks.

He was about to ask if she'd like dessert, when she tossed her napkin on the table and said, "We have to go."

Her voice didn't quite sound like hers. "Ellie?"

"She's getting annoyed," she whispered.

"How do you know?"

"She's talking inside my head." Ellie's face contorted with that confession.

If Lydia was inside her head, who knew what else she might do to Ellie. He paid their bill quickly.

As they left the hotel, Percy asked, "Should I hail a carriage?"

"It's a fifteen-minute walk." She headed down the street.

Percy rushed to catch up to her and grabbed her hand. "Don't lose me."

She giggled. "We won't." Her eyes turned the same silvery green as Lydia's.

The hairs on the back of his neck stood up like they were preparing for battle.

Ellie blinked and her eyes were moss green again, but the star sapphire glowed brightly in his dagger's sheath. He was walking into a supernatural threat without the Langley heir. And the person he'd sworn to protect was under the control of someone he couldn't trust.

Chapter 27

Percy stood in front of the formidable oak door of a three-story brick terraced house. He rang the bell and waited. Ellie's hand felt so little in his, like at any moment it could be snatched away.

A butler opened the door, looked them over with an air of disdain, and requested their names. After Percy replied, the butler said, "Follow me," in an indifferent voice.

Ellie squeezed Percy's hand. "She can't wait to see you." Then she pointed to the third door in the hallway and whispered, "She's in there."

The butler stumbled, but recovered quickly. He made his way to the door that Ellie had indicated and opened it. "Madam, your guests have arrived."

"Excellent. Please, show them in." Lydia's voice sounded as sweet as it always had.

The butler left the door open and gestured for Percy and Ellie to enter.

From the doorway, Lydia was the first thing Percy saw. She probably planned it that way. She sat on a couch with a tea tray and a tiered plate of assorted pastries set out before her. Her honey blond hair was piled atop her head. Several curls lay on her bare shoulders. A few brushed against her cheeks. Her dress had a delicate floral pattern of pink roses and pale green ivy. The same shade of green as her eyes. She didn't look like she'd aged more than five years since he had seen her, even though twenty years had passed.

The walls were a pale green silk that matched her eyes. There was an oval writing desk in the far corner, facing the window. Clearly, being banished from the four families hadn't diminished her—financially, at least.

Percy didn't see any auras but hers. As far as he could discern, there was no one else hidden in the room, prepared to harm Ellie or him. Of course, someone with Lydia's powers hardly needed to rely upon brute strength. He squeezed Ellie's hand one more time, as much to comfort himself as to reassure her.

He walked into the room, pulling the little girl with him. "You've certainly made a nice home for yourself, Lydia."

"Do you like it?" She sounded mildly pleased. "I moved here a few months ago. The previous owner was a count who lost his fortune and killed himself. His widow sold it quite cheaply."

Percy assumed that Lydia had had a hand in that series of events, but he chose not to comment. "The room reflects your tastes. As I remember them."

"Yes, it has been a long time, Percival, but it's so lovely to see you again." Her voice remained sweet but she gave him a savage smile—teeth that promised torment. Then she extended her hand for a kiss.

"Lydia." He bent over her knuckles and barely brushed them with his lips. "I go by Percy now."

"Percy." She tested it aloud. Then she released his hand and slid her gaze to Ellie. Lydia's smile disappeared. "Ellie, look at you. The spitting image of your dear mother." Loathing lingered in each word.

Ellie squeezed Percy's hand and pressed against his side.

"I was a little worried about you. What took you so long?" The slightest wrinkle marred Lydia's brow.

Ellie trembled beside him. "I'm sorry—"

"Ellie was exhausted. Then we needed to eat." He kept his tone somewhere between contrite and practical.

"A locator spell can be hard on one so inexperienced." Lydia almost sounded sympathetic, until she added, "Of course, I was doing them without difficulty by the time I was six."

Ellie blanched and looked down at her shoes.

"Not everyone can be like you, Lydia." Percy tried to keep the edge out of his voice. He couldn't afford to alienate her.

He gave Ellie's hand a few quick squeezes, trying to reassure her. They remained standing. He cleared his throat and looked at the chair, waiting for an invitation to stay.

"How rude of me, please sit." Lydia patted the spots on the couch to her right and her left, indicating exactly where they were expected to sit.

Ellie dropped Percy's hand and went to sit beside Lydia without hesitation. He would have preferred to take a chair a few feet away from Lydia, but he couldn't leave Ellie in her grasp, so he sat where he had been directed.

"Lydia, let the child go. We can talk, just the two of us," he said.

"But I'm having fun." He hated that devilish sparkle in her eyes, as she asked, "Will you amuse me instead, Percy?"

"I can't make any promises."

Lydia poured their tea. Steam rose from the cups. "Drink up, poppet," she said to Ellie.

Ellie's hand shook. The tea was too hot for drinking, but the child couldn't stop herself from lifting the cup to her lips. Her eyes went wide with fear. She was going to scald her tongue, her mouth, her throat—and she couldn't stop herself.

He knocked the cup out of her hand. The porcelain shattered on the hardwood floor. "That's enough. Release her."

"See? I knew you could keep me entertained if you tried, Percy." Lydia whispered a few words and Ellie slumped against the cushions. "I do enjoy this grown-up version of you." Lydia brushed the shoulder of his frock coat, like she was polishing a new trophy. "Though I was sorry to see you lose that eye."

"See or foresee?" He had no memory of her being there, but she did like to be there to witness the misfortunes she predicted.

Lydia laughed. It sounded like tiny bells. Everything about her drew him in, and he knew what she was like. He could hardly imagine her effect on those without his knowledge and his strength.

"Both, dear." She rested her hand lightly on his arm. "If I hadn't been exiled, I might have let you know more about it."

"Thanks." She wouldn't have provided enough information to stop it, just enough to make him fear it.

"Though seeing you now with that eye patch." Her voice trailed off.

"So handsome, with the perfect dash of danger." She smiled and the whole room brightened. "And that dagger, I knew you would get it."

"You can see it?" He tried to keep the surprise off his face, but it slipped into his voice.

"Did you really think a little cloaking spell would work on me?" She sipped her tea.

"Can you, I mean, will you help us?" Ellie's voice was small and tentative, like a mouse pleading for a crumb of cheese.

Lydia tilted her head to the side. "Why would I help you?"

Ellie looked to Percy.

"I'm sure there is something you want. Something we can trade for your assistance," he said.

"Depends on the assistance you need."

"You don't know?" Percy asked.

"I know many things. Tell me which one I'm supposed to help you with today."

"Sarah," Ellie said.

"The poisoned Langley heir. She should have known better. Foolish girl. There were other spells. Ways to extract the poison from Harrison without poisoning herself. A little more risky for the Radcliffe heir, but still..."

"Can you help her?" he demanded.

"She's dying," Lydia said.

"But there's a way to save her." Percy pushed onward. "Jonas told me."

"How is our keeper doing? I hope you got what you needed from him. He's not long for this world." She said it with such calmness, like she was talking about a style of dress falling out of fashion, not the death of the only person who tried to reconcile her with her family.

"How can you talk about him like that? He cared about you."

"Mallorys don't have friends. They have specimens they study. I was just his favorite specimen. He didn't want me to escape from under his lens."

Percy tried to steer the conversation back where it needed to be. "Can you save Sarah?"

"There are always ways to cheat death. None of them are easy."

"You're our cousin," Ellie said softly.

"Not anymore. Your mother banished me from the family. I am dead to them and they are dead to me." Lydia said the words brazenly, but something flickered in her eyes.

"So, you won't help us?" he said.

"I didn't say that."

Her silver-green eyes were mesmerizing. Percy resisted the urge to touch the curl on her cheek. He blinked and looked down at his dagger. The star sapphire winked back at him, reminding him how much danger he and Ellie were in.

"You cannot just walk in here asking for something. It's been two decades. There's so much we should catch up on first." She extended her hand toward the pastries and cookies. "You must try these. They are the best that Demel has to offer."

Ellie looked to Percy for permission. The star sapphire still shone because being around Lydia was a constant supernatural threat. The emerald, however, was dark. No physical threat. But Lydia could have put a spell on the food. He shook his head.

Lydia caught their silent exchange. Her eyes slitted. She grabbed a piece of marzipan and took a bite. "Perfectly harmless. If I wanted you dead, you would be. Don't be ungracious guests." The venom in her voice reminded Percy that he could be sent away at any moment by her. And he still needed her. Sarah still needed her.

Lydia sat back with her tea and waited for them to respond. Ellie took a tart. Percy, a piece of apple strudel.

For half an hour, Percy did as she asked. He talked about some of the sights in America. She found that fascinating. Lydia didn't say much about her time in France or anywhere else, but Percy got the sense that she seldom stayed in one place for long.

Percy was reaching the end of his patience when Lydia clapped her hands once and announced, "You've indulged me enough." She shifted to face him on the couch. "You want me to save Sarah's life."

"Yes."

"Exchanging a life for a life requires some powerful—and dangerous—magic." She paused. "What will I gain from working such a difficult spell?"

Percy leaned closer. "You want the Langleys to say they were wrong. You want them to apologize and beg for your return."

"I don't want them to take me back. I want to see them destroyed.

They didn't just cast me out. They left me alone and penniless. If I hadn't found my husband, I would have died." There was a starkness in her voice. A vulnerability he'd never heard before. She really thought her family wanted her dead.

"You always land on your feet," Percy said. "They knew that. We'll find a way to get you back in the family."

"I don't need you for that. They will welcome me back when the ring destroys Ellie. It will choose me next. It has to."

Her conviction confused him. Didn't she know why the ring skipped her? "Jonas said it will never choose you."

"Jonas doesn't know everything. I've always been very patient when it comes to what mattered."

"So, you won't help us?"

"I don't really have a reason to now, do I?"

"But my sister will die," Ellie said.

"Oh poppet, she doesn't matter to me."

"You could do that spell easily," he said.

"Of course I could. But I won't. Not for you, or your precious Sarah." Lydia poured some more tea and took a sip. "But Ellie could try. Yes. I'll even give her the spell. She just has to decide who dies in place of Sarah."

Lydia leapt up, almost cheerfully, and went to her desk. She sat down, grabbed some paper and a quill, and began writing.

"Don't do this, Lydia. She's just a child."

Lydia ignored him and kept writing.

"I'll do it," Ellie whispered.

"You can't," Percy said.

Lydia's quill scratched across paper. It was a few minutes before she came back and handed the paper to Ellie.

He glanced at the paper. The spell was written in red. "Is that red ink?"

"The darkest spells must be written in crow's blood," Lydia said.

Ellie snatched the paper and read it. "I have to swap someone as beloved to me as Sarah." Her voice trembled.

Lydia's eyes danced with amusement. "Percy, or perhaps your dear mama. Either would do. Of course, if you aren't dark enough to make this kind of decision, you can't cast this kind of spell. You must commit to it. And the darkness you fear in me? It will live inside you, too."

Ellie shrank back. "Percy, I don't think I can work this kind of magic."

"You don't have to." He switched his tone from comforting to commanding. "Go out in the hall for a moment. I need to talk to Lydia privately."

Ellie clenched the spell in her hand and fled the room.

As soon as Ellie shut the door, he demanded, "Was that necessary?"

"Not at all. It was solely for my amusement." Lydia brushed a stray curl from her cheek.

"Just tell me what you want."

Lydia seated herself beside him. Close enough for her thigh to brush against his. "Exactly what is happening. Sarah's death. Ellie's death. I want all of this and it's happening." She licked her pink lips. "It's delicious to watch you destroy yourselves with your noble intentions. I've never tried to save anyone. And I've always survived."

Tired of her games, he stood up. "Did you just bring me here to toy with me or is there something you want?"

Her eyes slid to his belt.

He quirked an eyebrow.

She giggled. "Not that. I want your dagger."

"I can't give it to you." It was his family's strength. It was what made them who they were.

"Then I can't help you with this spell." She added, "Ellie's too weak, you know. Too green. She's going to be slaughtered. You can only protect her a little longer, Percy."

"You've seen her future?"

Lydia nodded. "Sarah and Ellie will die. And you will live with the knowledge that you could have saved them both, but didn't."

"What would you do with my dagger?" It didn't just warn him of danger or protect him in battle. A single cut delivered by him severed the connection between soul and body. In her hands, it would become twisted.

"The question you need to ask is: What will you do if you fail Sarah and Ellie? How will you go on knowing that a silly family heirloom was all that stood between you and your darling Sarah?"

Rage ran through him like a deer's antler—sharp, twisted, and impossible to pull out. His fingers twitched. He'd never wanted to wrap his hands around someone's throat and squeeze, squeeze, squeeze the life out of her more than he did in this moment. But that wouldn't save Sarah or Ellie.

"I need some time to think." He moved toward the door.

Lydia followed him. "Don't take too long. Lives are at stake."

And it didn't matter to her. He swiveled to face her. "What happened to you?"

She stepped close enough to share a breath and whispered, "Everything."

For a second, he glimpsed a world of pain in her eyes. A world she masked from everyone else. A world that frightened even him.

She caressed his cheek. "Don't go like that." Her voice was so hard to resist. He felt her power tugging him toward her. His hatred turning to another burning emotion: desire.

She tangled her fingers in his hair and pressed her body against his. "You always wanted me. You can't help it."

She was right. Her darkness called to his. The best in him knew that he shouldn't, but that only made her more tempting. She wrapped her arms around his neck and stood on tiptoes, offering her lips, but they remained inches away from his. He couldn't resist. He lifted her up and kissed her. She still tasted of strawberries.

When he put her back down, he couldn't help touching the curl on her cheek. Just as he thought—it was softer than a rose petal.

"Take the night," she breathed. "But remember Sarah doesn't have many more left to waste."

With those words, the spell she cast over him shattered. He was the Kingsley heir again. He released her and stormed out the door. Her laughter echoed behind him. He grabbed Ellie's hand and stalked out of the terraced house.

Lydia's laughter still rang in his head.

Chapter 28

"Please slow down, I can't keep up." Ellie gasped and clutched at the sleeve of Percy's frock coat.

He hadn't realized how fast he was walking. He hardly noticed anything since he'd kissed Lydia—beyond his need to get away.

He forced himself to shorten his strides for Ellie's sake.

While they had been at Lydia's, evening had fallen. He and Ellie made their way back to the hotel under the light of the streetlamps. Carriages rumbled past them with horse hooves clomping over the paving stones.

He'd already put a few streets between Lydia and himself, but it wasn't enough. He could still feel her lips on his. His body still wanted her. And he hated himself for it.

An image of Sarah's wan face rose up in his mind. There was trust in her spearmint green eyes. And he'd replaced her last kiss with Lydia's. Guilt roared inside him. He wiped the back of his hand across his lips, but he couldn't wipe away what he had done.

"I had to get away from Lydia." He'd never say it out loud, but she had shaken him. Made him doubt himself.

Ellie still clung to his sleeve. "There's something dark in her soul. I can see it clawing its way out." The child sounded breathless, so he slowed his walking even more.

"That's why the family exiled her."

"What did she do?"

"I don't know." Beyond what Jonas had told him, he only knew rumors.

Some said she communed with the shadows, welcoming them into her life. Others said she cast death curses for her own amusement. Now, he suspected that she had done something worse. Something unforgiveable. Maybe harmed one of the heirs, or at least tried to. That would be a betrayal of everything their families stood for. A reason to be exiled forever.

Ellie's breath was coming in gasps.

Percy stopped. Her cheeks were flushed and her brow was sweaty. He should have noticed sooner. Blast Lydia for distracting him. "Are you all right?"

"I think so." Her voice shook like an unstable cliff about to give way. "She's strong, Percy. She almost made me drink that scalding tea."

It wasn't sickness, but fear and overexertion that were affecting Ellie. He should have realized how much Lydia would scare her. He tried to reassure her. "She's bewitched most of us at some point."

"Even you?" Ellie looked up at him with a mix of relief and worry.

"Even me." He wasn't that little boy that Lydia had toyed with years ago, but, still when she'd kissed him… Even now, he couldn't be sure how much was her bewitching him and how much was him wanting it.

Ellie bit her lip. "I could try the spell."

"You don't have the power or the darkness in you for it. Whose life would you trade for Sarah's?"

Ellie didn't respond.

She was too young to make a choice like this. "You're too good to ever do something like that. You couldn't."

"Mine." Ellie's voice was so soft he almost didn't hear her.

"What?"

"Mine. I'd trade my life for hers."

Percy dropped down in front of her and gripped her arms. "Ellie, no. Sarah would never want that."

"It's the only life I could take." She spoke quickly, like she had to get the words out or she never would. "You heard what Lydia said. She's right. I'm not strong enough to be the heir. I'll die soon anyway. This way, at least, my death can save Sarah."

The vulnerability in her voice called to every protective instinct he had. "Ellie, your life matters too much to throw it away. Don't you realize we are fighting to keep you alive and safe?"

"I can't let Sarah die, Percy." Tears filled her eyes.

He hugged her. "We'll find a way to save both of you." He stroked her back and prayed that he wouldn't become a liar.

Chapter 29

When we got back to the hotel room, I fought Percy for control and won.

Ellie leaned against the door, but the decisive look on her face was Evan's. "That's it. We're out of here."

I dropped down on the couch and stared into the empty fireplace. I couldn't help shivering. I wasn't sure if it was the lack of a fire or what Percy had decided. I knew that he was going to give his dagger to Lydia. I knew that he thought that he could win it back. And I knew that his plan wouldn't work. Because I knew that he was about to die in this very hotel room. He had one more day to live.

"You're right, Evan." The words hurt to think. They hurt worse to say.

"Kat, listen to me." He marched over to me like he was marshaling his energy for a fight—arms crossed and eyes full of fire. "Wait, did you say I'm right?" His voice stumbled, like someone had called a ceasefire in the middle of an attack.

"I don't know exactly what's going to happen next, but I feel like we have to get the dagger back to our time before it's too late. I want to help them, but I don't see how we can." The muscles in my neck tugged at the back of my head. I rubbed them, but it didn't help.

"So, we're agreed—"

"It's an awful choice. I hate making it." All my frustration and fear got tangled up in my voice. "But Lydia is so strong. Without my ring and my blood, I can't stop her. If she gets the dagger, we're all doomed." The admission slashed at my heart. The powerlessness I felt was a physical pain. "I have to try to save us—in our time. I have to face the danger there. There's nothing else I can do here." I hunched over, hating how right Evan was about everything. "Let's go home."

"Good." I could hear Evan's relief in Ellie's voice.

I untied my cravat and popped the top buttons on my shirt. I reached for the locket, but I couldn't find it. "My necklace." I ran my hand around my neck searching for the chain. It was gone.

"Kat, don't play games."

I exposed my bare neck. "Do you see it?"

"Check inside your clothes." I heard a note of panic now.

"Turn around." It might seem silly since I was in Percy's body, but I wasn't exposing myself to Evan.

He turned to face the door. "Hurry up."

I searched inside my shirt and even checked my pantaloons. Nothing. "I don't have it."

We turned over every pillow and looked under every piece of furniture, but we didn't find the locket.

"It's gone. Our only way home is gone." Horror overcame me and I sank to the floor. "If I stay here another day, Percy and I will die." My chest constricted. Suddenly, there wasn't enough air in the room. My breath came in tiny, terrible gasps.

"Kat, try to calm down. When was the last time you noticed it?" Ellie's small body sat next to mine, but I recognized the soothing, rational tone of voice as Evan's.

"This afternoon." I remembered adjusting it before we had gone down to dinner.

And then it came to me.

"Lydia." Her name stole my breath away again. "She kissed Percy goodbye. She must have stolen it when he was distracted."

Ellie's forehead creased with Evan's disapproval.

"I'm sorry."

He wouldn't look at me.

I didn't blame him. If I'd have listened to him earlier, we'd never be in this position. "This is all my fault, but I'll get it back," I promised.

"How? The minute we're in a room with anyone from this era, we revert back to Percy and Ellie."

"We'll wait until everyone is asleep and then we'll sneak into Lydia's house."

"Into that fortress?" Disbelief doused his words. "How do you propose we find the locket in all those rooms before we're discovered?"

I rubbed my lips together and tried to think of something. "Can you tap into Ellie's powers?"

"Ellie can barely tap into her powers," he muttered. "She only knows a few spells."

There had to be a way to use what she knew. I thought back to how Toria had explained that my magic was connected to my blood and my soul. "But you have a bit of my soul in you from when I healed you. Maybe you can use it to help Ellie? Sort of like how Toria's ghost slipped into my skin and helped me break the curse on the Radcliffe rubies."

"You think I could help Ellie?" He sounded skeptical.

"She knows how to do a locator spell. She can find the necklace for us if you help her." Evan's this-will-never-work look was less convincing on Ellie's face. "It's possible. Just try. Please."

"What if Lydia sees us coming?"

"No matter how powerful she is, she can't see everything that is going to happen. Toria couldn't and she was one of the most powerful Langley heirs. Ever." I thought about Percy's memories. "Lydia seems best at predicting harm to others. This is the opposite, right?"

I could see Evan's skepticism shining through, but I also saw resignation. The truth was, we didn't have much of a choice except to try.

Evan did not enjoy casting a spell. I could tell from the looks he was shooting across the hotel room at me. They ranged from doubt to frustration to annoyance and circled back again. I understood the array of emotions. This was usually my task, and it still felt weird to me.

For this locator spell, we'd had to improvise. We still had the basic ingredients from the spell that Ellie had cast to find Lydia, and Evan was able to probe Ellie's own memories a bit for guidance. We added a lock of Ellie's hair and a nail clipping from Percy because the locket was tied to both of them. We had to hope that this would be enough.

The piece of my soul that Evan carried helped power the spell even more than I had guessed. We figured that it might be because I was the Langley heir and stronger than Ellie. In any case, despite Evan's initial misgivings, we had a precise location. The locket was in the drawer of Lydia's writing desk.

All we had to do was get it.

Had Evan and I been on our own, we wouldn't have had a chance. Luckily, we weren't.

The locket wasn't just a piece of jewelry. It was an ancient and powerful piece of magic. With Lorelei's mirror and her own Langley blood, Lydia could travel to Dumbarton and, from there, to any of the four families' homes in Connecticut. Percy would never let that happen. He would want the locket back, and he would know how to burglarize a townhouse without getting caught.

After a quick discussion, Evan and I decided to recede into the background so that Percy could concoct and execute a plan to steal back the locket.

Percy blamed himself for losing the locket. He had let Lydia get to him. He'd been a fool. But he didn't have time for anger or self-loathing now. He had to fight and he couldn't be at war with himself. He had to reserve all his focus for the task at hand.

As he and Ellie stalked towards Lydia's house, he couldn't help thinking about how he'd been sneaking in and out of rich men's houses most of his life. Their wives and daughters had a weakness for him. It might have been the lure of the Kingsley name or his dangerous reputation or simply the eye patch. Whatever drew them in, he'd exploited it. Sometimes for Harrison's benefit. Sometimes for his own.

He might have carried on like that indefinitely. But now he wanted something more. Better. He wanted Sarah.

As he thought of her, he cast a glance at Ellie. He hadn't known whether to bring her or not, but, ultimately, he'd decided that he wanted to keep her close.

While Percy worried about Ellie, I lurked in the back of his mind and worried about Evan. I should have listened to him. If we'd used the locket to go home as soon as we had the dagger, he'd be safe now. And, with the dagger, he might even have been able to save me.

Ellie and Percy crouched in darkness, watching as the lights inside Lydia's townhouse were extinguished, waiting for the servants to go to bed. Percy checked his pocket watch. It was just after midnight when the last candle was snuffed. They waited another half hour. Then he scooped Ellie into his arms and crept silently towards the kitchen door.

He set Ellie down gently. "Don't move," he whispered.

She nodded.

He pulled out his tools to pick the lock. Just one of the questionable skills he'd acquired in service to Harrison. So much of who Percy was came down to being the Kingsley heir. Duty to Harrison had always come first, no matter what that duty required. Tonight, though, he was choosing Sarah over the Radcliffes and he didn't care about the consequences.

He heard the delicate click. The lock had released its hold on the door. Slowly, he opened it. He took a few steps inside and motioned for Ellie to follow him. It was so dark inside, Ellie stumbled. He caught her before she fell.

He couldn't carry her through the house. He had to be ready to fight if someone discovered them. He grabbed her hand. "Stick close to me, and don't let go of me," he whispered.

Her head bobbed in the darkness.

He skulked through the house, seeing the auras of objects and scooting around furniture as he made his way to the drawing room. When they stepped inside, he scanned the room. Nothing living. He shut the door behind him and locked it.

He noticed a faint orange aura emanating from the bottom drawer of the desk. That had to be the locket.

"Stay here, next to the door. I'll be right back."

He skirted around the coffee table, passed the fireplace, and went around the couch toward the desk. It took him just a moment to pick the lock. He slid the drawer out and found the locket lying inside. He was about to reach for it when he saw the glow from the star sapphire in his dagger's sheath. A supernatural threat.

He had faced assassins, thieves, and marauders on his own, but it had been years since he'd faced off with something supernatural without Sarah. The blood rushed through his veins, readying him for the fight.

He looked back to the door, where he'd told Ellie to stay. Her aura had disappeared. He whispered, "Ellie?"

No reply.

Blast it. He slid the locket into his coat pocket and looked around the room. There were no living auras anywhere. No sign of any other person there. But of course there wouldn't be. The realization made him feel sick. And disgusted with his own stupidity.

"Lydia." She'd lured them there. Of course she had.

She chuckled. It sounded like it came from everywhere. His heart pounded against his chest, trying to beat down the fear. He pulled his dagger out and held it in front of him as he spun around, but he couldn't find her. She was masking her presence.

"Where is Ellie?" he asked the darkness.

Lydia's voice echoed around him. "She's right here beside me."

"Ellie?" he called out again.

"I'm here." Ellie's voice came out in a high-pitched squeal.

Lydia was cloaking both of them. "Lydia, let her go."

"Don't break into my house, pull a knife on me, and give me orders." Her voice was so cold that he almost shivered.

Ellie gasped just before all the candles in the room flared to life.

Lydia stood by the fireplace in a dressing gown of pink and blue. Such gentle colors on such a cruel woman. Her long hair hung around her shoulders. Her eyes glittered with anger. She kept Ellie in front of her and held a small knife to the girl's throat. It glinted in the candlelight. A drop of blood seeped up from where she'd pressed the blade too hard against Ellie's neck.

Ellie's lower lip trembled. He'd never seen such fear in her eyes. It sent a terrible sensation tumbling down his spine and slamming into his stomach. He tried to keep his voice calm. "It'll be fine, Ellie."

Lydia made a noise in her throat like a bobcat mauling a rabbit. "Depends on your definition of fine. And I'm going to need for you to return that locket."

"It doesn't belong to you," Percy said.

"It doesn't belong to you. It belongs to the Langleys," she hissed.

"The Langley heir, Lydia." He needed to keep her talking while he found a way to get Ellie away from her. "It must sting to be reduced to picking pockets."

"I've always done what I must."

"Did you learn that skill after your family banished you?" He wanted to incite her anger. He hoped that emotion might cause her to make a mistake. "Is it something your husband taught you? Or another man, perhaps?"

She lifted her chin and taunted him. "Are you jealous? That the great Kingsley heir was outmaneuvered by a Langley, and not even a Langley heir?"

"You think this is about my pride? You don't know me at all."

She pressed the knife harder against Ellie's throat. A thin stream of blood was falling toward her collar. She looked terrified.

His stomach twisted. It had been a mistake to try to provoke Lydia into a misstep. He slid his blade back into the sheath.

"I know you, Percy." Lydia's eyes narrowed like a hawk siting its prey. "You will always do the right thing. And that means saving Ellie at any cost."

He folded his arms and leaned against the desk, trying to appear indifferent. "But you already told me she's going to die soon. At least this will be quick."

"Who said it would be quick?" Lydia slashed Ellie's neck. Blood poured out, drenching her dress.

"No!" He leapt toward them.

Ellie's aura faded from red to orange to a faint yellow. She was dying. As Percy was striding toward her, Lydia whispered ancient words and the wound on Ellie's neck healed. The life came back into her eyes. Her aura glowed again.

Stunned, he froze in place.

Lydia pulled Ellie close again and the child cringed. "I can do this all night. Kill her and bring her back. Or I can start summoning servants. I can sacrifice people in her place until it turns her very soul."

"You can't. You don't love them."

"I don't have to." Her laugh sounded almost merry. "Oh, I know what Jonas told you. But that spell only requires that I love the person I'm killing as much as the person I'm saving. And I love the girl who arranges my hair at least as much as I love this little thing."

Percy couldn't keep the look of horror off his face, even though he knew that Lydia would relish it.

"In any case, I know all kinds of spells to save lives and trade lives. Spells that extract a brutal price from those they save. There are so many ways we can do this." An unholy fire burned in her eyes. "But those spells are exhausting, even for me. Eventually, I might become too weary to bring her back again."

Percy was desperate now. He just wanted to keep Lydia talking. "Why do you want the locket? It's a doorway to the families you despise."

"That's no concern of yours. All you need to understand is that I want it. And I've already explained what will happen if I don't get it." With that, she stabbed Ellie in the stomach, pulled the knife out, and let the child fall to the floor.

Ellie's blue dress turned red at the center. "Don't do it, Percy," she whimpered.

He didn't have a choice. "Heal her first."

A smile slithered across Lydia's face. "I thought you'd see it my way."

She whispered words of healing again. A few moments later Ellie stood up, shaking. Her eyes were haunted by what had happened.

"Put the locket on my desk."

If he conceded to her now, he might have one more chance to best her. He doubted that he'd have more than one. He pulled the locket out of his pocket and placed it on the desk.

"This has almost been too easy. You were all so eager to abandon Harrison in order to help Ellie. I had assumed that you'd have more of a sense of duty. Ah, well."

"Was Ellie really in danger?"

"Of course. But Sarah was a fool to not see through the vision I sent her."

Percy struggled to understand what he was hearing. "Did you really even want my dagger?"

"Oh, you know how negotiations work. Ask for more than you can imagine. Settle for what you want."

"Which was the locket." He'd been so stupid. She could get to everyone now. Because of him. "Are you going to kill them all?"

"We need to start over. The four families need a fresh set of heirs." She spoke with a feverish intensity. "The ring will be mine."

"The ring passed over you once, and it will do so again. It will never choose you, because you killed your mother."

Her face contorted with anger and she tightened her grip on Ellie. "That wasn't my fault. She was killing me. I had to survive."

"That doesn't change the fact that the ring will never choose you."

"Do you know what happens if all the heirs die at once?" she asked. "I don't."

"Neither do I. Nobody does. But I, for one, am eager to find out."

She thought she could manipulate the ring into picking her. And it didn't matter how many people had to die. She was willing to do anything to make it happen.

No. That wasn't right. She'd already done things to make it happen. The truth was written across her face. Somehow, she had gotten close enough to poison Harrison without Sarah or Percy realizing it. She was the reason Sarah was dying. She'd used Ellie to get Percy here and to lure out Jonas. She was behind everything bad that befell the heirs and she had used him to advance her plan.

Lydia was the reason everyone he had sworn to protect was in danger. In that moment, his hatred for her flash-flooded his mind. Lydia had to suffer. Every inch of his body cried out for her death. He took a step toward her intent on ending her, even if it ended him.

I couldn't let this happen. Lydia would kill Percy and Ellie. I had to do something. I struggled to take control. I shouldn't have been able to do it in Lydia's presence, but, somehow, I did it. And I had a plan.

If Langley blood and Langley souls powered spells, maybe getting some of Ellie's blood on my hands would help me work magic, even though I was in a Kingsley body. "Release Ellie. Let her come here, to me, and I'll leave the locket on the desk, just as you asked me."

Lydia eyed me curiously before saying, "Take a few more steps away from the desk."

I had to put several feet between me and the desk before she would release Ellie. When Ellie rushed to my side, I touched the blood on her dress. I felt the energy. The connection. The Langley power pulsing in my soul.

Lydia's face contorted. "Who are you?"

"Someone you shouldn't have messed with." It was Percy's voice, but my words.

"You're a Langley, aren't you?" She stared at me and for a second I swore she could see into my soul. "Are you from the future, or the past?"

The question caught me off guard, but I refused to answer. "That's my locket now." I managed to keep my voice level, even though I was terrified.

"No, actually, it's mine now." She grabbed it off the desk and slid it into the pocket of her dressing gown.

"I won't let you hurt them."

"You think you can stop me?" Her tone was dismissive. "Your magic won't work here. Wherever you've come from, you're in the wrong time, girl."

"The heirs are stronger than you, aren't they?"

"I don't see a ring on your hand," she said.

"But I'm not the Langley heir right now. I'm the Kingsley heir, and I have my dagger." I slid my hand to the hilt, grasping it.

Her gaze followed my movement.

In her moment of distraction, I gripped Ellie's hand and imagined my soul's power flowing into her. Words, ancient words that I'd never spoken, came to me. To us. Ellie and I said them together. Lydia's eyes widened. I didn't know what we were doing, but it seemed that she did.

I thought she was frozen in place until I noticed her lips moving. A counter spell or a curse. Whatever she was saying, I couldn't let her finish. I didn't think, I just acted on Percy's instincts and threw the blade at her. The Kingsley dagger hit her in the belly. She stumbled backwards, but she had enough strength left to send her own knife hurtling toward Ellie. I shoved Ellie to the ground and an incredible pressure spread through my side.

Chapter 30

My first instinct, after assuring myself that Ellie was safe, was to pull the knife out of my side. But then I wondered if it might be the only thing keeping the blood from pouring out of me. If I had been in my own body, I would have fainted at the thought. But Percy wasn't squeamish.

I heard a rough, wet gasping and turned my attention to Lydia. I rose, ignoring the burning pain of my own wound, and started across the room. I swayed on my feet, weakened both from the injury and the spell casting.

Suddenly, Ellie was underneath my arm, trying to support me. "Are you really a Langley? Have you really traveled through time?"

"Yes." I panted around the pain.

"Why?"

"To save you." That was all of the truth I could manage to get out at that moment, and, for Ellie, it was the only thing that mattered.

"Thank you."

I heard the gratitude in her voice and my heart swelled. I had changed the past. I had saved Ellie from Lydia. "You're—"

Before I could finish the sentence, Percy took control of his body and swung around to put himself between Ellie and Lydia.

"Are you all right?" he demanded.

"I'm safe. Pppercy?"

"Yes?"

"You're bleeding. Badly."

His side ached and his coat was soaked in blood, but he'd suffered worse. He wondered why the blade was still lodged in his flesh. He yanked it out and dropped it, letting it clatter on the floor. "I'll be fine. I'm healing already."

He looked at Lydia, crumpled on the floor, and said to Ellie, "Stay right here. Don't move."

There was a blank space in his recent memory. He remembered Lydia saying that she planned to kill all the heirs and realizing she had already begun her plan. Anger blinded him. Then nothing, until he had discovered her knife in his side. He saw the Kingsley dagger was buried in Lydia's belly, but he had no recollection of how it had gotten there. And—

"Ellie, where's the locket?"

"Lydia has it. In the pocket of her dressing gown."

Lydia moaned as Percy searched her pockets. He ignored her. Once he had the locket, he fastened it around his own neck again.

Lydia was dying—she was strong, but not stronger than the Kingsley dagger. His dagger was a death sentence. Percy needed for her to live just a bit longer, though. She was still Sarah's only hope.

If only he could trade Lydia's life for Sarah's. But that wasn't how the spell worked, at least not the spell that Jonas had described, the spell that Lydia had given Ellie. That spell required a sacrifice: someone you loved for someone you loved. Ellie was willing to pay that price. And so was he. It was the only way.

Ellie touched his shoulder. "It wasn't your fault."

"I asked you to stay put," he said, more roughly than he intended.

"You can't protect me from this." Ellie sounded much older than her eleven years.

He stared down at Lydia, wondering how he could convince Ellie to do the spell for him.

"We've got the locket back. And she'll never help us."

"I know."

"Percy..."

And then an idea began taking shape in his mind. Langley blood was powerful. Lydia's blood must be *very* powerful. He looked around for a cup, a vase, an inkwell. Something. Then he heard people stirring upstairs. They didn't have much time.

He couldn't possibly leave without the Kingsley dagger, but, the moment he pulled it from Lydia, it would sever the bond between her body and soul. Once she died, her magic would die with her and her blood would be useless. If he and Ellie were going to use it to save Sarah, they had to act fast.

Once more, I pushed myself to the surface.

"Ellie, it's me again. I'm a Langley heir from the future, and I need for you to listen to me. The Kingsley heir from my time traveled with me, and I need you to let me talk to him. If I call to him, do you think you can let him answer?"

She didn't understand, but she nodded. Her trust broke my heart.

"Evan."

The look of confusion in Ellie's eyes was replaced with one of determination.

"We've got to get home, Kat. Take the dagger. Now." Evan pulled a pin from his pocket and pricked Ellie's finger.

As soon as Ellie's blood touched the mirror, the portal would open and we could go home. I clutched the hilt of the Kingsley dagger as Evan took the locket and—

I saw Ellie's hand falter. She pulled away. And Evan was gone.

And I was, too. Percy had taken control of his body again.

Percy held out the locket. "Ellie, take this. Use it to go back to Dumbarton. After you do the spell for me."

Ellie shook her head. "I won't."

"We both want to save Sarah, and I promised her that I would save you. My life for hers. It's the only way."

"I can't kill you."

He gripped Ellie's small, delicate hand in his large, callused one. "I'm not asking you to take my life. I'm asking you to help me give it to Sarah. It's my duty, as the Kingsley heir, to protect the others."

Ellie started to cry. "Don't ask me to do this. Please, Percy. Don't ask me to be a murderer."

He pulled her close. Her warm tears soaked his shirt, dampening his chest. Percy stroked her hair and tried to comfort her. "You will be saving your sister and yourself. Two lives for one. That's not murder. That's a miracle."

"I'm not strong enough to do that spell on my own." There was a stubborn note in Ellie's voice now.

"You don't have to. We can use Lydia's blood for the spell. She's still alive. Add her power to your own."

"And if I don't?" She sniffed.

"Then Sarah dies. The ring chooses you, and you die, too. And all of this will have been for nothing."

Ellie sighed and sank into herself.

"It's the only way. Please, Ellie. I need you to help me."

"All right, Percy. I will."

He leaned over Lydia and her long blond eyelashes parted. Her silver-green eyes bored into his. "Don't." She could barely whisper.

"Why?"

"I can save Sarah." Lydia's voice was a wisp.

"And you will. Ellie is going to use your blood to help her work the spell you gave her."

Ellie touched Lydia's wound with her palm and let her hand rest there to absorb the blood. The red aura around Ellie intensified, thickening and brightening until she was filled with Lydia's power.

No one without Percy's heightened senses could have caught what Lydia said. "But you don't…"

And he didn't care. "You can do it, Ellie," he said.

Fat tears rolled down her cheeks and her voice shook like a glass about to shatter, but she didn't falter as she whispered words Percy couldn't understand.

And then she grasped the hilt of the Kingsley dagger and spoke in English, her words clear and strong. "In the place of Sarah Langley Harding, our priestess, I offer our weakest. I offer myself."

It took Percy a moment to understand what she had said. "Ellie, no."

"I have to."

She had the dagger pointed at her own midsection now. Percy struggled to grasp her wrists.

She fought him as best she could, but she was a child, and he was a grown man, and a Kingsley.

He had the dagger now, point pressed to his own belly.

"This is for you, Ellie. And for Sarah. Tell her that I love her, please." His voice filled with all the feelings he'd hidden away for years.

He took a breath and thought of Sarah—how her hair smelled of spring and how her spearmint green eyes always felt like home to him. Then he plunged the knife into his belly.

Ellie stumbled through the rest of the spell with her face pressed into his shoulder. When she finished, she touched his face. "Oh, Percy, I'm so sorry."

Percy was dying.

And I was dying, too.

As Percy surrendered himself to his fate, I was able to resurface. One word slipped from my—our—lips. "Evan."

Ellie's expression changed, and I saw him. Evan.

"Hold on. I'm going to get you home." He opened the locket, smeared Langley blood on the mirror inside, and gripped the dagger that was lodged in my stomach. "Think of home. Think of Dumbarton. Think of Vivian waiting for us there. Please Kat, just hold on."

I tried to conjure up the chamber of mirrors at Dumbarton. I saw stone walls, and the dull flash of torchlight reflected in the mirrors, and… Then I lost it. I tried to see the Langley coat of arms, traced out on the floor, but I couldn't focus. My mind kept fading to blue.

Death was dragging me into oblivion.

My thoughts and Percy's intermingled. Sarah and Harrison flashed through his mind. All the things he had to do to keep them safe. It was worth it. He glanced at Lydia. Her eyes were glazed over in death. At least, he could protect everyone from her.

"You're safe," Percy whispered to Ellie.

Her sad green eyes were the last thing he saw before his eyes slipped shut forever.

Chapter 31

Percy's life flashed before his eyes. Not as a beautiful tapestry of memories, but as a chaotic mix of thoughts, sensations, and images. His mother's hugs. His father's disregard. His brothers' backs as they walked away from him, refusing to wait for him to catch up.

There was the shock of a broken bottle slammed into his eye. And then the pain was gone. He was talking, softly, to a woman. His voice was husky, and he was promising her things he'd never give her.

And then he saw Sarah, lying in her bed, close to death. Her eyes opened and—

She gasped.

Her eyes were clear now.

"What have you done?" she whispered.

Percy tried to answer, but he couldn't because he was suddenly pulled back to Lydia's drawing room. Ellie sobbed over his body. Incoherent noises that weren't quite human.

He tried to get to her. To climb back into his body, to protect her, but it was too late.

If I was dead, then why did everything hurt so much?

Ghosts didn't have physical pain, yet I had throbbing joints and aching muscles.

And a pain in my belly that was unlike anything I'd ever felt. It twisted everything inside me until all that existed was the pain.

The blood pounded in my veins, finally convincing me I was alive. But I couldn't open my eyes or speak. Then I heard voices. Distant. Garbled. Slowly, they grew clearer. Eventually, I sensed movement nearby.

"The fever is getting worse." I recognized Vivian's gentle tone.

"She was too weak." Jacqueline's judgment wove through every word.

"She can't die. You have to do something." Hope and fear fought for control of Evan's voice.

"She saved your life, but she may have sealed her own fate," Jacqueline said.

"But her body looks fine. Why is she so sick?" Evan asked.

Voices and words began to intermingle and I no longer knew who was talking.

"It's her soul. That's where all the damage was done."

I floated among the clouds. Weightless. Each moment felt like an infinite number of moments. Then the clouds parted. I saw Toria standing on the cliffs on the Isle of Acacia, staring out at the ocean. And then I was right beside her.

Her expression reminded me of the sky before a storm breaks—dark and threatening. "Why couldn't you just get the dagger and come back? Such simple instructions."

"I had to help Ellie."

Her eyes seared mine. "No, you didn't."

"I couldn't let her suffer. Her ghost asked me for help." I rubbed my arms, trying to soothe myself.

"You changed the past, but you didn't save her. Not really."

"What do you mean?"

Toria's gaze grew distant, like she was looking into the past, trying to sort its new configuration from the old.

"Sarah lived, didn't she?"

Toria nodded.

I felt Percy's relief in my soul. "And so did Ellie?"

Toria nodded again, and then she added, "But Sarah never forgave her little sister for her role in Percy's death."

I shook my head, trying to void her words. "But it was Percy's choice. None of it was Ellie's fault."

"Ellie never told Sarah exactly what happened. She felt guilty about not giving her own life, and she was happy to let Sarah blame her."

I didn't know what to say. The sound of the waves crashing against the rocks below filled my ears. All I could think about was how Ellie's heart must have shattered at Sarah's rejection.

I scrambled to find some good in what Toria was telling me. "But Ellie got to live."

"Yes, but Sarah convinced their parents to send Ellie away, to England, to live with distant relatives." Toria squinted at the horizon. "Ellie lived a life she didn't want. Sometimes, it's impossible to live with the sacrifices of others. It's too much."

Toria fell silent for a while.

"Percy should have accepted that. Ellie wanted to die for Sarah. If she had, her life would have been short, but meaningful." Toria's voice was full of reproach.

"I wanted to help them. Did I make everything worse?" Guilt crushed my heart to a fine powder.

Another eternity passed before Toria spoke. "You didn't make everything worse. You made some things different."

I didn't want to ask my next question, but I had to know. "Am I dead?"

She gave me a sidelong glance. "Do you want to be dead?"

"No." I was certain of that.

"Well, then you are going to have to fight." She grabbed my hand in her own. For once, her touch felt warm. "This is going to hurt. All of it. Don't let it break you."

With that warning, Toria disappeared.

I prayed I'd wake up at Dumbarton. Instead, I found myself in total darkness. Except this time, I was standing in it, like I'd been tossed into another body in the middle of a moment in someone else's life. I bumped into something solid and grabbed on to steady myself. A chair.

I didn't know who I was, but the Langley sapphire glowed on my finger. I sensed I was in my apartment. And then I became her completely. I took two steps toward the wall, but my hand never made it to the light switch.

My only warning was the sudden unbearable weight on my chest. It's strange how calmly the realization hit. *Time had run out for me.*

My eyes darted around the darkness.

He was here.

My body fought a pointless battle. Every muscle strained to pull the air into my lungs, while something unseen pressed down on me, forcing the air right back out. I tried to remain calm—it's what you're supposed to do in a crisis. My heart refused to listen, beating faster and faster, running the most important race of my life.

It didn't matter. He'd found me.

They say before you die, your life flashes before your eyes. Mine didn't. All I saw were the moments left undone. The people who would suffer. My brother Maxmil living in the shadows. My niece Kat having her world ripped apart.

The images faded. I forced my eyes back to the darkness.

Something stirred in the void.

He was coming for me.

The blood singed my veins. There wasn't much time left.

His voice was in my head. He was circling his prey.

A shrill sound filled the room, startling me. Then I realized it was me. My breath was coming in sharp, painful gasps. Cold sweat trickled down my back. Tiny tremors ripped through my body.

A fire started inside my feet. The burning spread to my legs. The flames were devouring me from the inside out. I could hear my screams, the pain pushing me to the edge of sanity. My mind tried to clamp down on the horrific sensations. If I let it win, I'd become an observer to my own death.

My voice broke, begging him to stop.

There was no escape. Blue flames licked at my heart. A strange warmth enveloped me. I couldn't give in. Not yet.

I was dying. Not some heroic last stand, but a meaningless coward's death. My aunts' warnings rang out in my mind. *Never go into battle alone. Always bring the Kingsley heir with you. Even without his dagger, he can help.* But I didn't listen. I wanted to spare Evan a little longer. I thought this was something I could handle. I thought wrong.

Now, I was paying with my life.

I wasn't alone though. The hunter was laughing at my pain, delighting in my agony. He wasn't just here for my soul. No, that wouldn't be enough for him.

I had miscalculated there. He wanted the ring, too.

A floor lamp flared, like he wanted his face to be the very last thing I saw before I died. He smiled down at me with blinding indifference. I searched the merciless obsidian pools where his eyes should have been. I'd better make this count.

He reached for me.

I felt the delicate tearing—the remains of my soul being torn from my body. I clawed at my executioner.

In that split second, he looked surprised as though I was the one who wasn't playing fair. His icy touch encircled my finger. I couldn't let him have the ring. It was all I could do. Please forgive me, Maxmil.

Now, I was just a piece of the giant Langley tapestry. A mere moment in all of it. I had to hold on to something or I'd disappear. Morgan was a hazy memory. Mom. Mom was real. I loved the way she smiled on a dig, like she was exactly where she was always meant to be. It was the only time she ever looked truly happy.

Her face started to slip away. I needed someone else. Evan. Something anchored me. I felt myself coming back together. I thought of all we had been through and how hard he fought to get me back here. I couldn't let him down. I had to find a way back.

My self came flooding back to me. I was Kat Preston. Kat Langley. Katarina Preston Langley. I saw myself as a little girl secretly helping the ghosts.

Suddenly, a thick fog swirled around me. I couldn't see anything. I took a few deep breaths and waited for the fog to part.

When it did, a grave stood in front of me. Mist shrouded everything but the black marble headstone. I expected it to be mine. I stepped closer to read the names: Joshua Radcliffe and Olivia Mallory Radcliffe. No. They weren't even married yet. I couldn't see the dates on the headstone, but the headstone was cold and unyielding beneath my fingertips.

Tears clogged my throat, making it harder to breathe.

The fog receded further, revealing a line of headstones like notches on a belt. My stomach turned over, trying to escape the sight. I didn't want to look at the names, but I had to. The next gravestone was pink granite and the name engraved on it was Morgan Sanchez. No, not my Morgan. Please not Morgan. Tears burned my eyes and trickled down my cheeks.

I stepped toward a gray granite headstone. The name read Dr. Valerie Preston, Beloved Mother and Brilliant Archaeologist. My mom was gone. I collapsed on the ground and sobbed for her.

I don't know how long I cried—time had no meaning here—but when I looked up, another gravestone waited. The fog was relentless in its revelations. I wiped my face on my sleeve. I couldn't bear to see the next name. I crawled toward it with one hope in my heart: Please, let it be mine.

But the name on the headstone was Maximillian Langley. My heart stuttered, *Daddy, Daddy, Daddy.* I didn't want to go on. I couldn't.

I felt a hand on my shoulder. I jerked away, expecting an attack. But it was Evan.

"You aren't alone. All you have to do is reach out. We're all here for you," he said.

Sadness strangled me. All I could do was point at the graves. A weird keening came from my throat. Morgan was gone. My parents were gone. Joshua was gone. Everyone I should have protected was gone.

I blinked and Evan disappeared. Another gravestone appeared. I didn't want to look at it. To see the name that was there. But I had no choice. I stumbled to this last grave, praying it was mine. That I was done suffering.

It said, Evan Kingsley, a fearless fighter.

He was gone too. Just like everyone else. They had all left me.

I was the only one that remained.

I curled into myself and prayed for my end.

When I had found out about the Langley legacy I had been so afraid to die, but this, this was far worse. Not dying to save the ones I loved, but being the only one still alive when all the battles were done.

Chapter 32

I awoke to darkness that was punctuated by a soft snore. I was lying in bed and my skin was so clammy that my pajamas clung to me. The comforter felt satiny with bits of scratchy metallic thread, like the one on my bed at Dumbarton.

I tried to sit up, but pain shot through my stomach. I clenched my teeth and sucked air around them. My hands covered the tender spot as if that could protect me from more pain. I stayed as still as I could. Deep, deep inside me, it ached like something had tunneled through my stomach on its way to my spine.

Something stirred in the chair beside me. Fabric rustled and the snoring slowed.

My mouth was so dry I could barely speak. "Vivian?"

No response.

"Jacqueline?"

Nothing.

"Evan?" A terrible tickle started in the back of my throat. I couldn't swallow it away. I coughed and it tore at my stomach. I yelped in pain.

"Kat?" Evan sounded suddenly alert.

He must have flicked on the lamp because brightness blasted the darkness away. I winced as my pupils adjusted. Everything was blurry. I reached for my glasses, but Evan was already sliding them onto my face. I could see the desk and the armoire at the end of my bed at Dumbarton.

Dark circles rimmed Evan's eyes. "You're all right." His relief told me how close I had come to dying.

I didn't know what to say. My mouth was dry, and I struggled not to cough again. "I'm thirsty."

He poured me some water and propped me up with pillows so I could drink.

My throat burned and throbbed. I grabbed the water from his outstretched hands. It tasted wonderful, cooling my mouth and soothing my throat. I gulped the first glass down. He refilled it.

While I sipped it, he perched on my bed. "When Percy stabbed himself with the Kingsley dagger, he stabbed you too. Well, your soul, anyway. That's what Jacqueline said. When you came back to your body, your soul was deeply wounded."

"The Kingsley dagger is a mortal blow. How did I make it through?"

"You saved yourself. When you gave me a piece of your soul to save my life, you made it impossible to kill you without killing me, too."

I was happy to be here until he said that. "I didn't mean to put you at risk. Give it back."

"No." He gave me a tired, but determined smile. "According to Vivian, it makes us harder to kill. We're linked. No one can kill me without killing you. It works both ways."

"So, you could say I saved us twice?"

His laughter sounded exhausted. "Are you keeping score?"

"Not really." Though, I was still ahead. I handed him my cup for another refill. "How long was I out?"

"Two days."

Two days. No wonder those nightmares felt like they went on forever.

He pressed his hand to my forehead. "Your fever finally broke. You were delirious for a while."

"Did I say anything?"

"You cried out for Ellie. And you begged me not to leave you alone."

Heat crept over my cheeks. "Must have been the fever."

"What were you dreaming about?"

"Those weren't dreams. They were awful nightmares." I told Evan about my conversation with Toria, my aunt Shannon's death, and the graveyard.

"Try not to let the graves get to you. You can't see the future."

"I know." But the memory of those gravestones still haunted me. Everyone was dead, everyone, except me. A shiver zigzagged down my spine.

"Are you hungry?"

"I probably should be, but no."

He reached for my wrist and checked my pulse. "Nice and steady."

"It wasn't before?"

He rubbed his hand over his lips, like he was unsure how much to tell me. "Your heart stopped. Vivian and Jacqueline cast every healing spell they knew to help you."

"They must be exhausted."

"They need a few nights' rest. That's why I offered to stay with you."

Without thinking, I shifted and a sharp pain ripped through my stomach. I hissed and pressed my hand over the wound.

"Stop moving. You're going to be sore for a bit," he said.

"Will I have a scar?"

"Not on your body."

"On my soul?" I said, half-kidding.

"That's what Vivian said. A badge of courage, she called it."

I didn't know what to say to that, so I asked, "Did we bring the dagger back?"

He stood up. The dagger hung from its sheath on his belt. When I looked at it, I remembered the heat and pressure as it sliced into me. I never wanted to feel that again.

I rubbed my stomach. "How long until the pain stops?"

"They said it's going to take a week to heal completely."

"A week?"

"What part of mortal blow are you not understanding? You should be dead. It takes time to heal that kind of supernatural injury."

I flicked at a pull in the comforter. It was my fault that I was injured. My fault that the Langleys were exhausted. My fault that we almost got stuck in the past. "Evan, I'm sorry."

He brushed the hair off my forehead and tucked it behind my ear. "For what?"

"For staying in Vienna. For risking your life."

"My life was barely at risk. You made sure of that with the protection spell." His eyes were a storm of brown and green coming for me. I couldn't look away.

He cupped my chin. His palm was warm, comforting. "You risked your own life too many times."

"I should have listened to you. I think I made everything worse."

Evan gently slid onto the bed and wrapped his arm around me. "You didn't. Ellie lived."

"Miserably."

"Sarah?"

"She never forgave her."

"Why?"

"Ellie let her think it was all Ellie's fault."

He rubbed my arm. "You did your best. You were brave and strong."

"But it wasn't enough." I turned my head into his shirt.

"Kat, you helped Ellie. You saved me. I've got the dagger. I'm already stronger. And now we have a fighting chance."

"I'm so glad you're okay." I reached for his hand, grateful to have him here.

He laced his fingers through mine. "Me, too. You really scared us."

He reached over to turn the lamp off, but I asked, "Can we leave it on? I hate waking up to darkness."

"Of course." There was a roughness to his voice.

I didn't think I'd sleep for a while, but I nodded off a few sentences later.

In the orchard behind Castle Creighton, I rested my back against the apple tree and bit into a Granny Smith. The tartness tickled my tongue and the juice ran down my chin. The sun snuck through the branches to warm my skin. A breeze rustled the leaves above me. The grass tickled my bare legs. I closed my eyes and breathed in the warm air.

I didn't hear her, so much as feel her presence. When I looked up, a semi-transparent Lorelei stood in front of me. Her long raven-colored hair hung around her shoulders. Her dress was dark green with a gold cord tied around her waist. She was barefoot and her silver toe rings glinted in the sunlight. There was a grace and a calmness about her. I wasn't sure if it was an ancestor thing or just who she'd always been.

"You did better than I expected." Her voice had a thick Scottish brogue.

"But I wasn't strong enough to change the past."

Lorelei sat beside me and arranged her skirts. "You're wrong. You did so much."

"Percy's still dead."

"But he didn't die in his hotel room. Lydia didn't murder him."

"Ellie still was blamed."

"You don't know what you averted." Her expression radiated appreciation at me. "If you hadn't gone back, Lydia would have had the locket. She would have hurt the families more than you can imagine. Originally, she let everyone think Ellie was behind Percy's death. Sarah died. Ellie inherited the ring and died horribly. Lydia didn't inherit the ring, but she lived a long miserable existence and harmed countless people before her death. Lydia won last time."

"And this time?"

"She died a few moments before Percy did. She never got her revenge on the families."

"And Jonas?" Lydia made it sound like she'd poisoned him too.

"Sarah was able to save him."

Lydia hadn't won. Three of the heirs survived her attacks.

"How do you know all this?" If I had changed things and it hadn't happened that way, how could she know?

She gave me a mysterious smile. "I've always seen all the realities— what was, what is, and what could be."

"So, I helped?" Hope stirred within me.

"You changed so much for the better. In the past, and in the present. You prevented a horrible tragedy from befalling all four families. Evan has the dagger now. The Kingsley family heirloom has been restored." The pride in her voice eased the ache in my stomach.

"Then why was Toria upset with me?"

"She's very protective of you. She couldn't bear the thought of you dying this young."

"But that's my fate."

The intensity in Lorelei's eyes stole my breath. "Those who see the future, they think fate cannot be changed, only deferred. Those whose powers are connected to the present believe the future is of their making. But the few who can go to the past, they understand that it's much more complicated than that. Everything ties together. You see that. Trust yourself."

I wanted to ask her more questions, but she whispered, "I've stayed too long. I don't want to tire you out. Rest, dear girl, you've earned it." She kissed my cheek and disappeared.

Chapter 33

I woke up without Evan, but he'd left me with daylight streaming through an opening in the curtains. I stayed in bed until I realized I was hungry. Ravenously hungry. Hungry enough to dare to get up.

I tried to avoid twisting my torso, which meant I moved like a ninety-year-old woman. After I tugged off my nightgown, I stood in front of the mirror, staring at my bare stomach. Evan said there was no scar, but I swore I saw a faint silver line across my belly. When I tried to trace over it with my finger, the scar disappeared and felt like smooth, normal skin.

I had almost died.

I stared at my reflection, trying to see if I looked different. My face was still my face, but my eyes seemed older somehow. Maybe it was the weight of what had happened. Maybe it was the pain I was still enduring. Either way, I wasn't the same girl who had gone back in time to get the dagger. Sadness and relief wrestled for control of my heart. Neither won.

By the time I had struggled into a pair of jeans and a shirt, the pain in my stomach was unbearable. I lay back in bed and fantasized about breakfast.

My bedroom door creaked open and Evan came in. Vivian and Jacqueline followed him. A maid came last, carrying a tray filled with breakfast foods.

"How did you know?" I asked.

"I've seen how bad you are at taking it easy. I cast a spell to warn us when you got out of bed." Vivian put a bunch of pillows behind me to keep me propped up.

The maid placed the tray beside me and left. I started with the Danish and coffee.

Evan sat at the end of my bed. He wore a white button down shirt and khakis. He looked good. Self-consciously, I reached up to push my snarled hair back.

"I'll do your hair later. Just eat." Vivian sat in the chair next to my bed. Despite all her work casting spells to save me, she looked well.

Jacqueline remained standing by my desk. Her eyes were dull and additional white streaks had appeared in her hair. Her face was sallow and new wrinkles clung to her eyes. Healing me hadn't just sapped her energy, it had aged her. I felt awful. When I was better, I had to find a way to repay her.

I summoned my courage and said to Jacqueline, "Thank you for saving my life."

She crossed her arms like she had to hold herself together. "If you'd have just followed instructions, none of this would have happened."

She was right. I bit my lip. "I had to help Percy and Ellie." Seeing the new lines on her face made my words so feeble.

"You barely survived," Jacqueline said.

"But I'm here." I took a big bite of my Danish.

"Look at me, Kat." Jacqueline gestured at her face. "Saving your life cost me years of my life. Aged me like this in a day. Was it worth it?"

Before I could answer, Vivian *tsked* at her. "It was worth it to save Kat. Without her, we wouldn't have won this round."

"Evan's safe now?" I asked.

Jacqueline looked at Vivian. They exchanged one of those glances that communicated so much between them and so little to me. "For now."

"Just tell me the truth. I think I've earned that." I shoveled eggs into my mouth.

Vivian folded her hands together in her lap and leaned forward. "Let's focus on getting you healthy. Once you've healed, you need training. So does Evan."

Those were short-term goals. "And then what happens?"

"Why don't we deal with that then?" Vivian tried to steer me away from my future responsibilities.

But I was done running from them. "What do we have to do next?"

"The Mallory amulet still remains lost. After your training, you will need to find it," Vivian said.

Disgust flared in Evan's eyes. I felt it, too. "So, we will risk our lives for someone who doesn't ever risk anything."

"It's not fair." Vivian leaned closer like her proximity could ease our anger. "But you remember Shannon's letters? Well, they got me thinking and I contacted the ancestors. They told me that when all the families have their amulets, we will all be stronger and better able to face the Dark One."

So we had to get the Mallory amulet back to them for our own sake. "And what is the Dark One doing in the meantime?"

"He's amassing more power," Jacqueline said.

"It's a bloody magical arms race," Evan muttered.

"What about my training? How long will I have to stay here?" I clutched at my coffee mug, fearing I'd have to leave McTernan Academy and everyone I cared about behind.

"A couple weeks," Vivian said.

"We can't send you back out into the world without teaching you some defensive magic," Jacqueline said.

I opened my mouth to object, but Evan talked right over me. "I'll ask Professor Astor to get our assignments emailed to us."

"But classes..." I said.

Evan patted my leg through the comforter. "You can get the notes. I'll help you catch up. Don't worry about school."

When he said it, I wanted to believe it. But school and my Preston family were all the normal that remained and it felt like they were slipping away.

"After you go back to school, you'll come here whenever you can." Vivian pointed to my locket. "That will allow you to come here instantly. No need to take a train or bus. We'll teach you spells and everything you need to know to fight. You will be trained properly. Evan will continue learning how to use the dagger. Eventually, he will have to make his way to Ravenhurst. There are things only the Kingsleys know about that dagger and their powers."

"How will I get there?" Evan asked.

"When she's better, Kat will help you find it," Vivian said.

A look of confusion passed over Evan's face. "Why can't I just go through the mirror?"

Vivian gave him a patient smile. "The first time the Kingsley heir goes to Ravenhurst, he must find it. It's part of the wards that protect the place."

"So, I should be able to help him in a few more days?" I asked.

"Weeks," Jacqueline said. "You cannot cast spells until you are healed."

"What if I cast a spell? What happens?"

"Magic doesn't just draw on your body's energy. It draws on your soul's energy," Jacqueline said. "You would be reopening the wound on your soul and undoing all the healing Vivian and I have given you. You wouldn't die, but you would weaken Evan. And healing you again would age me further."

"I'll be good. For all of us." I tried not to squirm under Jacqueline's piercing gaze. "What else can I do to get better?"

"Eat well, sleep well, no magic, no strenuous activity," Vivian said.

I stuffed down another poached egg with hollandaise sauce, three strips of bacon, and a corn muffin. Then I tackled a bowl of berries. Another glass of orange juice and a second cup of coffee. Anything to help the healing process along.

Jacqueline moved closer to Evan. "There is something Vivian and I have to do before you leave."

"What?" he asked.

"We want to bond you to your amulet," Jacqueline said.

"Is it dangerous?" The Langleys were the only ones who ever bonded to their amulet. Something told me there was a reason for it.

Vivian avoided my gaze. *It was dangerous.*

"That bond is why Langleys lose their minds if they don't save the Radcliffe heir. That's the cost of the amulet bond," Jacqueline said.

"No." I shifted my leg and the tray rattled beside me. "Absolutely not."

"It's not your decision." There was an unexpected firmness to Evan's voice.

"I haven't done everything to save your life for you to sacrifice it," I said.

"It will make me stronger," he said.

"You're strong enough."

No, I'm not." Pain flared in his eyes. "I watched your heart stop, Kat. I will do anything to keep that from happening again."

"I won't help you."

"You can't," Vivian said.

My gaze never left Evan's face. "Please, don't do this."

"Kat, we've always been in this together." There was such conviction in his words.

"Not like this."

"Why is it okay for you to risk your life for me? Why can't I do the same?" he asked.

"Because I need you alive and safe," I blurted out.

"And I need the same for you." His voice was so warm, it sent heat rushing to my core. But that heat couldn't eclipse the fear I felt for him.

Chapter 34

I didn't want to follow Vivian, Jacqueline, and Evan into the library and through that metal door again, but I wanted to be there when Evan bonded to his dagger. And if I was being honest, a part of me was hoping something would stop this from happening.

Vivian and Jacqueline went down the stairs first. Torches flared to life in the stone walls as they went deeper and deeper underground. I paused at the top of the spiral staircase. Had there always been so many steps? After three days of rest, I felt better, but I still hesitated. Evan didn't. He scooped me up like a child and started down the stairs. I was 5'9" and a size 14, but somehow in his arms I felt tiny.

"Are you sure I'm not too much to carry?" I asked as we went down the stairs.

"I could do this one-handed." He didn't sound the least bit winded.

"Really? The Kingsley dagger already made you that much stronger?"

"It's bloody amazing, Kat. I can do things I've never done before. And my vision. It's like being a snake and seeing heat waves."

"It's pretty cool, right?" I'd experienced that ability when I was Percy. "It was a little disorienting after the time travel, but I never stumbled in the dark." One of the few things I missed about possessing the Kingsley heir.

"I get why you had to help Percy. I feel that pull now." His breath warmed my cheek and sent tingles down my neck.

"It's stronger than anything I've ever felt." Especially when it came to protecting Evan. I leaned my head against his shoulder and listened to the *thunk-tunk, thunk-tunk, thunk-tunk* of his heart beating in his chest. I drifted off to sleep.

Suddenly, I stood alone in a field of heather. The mossy herb-like scent enveloped me. The summer sun heated my skin. The sky was a brilliant azure blue. A knight on a gray horse appeared across the field. He rode straight at me, but I wasn't afraid. I had been waiting for him for so long. Before he could lift his helmet, everything faded away.

Evan nudged me. "Kat, we're here."

I opened my eyes. Somehow, he'd gotten down the stairs, through the twisting corridors, and all the way to the door with the hourglass on it without waking me. He set me down gently.

I stared at the hourglass. I didn't want him bonding with his amulet, but he was doing it. Since he'd gotten the dagger, he had a quiet strength about him. A certainty. A new power that I would have to learn to understand.

Vivian pressed her hand to the door and the hourglass came to life with the sand slipping upward. The door popped open and we headed inside. The chamber of mirrors smelled of hope—a faint citrus smell. My sandals clacked against the stone floor.

Evan stood beside the Langley mirror and waited for Jacqueline and Vivian to begin the spell.

I took a seat on the gray stone bench, watching Jacqueline and Vivian mix herbs and anoint candles with oils, preparing to call on the Kingsley ancestors. The ancestors had to agree to the bond because they were the ones who decided on the dagger's heir. I prayed they would side with me and keep the dagger unbonded.

The air beside me darkened and sparkled. White smoke emerged and took form. Toria appeared beside me in her Victorian finery. I jerked and my stomach muscles spasmed. I pressed my hand to the spot like it could somehow stop the pain.

Toria's brow wrinkled. "I didn't mean to startle you."

"I wasn't expecting you." The great aunts had forbidden me from doing any magic, even summoning a ghost with my ring.

"I sensed you needed me." She gave me a confident smile. "Don't worry I'm not drawing energy from you. I can draw it from this room."

Toria sat beside me on the bench.

I looked at Evan and a wad of fear lodged in my throat, making it hard to speak. "I can't shake the feeling that this is sealing his fate."

"It is. But it may save all of you."

"How?"

"The blade will never be taken by another again. That much power in the Dark One's hands could do serious damage to the families." Toria gave me her serious face.

"But Evan…" I didn't want him hurt. Ever.

"If his bond to the weapon is permanent, it makes him stronger, which in turn, makes you stronger."

"Why?"

"You were the last heir with her amulet. That was a terrible responsibility. Everyone was counting on you. If you fell to the Dark One, all the other families would fall. Once Evan bonds with his amulet, you won't ever carry that burden alone again."

"But his sanity matters." I didn't want this for him. And he had a choice. I didn't. "Why would he choose this?"

"For you."

I tapped my fingers nervously on my knee. "I don't want him doing this for me."

"And he didn't want you risking your life for him, but you kept doing it." She leaned closer and softened her tone. "Don't you see how much you matter to him?"

Jacqueline cleared her throat and looked pointedly at Toria and me. "We need to start the spell. Try to keep it down over there. And Toria, you're not needed here."

"Kat needs me. I'm here for her. When the spell is done, I'll go." Toria sounded tart.

Jacqueline turned her back on Toria, but Vivian mouthed a "Thank you" to Toria.

The candles burst to life throughout the room. Vivian spoke in Scottish Gaelic to summon the Kingsley ancestors to this room. They came slowly. Some looked like faded photos. Barely visible. Others were almost human, except for their blue-gray flesh. Their clothing marked them as years dead, decades dead, and centuries dead. Most of them were men, but I spotted a few women, too.

I recognized Alistair by his wavy, brown hair and labradorite eyes. His skin, however, had a tinge of gray-blue. He glanced at me, but he didn't seem to see Toria right beside me.

"He still can't see you? Even in here?" I whispered.

"It's our punishment," she said softly.

I couldn't imagine how I would feel if I could never see Evan again. I had to find a way to fix this for her. I was about to say that when another Kingsley materialized and caught my attention.

Percy.

He looked dashing with his black pantaloons, black double-breasted frock coat, and gleaming boots. His eye patch made him stand out among the Kingsleys, just as it had in life.

So many Kingsleys encircled Evan. My gut ached. Not just from the dagger wound, but from my growing fear for Evan.

An old man stepped forward. He had bushy gray eyebrows and a mustache.

Evan looked startled and stepped back. "Grandfather?"

"I'm sorry this has fallen to you. I had hoped that I'd live longer and save you from being the Kingsley heir. When the ancestors picked outside our family for my successor, I thought you would be spared. But he died young." He sounded as if he blamed himself for what would happen to Evan.

"It's all right," Evan said. "This is my choice."

His grandfather glanced at me. So much knowledge festered in his eyes. I wondered what he knew. "She's strong. You're strong. Trust in your bond." He stepped back into the sea of Kingsley ancestors.

Jacqueline asked their permission to forever tie the dagger to the Kingsleys and to accept the consequences of the bond. Insanity would come to any Kingsley heir who failed to save the Radcliffe heir.

One by one, each Kingsley agreed.

I prayed Percy or Alistair or Evan's grandfather would say no. Just one *no* could stop this ceremony. But none of them did.

Toria rested her ghost hand on mine. It was cold and somehow soothing. Her thoughts filled my mind. *This has to happen. It's not your place to interfere.*

I didn't agree, but I believed her, so I kept silent.

Jacqueline handed Evan a potion. After he drank it, he pulled the dagger from its sheath and cut his palm with it. She used his blood and

Vivian's blood to forge a bond between him and the dagger. A bond that would change the Kingsley family forever. Vivian and Jacqueline chanted in Scottish Gaelic. I didn't know what they were saying, but I felt the power rising in the room. I could almost taste it on my tongue, sweet and tangy. It swirled around Evan.

A bright light burst up from the Langley mirror, blinding me. Then the light was gone. All the Kingsleys were gone. Only Evan remained, lying on the mirror.

I gasped and leapt up, ignoring the sharp pang in my stomach. I rushed to his side.

I was a few steps from the mirror, when Jacqueline said, "Don't touch him."

I hovered at the edge of the mirror. "But..."

"This is part of the bonding process. He'll wake up when it is done." Her tone held me back.

I knelt next to him. My heart pounded in the back of my head. I felt disconnected from my body, like my soul might float away. I almost wished I'd pass out because this waiting was brutal. It felt like hours passed, but it was minutes. Five, ten, fifteen, twenty. Didn't matter how many passed, each one felt like an eternity. The time when I thought I'd lost him to when he came back to me. There were no numbers to measure those moments.

Finally, his eyes blinked open.

Relief coursed through me like a shot of vitamins for my soul. His eyes were green and gold and amber. Mesmerizing. My heart stopped and did a double beat to catch up. "Are you okay?"

He nodded. "Bloody difficult doing that bond thing."

I looked to Jacqueline. "Can I touch him now?"

She nodded.

I reached out to help him up, forgetting about my own wound. The stabbing pain in my stomach made me double over. I curled into myself, trying to contain the hurt.

Evan scooped me up and cradled me in his arms. He was so much stronger than he had been moments ago.

"Evan?" I asked.

"Yeah?"

"Can you put me down?"

"You need to heal. You're going to rest and that's it." His voice was deeper with an undeniable power behind it.

I couldn't help listening to him this time.

Chapter 35

I spent the next few days resting, healing, and lying. Lying to my mom and grandparents about how a terrible stomach virus kept me at Dumbarton. Lying to my teachers about why I wasn't back at school yet. Lying to Morgan about what I was really doing at Dumbarton. I was lying to everyone I loved.

And I hated it.

I shifted on my stool at the worktable in Jacqueline's conservatory. I tried to listen to her lecture on plants, but she was in the fourth hour without any break in sight. I couldn't help thinking about how lonely it was to be the Langley heir. Toria's only real friend had been Alistair. I bet my aunt Shannon couldn't keep a friend with all this deceit. I was starting to worry about me and Morgan. The lies were building a wall between us. I felt it every time we texted and I said nothing was happening when so much was actually happening.

Like today. I was learning about herbs and spells. At least fifty different leaves were scattered across my side of the cement worktable. Sunlight filtered through the windows and the plants and flowers gave off a fresh, earthy smell. Jacqueline opened a cabinet and pulled out a few more jars of oils and dried herbs and put them on the table.

Plants have a natural energy we could tap into to help fuel spells. Unfortunately, she was trying to teach me *everything* in one day. After four hours, my mind was mushier than oatmeal.

"Hand me that leaf." Jacqueline was too busy measuring out three drops of lavender oil to tell me which leaf she meant.

I leaned forward and studied the different leaves strewn across her worktable. "The round one?"

"The one for treating a wound." She snapped her fingers at me to hurry up, adding to the pressure.

The spearmint leaf was for stomach problems. The oak leaf was for a fever. But I couldn't remember which one was best for a wound. I bit my lip and hesitated over the pile of leaves.

Her brow snapped together. "I just told you about it."

Of course she had. In the past four hours, she'd gone over the healing properties of hundreds of plants. When to use the leaf vs. the bark vs. the flowering part. I'd been taking notes for a few minutes when she snatched up my notepad and tossed it in the garbage.

"It won't do you any good on paper." She tapped my forehead. "It has to be in there."

"Once I'm better, I won't need to know it all. I can just draw on my blood and the ring for spells."

From her rigid posture, I knew I'd said the wrong thing. "Your blood and your ring are not a limitless well of power. When you are doing defensive magic, you will sap your ring and yourself easily. You need to rely on the energy in nature to help. That's why this knowledge is so essential. It can be the difference between life and death on the battlefield."

"Right."

"Which leaf for a wound, Kat?" The impatience in her tone ticked away like a time bomb.

I picked up a maple leaf.

Her face twisted in disgust. "That's for a cough."

I dropped it back in the pile and rubbed my palms together. "I don't know."

"It's the birch leaf." The words ground against my skin like gravel.

I hunted for a leaf that resembled an arrowhead with slightly serrated edges. I grabbed it and passed it to her.

She shredded the leaf and then ground it with her mortar and pestle. "You have to focus the entire time. Push your intention into the spell and summon the power from your ingredients."

"Toria taught me that."

She put the mortar and pestle down, wiped her hands on a towel, and turned to face me. "I need you to pay attention to me, not Toria. I'm in charge here, not her."

"Okay."

She picked up the mortar and pestle and continued grinding the ingredients together.

My thoughts went back to my friends and family. I sighed.

"What?" She managed to communicate a lot of impatience in that one syllable.

"I hate lying to everyone I love."

"You'll get used to it."

"I don't want to get used to it," I muttered.

"Then tell them the truth and watch how quickly we all lose to the Dark One." She pressed down with such force her knuckles whitened and I thought the marble pestle might snap.

"I know why I have to lie, but I don't like it."

Jacqueline slammed the mortar on the table. "No one is asking you to enjoy it. You have to do things you don't like in life. That's part of growing up." She started putting the herb jars away in the cabinet. "I think this has been enough for today."

"But we didn't finish the healing spell."

"We've covered all you can. Go work on your homework." She dismissed me without a backward glance.

I shut my AP Calculus book and rolled my head from side to side, stretching my neck muscles. The clock on my desk told me two hours had passed since Jacqueline had tossed me out of her conservatory. I'd hoped a little math would clear my head, but the old problems kept creeping back in.

A restlessness that I couldn't control came over me. Moving around my room wasn't enough. The walls felt too confining. I headed outside. Behind the mansion, gravel pathways cut across the garden. Giant rose bushes bloomed in a riot of peach, pink, purple, orange, and red. They gave off a heady, sweet scent of summer.

I closed my eyes and took a big breath. And another. The season for roses was long past, so this must be some magic that Jacqueline worked. The gravel crunched beneath my feet as I headed farther into the gardens.

Movement always helped ease my mind. But there was one hurt it couldn't help: my father's continued silence.

The Langleys had passed down Sarah's lie about distance protecting a green-eyed Langley from the ring. Vivian and Jacqueline swore that was the reason he pushed Mom and me away. One lie told in 1831 had prevented my father from being in my life and forever altered my family. And now, seven days had passed since I'd arrived at Dumbarton. Seven days without a word from him. I wanted to believe what my great aunts said about him wanting me, but really, how hard was it to call? He could use magic to send a note. Something. Anything to let me know he cared.

I'd spent my entire life waiting for him. Why did I keep thinking this could change? Stupid and foolish. I had almost two decades of evidence to prove otherwise. But hope lingers in the face of certainty, especially a certainty I wished wasn't so certain.

The path wound toward a brook with an ornate stone bridge leading over it. When I got to the middle, I stopped and stared down at the water rushing over the rocks. The *blu-blu-blu* sound soothed me.

Over the years, I'd convinced myself that my father's absence wasn't so bad. I had to. Otherwise, it would have destroyed me. But right here, right now, I had to admit the truth: I would never be okay with my father's absence. The only thing I could do was keep ignoring it. Say it didn't matter until I started to believe it. I was good at lying to myself. I'd had years of practice because of the ghosts.

My feet took me deeper into the garden. On the other side of the bridge, I spotted a covered walkway with bright purple wisteria blooming over it. As I got closer, the smells of honey and vanilla teased my nose. I thought I glimpsed someone waiting in the shadows beneath it. Shielding my eyes from the sun, I realized it was a semi-transparent man. A ghost. He stood just inside the opening as if waiting for someone to join him.

I moved faster, needing to see if it was Alistair. Well, his ghost. I was several feet away when I knew it was him. He looked handsome in his white shirt and necktie with a dark blue single-breasted morning coat and loose fitting trousers. He carried a walking stick and a bowler hat. He stared off in the distance like he was trying to remember something.

I cleared my throat. He gave me a nod of acknowledgment.

"Are you looking for Toria?" I asked.

"Always."

"She's around. And she misses you, too."

He gave me the saddest smile. "It wasn't supposed to be like this. I was supposed to save her."

"No one could save her from the Langley legacy."

"If I were stronger, I'd have ended her life. It would have been agony, but we might be together now." His lips compressed with a century of regret.

"But you couldn't do that. You loved her."

"I loved her so much I let us have an eternity of misery."

His voice broke my heart. Before I could pick up the pieces, I heard footsteps behind me. I turned and saw Evan marching up the path to me. "Are you checking up on me again?" I asked him.

"Just taking a break from training."

He'd been holed up in the Langley chamber of mirrors with Percy's ghost the past few days, learning how to fight and use his dagger. Somehow, he always managed to take a break when something was bothering me.

"Alistair was just telling me about Toria and him." I turned back, but his ghost was gone.

"I must have scared him off," Evan said.

"I wish I could do something to help Toria and him."

"It isn't right. But what can we do?"

I studied the ground. I'd been kicking around a couple thoughts on this topic. "Find a way for them to see each other again. Let them say everything they want to say to each other."

"Would it really matter? They're dead, Kat."

I looked up in shock. "You sound like Jacqueline."

He grimaced at the comparison. "She does have a point there."

"Don't you remember what it was like to be Alistair?" I grabbed his arm. "He was so close to having everything he wanted before Sebastian died. All Toria and Alistair wanted was to be together. And they weren't. Not in life. Not even in death." It felt wrong to me. Not just personally wrong, but cosmically wrong. Like it had to be righted.

"I will never forget what it was like to be in Alistair's body. I know how much Toria meant to him." His tone echoed my frustration. "But how do we help them?"

"I don't know. But there has to be a way. Now that I'm better, maybe there's a spell I can do."

He muttered something that sounded like "Here we go again."

I crossed my arms and kept walking. "You don't have to help me."

Evan fell in step with me. "But I do."

I didn't know how to respond to that, so I kept moving. We followed the tunnel of wisteria. It opened onto a large white stone rotunda with pillars and a few steps to the landing. I felt the urge to go there. I wasn't sure why, but I followed my instincts and walked over to the building. I tapped my hand against one of the white pillars.

"Something about this building..." Something important had happened here. I wasn't sure what or when, but some part of me remembered.

I closed my eyes, hoping I'd get a better idea, but nothing came. When I opened them, Toria was sitting on the opposite side of the rotunda.

"Is that Toria?" Evan whispered.

All believers could see ghosts, but as Alistair just showed me, not all ghosts wanted to talk to believers. I shushed Evan. "Let me talk to her alone." I made my way over and sat beside her on the steps.

She stared out at the grass and trees without saying anything. I almost felt like I was intruding on a private moment.

"This place is special to you," I said gently.

"Alistair promised we'd be together. We'd beat the Langley legacy. We'd have children and grandchildren." Her eyes glistened with unshed tears.

"I just saw him. He wanders in search of you."

"I know." Her voice shook. "It's our fate."

"I don't believe that. There has to be a way around it."

"You can fight fate, Kat. But it always wins in the end." Her voice flattened under the weight of a century of certainty.

Then she faded away.

Evan came over and sat on my other side. "Do you think she's right about fate?"

"If she is, I will die. You will die. We will fail. And all of this," I waved my arms around and my voice edged toward hysteria, "is pointless."

"I don't really believe in fate then."

I dropped my face into my hands. "Fate. I hate that word. Like everything is written in stone and can't be unwritten."

"Not when you're involved," Evan said. "You've changed the past."

Evan's words triggered my memory. I lifted my face out of my hands. "Lorelei said that I see how the past and present and future are all tied together. Maybe fixing the past helps us in the future. I felt like I had to help Ellie, the same way I feel like I have to help Toria."

"Maybe having all the living and dead heirs at full strength could impact our battle with the Dark One."

I couldn't tell if he was agreeing or saying it out loud to show me how insane it sounded. "I know it sounds crazy…"

"I don't think it sounds crazy. Or any crazier than what we've seen and done to date. You could ask the Langleys. Maybe they'll know a way to help Toria and Alistair."

"And if they do, will you help me?"

He put his arm around me. "I will always help you, Kat."

Chapter 36

"Is there any way for Toria and Alistair to be together?" I asked.

Vivian put her book down and patted the spot beside her on the sofa in the living room. "That's the saddest part of the Langley legacy." Her face sagged under the weight of it. "Insanity leads to suicide and the ghost is punished for it."

"That's why Toria can't see Alistair, but why can't he see her?" Evan sat in the armchair.

"They say he sought his death out. He died in a duel." Vivian's lips compressed.

"How is that suicide?" Evan asked.

"He never loaded his pistol," she said. "I guess he couldn't bear living without Toria."

"So, if he'd have died naturally, he'd have been able to see her?" I tried to reason out this punishment.

"But she still wouldn't be able to see him. It would be a different torture for him." Sadness ravaged Vivian's voice.

"What happened to Percy and Sarah?" Evan leaned forward.

Vivian shifted to face him. "That's a bit more complicated. Percy sacrificed himself for Ellie. Unfortunately, she was holding the blade when he plunged it into his stomach. So, it's not suicide and it's not murder."

"So, Percy can see Sarah," Evan said.

"Yes, but he and Ellie can never meet," Vivian said.

"Why?"

She must have seen the frustration on my face because she reached over and squeezed my hand. "Kat, every religion speaks of judgment when we die. This is our judgment."

"When we are alive, courts sentence us to punishment for terms, not for eternity."

"Judgment for a lifetime punishes the ghost for the rest of its existence, but gives the soul another chance in its next reincarnation." She made it sound like that somehow balanced out. Maybe it did for the soul, but not for the ghost.

"What about something temporary? Not a pardon but a break from their eternal sentence?" I just prayed it wasn't one of the dark spells that Lydia worked. "Surely, there has to be something."

Vivian started to speak, but Jacqueline cut her off from the doorway. "Rules are there for a reason. Why can't you just follow them?"

"Because they are punishing the wrong people. Toria has suffered enough. She deserves to see Alistair and he deserves to see her. Their ghosts are wandering around here, walking right past each other. It's so sad."

"They're dead." Jacqueline said it as if the dead didn't have any rights.

"Those whose powers are grounded in the present, like Jacqueline, are particularly sensitive to the ghosts trying to syphon energy from them." Vivian rushed to explain. "Ghosts want to latch onto the present. It isn't natural for them to bond with her and it makes her ill."

"They tire me out, too," I said.

"Because you haven't learned the extent of your abilities. That will get better in time. You have a natural bond with the past and with them," Vivian said.

"They just want a reckoning." I heard myself defending the ghosts that I'd blocked out for half my life. The same ones I'd been frustrated with at McTernan Academy a week ago.

"At your expense," Jacqueline murmured.

"Toria and Alistair aren't just family. They're tiny pieces of what keeps reincarnating among the Langleys and the Kingsleys. Evan and I are attached to them; their souls eventually became ours. We have to help them."

Neither Vivian nor Jacqueline said anything. My argument wasn't swaying them. I bit my lip and looked at Evan. We had to tell them my theory.

"We think fixing the past will help us be stronger in the future," Evan said.

"Why?" Jacqueline towered over a seated Evan.

He explained my dream and how we thought living and dead heirs all needed to be at their strongest for the upcoming battle. While he spoke, I watched Vivian. Something shifted in her expression. She looked at Jacqueline, who shook her head. Vivian tilted her head. Jacqueline grimaced. It was like watching a silent film without the title cards.

"What?" My knee bounced up and down with nervous energy. "Is there a way to help them?"

"No." Jacqueline's voice came out harsher than bleach on silk. "You need to let this go." She turned and stalked out of the room.

I made my voice small and childlike, pleading for Vivian's help. "Do you know of anything we can do?"

"I know Jacqueline wouldn't approve of it." Vivian pushed her glasses up on her nose. "But there might be something in the spell books." She got up and headed to the door. When she got there, she stopped and turned around. "Aren't you coming?"

Evan and I leapt up and followed her.

Vivian led us through the stone corridors under the house. I thought we were headed back to the chamber of mirrors, but she took several lefts and rights, bringing us into side corridors I didn't even know existed. We stopped in front of a plain black metal door with no design or door knob.

"To open the door, you need a few drops of your blood. You smear the blood into the design that comes into your head when you touch the door," she said.

"Why blood?"

"To make sure a Langley opens the door. The design will only appear in a Langley's mind. We have to protect what's inside."

I looked around for something to prick my finger with, but she just took my finger and pressed it to the door. I felt a tiny sting. I tried to pull back, but she kept my finger there. Inside my mind, I saw a symbol. A simple rune. I traced it onto the door.

When we were done, I pulled my hand away. The tiny cut in my fingertip disappeared and the door swung open on a vault filled with books. Giant chandeliers hovered in the air, sending warm light over everything. They weren't attached to the ceiling. One swung down to us to light our way. The walls were lined with shelves from floor to ceiling. Bookcases formed rows up and down the room.

"This is our library of spells. It has every spell ever cast by a Langley in it." There was a note of pride in her voice. "Each Langley keeps a personal book of spells, a grimoire. We also collect spell books from all over the world."

"Even the dark ones? The kind Lydia cast?" My breath caught in my throat.

She nodded. "They are locked away. The darkest spells are the most dangerous. Their price is too high. They twist your soul and turn it darker."

I hoped I never had to cast one. My gaze darted around. I couldn't count how many books were here. It would take us months to search through them. "How are we ever going to find a spell to help Toria and Alistair?"

"Tap into your ring's power and think about what you want to do. The books that can help will come to you. Then you have to figure out the best spell to use."

"Can you help me?" This was too important for me to do on my own. What if I made a mistake?

"This is part of your training." Her eyes sparkled behind her glasses. "Find the spell, put together all the ingredients, and I'll meet you in the chamber of mirrors tomorrow."

She left and shut the door behind her.

Evan went to the shelf and pulled a book down. "This one's in Scottish Gaelic." He tried another one. "English." The third he held up for me to see. "French."

"These could take forever to translate."

"Maybe we'll get lucky and you'll only summon a couple books."

"Let's hope." I closed my eyes and turned my ring a few times. I concentrated on what I needed: a spell to help Toria and Alistair see and touch each other. To reveal what was invisible to each of them. I wanted them to connect again as ghosts.

I heard a flurry of movement, like books being yanked from their shelves. I opened my eyes and books whirled toward me. They landed softly at my feet. I bent down to gather them up. "There are eleven books here."

Evan came over to help me. "Not bad for your first time searching for a spell." The admiration in his voice sent a warm pleasant rush through me.

We brought the books over to a long wooden table in the middle of the room and sat down. The chairs were cushioned. Perfect for research. Three chandeliers moved to hang over us.

"Doesn't this feel familiar?" Evan reached for a book.

"Like Castle Creighton—when you were translating four lines, not eleven books." I stared at the pile of books on the table. I had thousands of pages to read, not all of them in English. I got a sinking feeling, like a giant chunk of cement was chained around my stomach and dragging it down, down, down to my ankles. "How am I ever going to find the right one?"

"Considering we started with tens of thousands of possible books, eleven is a much better pool." Evan flipped open the first book. I glanced at the pages, the letters were familiar but the words weren't. I pulled the book over for a closer look and suddenly the letters on the page made complete sense. It was in English. I skimmed down to the spell's purpose. "This is for recovering a lost object."

He leaned closer. "You read Latin?"

"No, it's in English."

"Not for me," he said.

He opened another book. "This one's Italian." He handed it to me.

As soon as I touched it, the words turned to English for me. "It's a love spell." My heart sped up. I didn't know how it worked or why, but somehow my touch allowed me to read each spell regardless of the language it was written in.

"You read Latin and Italian, right?" I asked him.

"I do."

I handed him back the books. "You work on these. I'll tackle the others."

Six hours passed with me skimming each page for the spell's purpose. Evan translated that section for most of the Latin book. It was in a book of Scottish Gaelic spells that something weird happened. Okay, weirder. The page gave off a faint glow when I touched it, like this was the best answer to my question.

It was a possession spell.

Memories burst through my brain from when I was a child and Leanna's ghost tried to possess me. Being sick in bed. Losing minutes, then moments. It was awful. If Toria hadn't helped me, I could have disappeared forever. I swallowed. But the fear wouldn't go down. It lingered in the back of my throat.

"It's a possession spell." My voice came out like I'd just swallowed glass.

Evan's forehead wrinkled up. "Who would they possess?"

I skimmed over the spell a few times to be sure. "A relative works best."

"So, us."

"But Alistair's ghost is a shard of the soul that eventually became your soul. A piece that was left behind long ago in the reincarnation process. If you let him in your body again, you might have trouble separating from him."

"But you do it with Toria all the time." Evan closed the book he'd been translating and ran his fingers over the cover.

"It's not easy. I want to let her stay."

"What would happen if they stayed?" he asked.

"There's a long warning about that, actually. They would either rejoin with our souls, which would change who we are, or they would take control and we would disappear. Even if they meant us no harm, they would want to stay and live. They can't help it."

His lips twitched and his eyes tightened like his mind was trying to make sense of it. "Will it feel like when we possessed their bodies in the past?"

"I don't know how aware we will be of what is happening. We can't trust that we will be strong enough to expel them or they will be kind enough to leave."

"Best-case scenario?"

"They take possession, they get their moment together, they make peace with each other, and they leave. We will get our bodies back," I said.

"Worst-case scenario?"

"We are lost. Toria and Alistair live again. It goes against the natural laws. I don't know what will happen to us. Our souls may be buried deep in our own bodies or cast out and wander for eternity, powerless to ever reincarnate."

Evan's eyes seared mine. "And you still want to do this, don't you?"

I gripped his hand. "I'm scared. But I do."

"You really think it's worth the risk?"

"To end a century of torment for Toria and Alistair and help us battle the Dark One? Yes. I trust Toria."

He put his other hand on top of mine. "And I trust you. So, I guess I'll have to trust Alistair, too."

Chapter 37

After breakfast, Evan and I met Vivian in the chamber of mirrors. We gathered around a stone worktable while Vivian read over the possession spell and checked all the ingredients I'd selected.

"Excellent work locating the right spell and gathering the right ingredients." Her words were full of praise, but her voice wasn't. "Now, you have to decide if you are willing to pay the price for this spell."

Evan gave me a what's-she-talking-about look.

"You mean some of our energy?" I asked.

"Spells always have a cost. Sometimes it's to your health," Vivian said. "This one has a different price. You can't pause Toria and Alistair's punishment without consequences. The cost of this spell is that you will lose your most treasured memory."

"I don't even know what my most treasured memory is." But it sounded like something I should hold onto.

"Neither do I," he said.

"Will we know we've lost it?" I asked.

"You'll feel an emptiness where it used to reside," Vivian said.

My throat was unbearably dry, itching in places that I couldn't scratch. I coughed a few times, trying to make it stop. I had so many memories of my friends and family. Could I give up the most important one for Toria?

Evan's face was a mix of curious and aghast. "What will losing the memory do to us?"

"Our experiences make us who we are," Vivian said. "To lose a memory is to lose a tiny piece of ourselves. And our treasured memories usually have a huge impact on who we become."

"It sounds like the beginning of a slippery slope," he said.

"It can be," Vivian said.

Her tone worried me. "So, we shouldn't do it?"

"That's your decision to make. But you should know the consequences before you do," Vivian said.

"Give us a moment." I pulled Evan aside and spoke in a low voice, barely above a whisper. "Are you still willing to do this?"

He rubbed his forehead. "I don't know what my most treasured memory is. But what if it made me who I am? What if losing it changes me forever?"

I couldn't help thinking of Lydia. She was willing to work the darkest spells, no matter what the cost, to get what she wanted. I didn't want to become like her, but suddenly I saw how easily I could.

My fingertips were suddenly ice cold, like the blood had scurried away, in search of safety. "It's a huge risk."

"You really think we need the dead heirs in the future?" He stepped closer.

"I do."

"And you still want to do this spell knowing what we will lose?"

"We were willing to risk losing ourselves to the possession, the only difference is now we know that we will lose a piece of ourselves to the spell." I stared down at my ring. These were the kinds of hard choices we were going to be facing for the rest of our lives.

"I trust you." He took my hand in his and laced his fingers through mine, warming my fingers again.

My throat clogged with emotions I didn't dare name. "I trust you, too."

When we went back to the table, Vivian asked, "What did you decide?"

"We'll do the spell," I said.

Evan squeezed my hand. "Together."

Vivian walked me through how to cast the spell. We even did a practice run to be safe. Vivian oversaw everything we did and tweaked a few elements along the way.

Once she was certain that I was ready, she said, "You've done a good job finding the spell and getting the ingredients together. When you work the spell, I want you to focus on pulling the magic from the mirror and your ring. I don't want you tiring yourself out."

I anointed purple, magenta, royal blue, and indigo candles with frankincense oil and arranged them on the cardinal points around the mirror. Evan and I pricked our fingers and smeared drops of our blood on the bloodstone. We put it in the center of the mirror between us.

I spoke the spell in Scottish Gaelic and felt the energy of the mirror flow from my toes to my scalp. It was gentle and warm and filled me with power. Something shifted at my core. A feeling of *moreness*. Toria was inside me.

I looked to the Radcliffe mirror on the wall. Where I should be standing, I saw Toria. She wore a beautiful gold and red striped walking-out dress. Her skirt was gathered with red ribbon at the side to expose the pleated gold underskirt. Her hair was piled atop her head under a bonnet that was trimmed with red feathers and a gold butterfly.

What am I doing here? I heard her ask inside my mind.

I thought back at her, *I'm helping you and Alistair like I promised.*

She took control of my head and looked around at the spell's ingredients and her reflection. Her face tightened. *Kat, no, not a possession spell.*

I know what I'm doing. So does Evan. But I need you to promise to give my body back as soon as you are done.

I don't want to possess you.

It's too late now. And you don't have much time. Use it. Use me.

All right. I felt her hope coursing through my veins.

I shouldn't still be this aware. You need to take complete control of my body.

I have.

But I'm still here, I thought at her.

Try to move.

I told my hand to touch my face, but it didn't move.

See? I'm in control.

Which meant I got to be an awkward observer. Again.

I looked at Evan and realized he was no longer Evan. Or at least he no longer looked like Evan. He was Alistair with wavy, brown hair and a strong nose. He still had his bowler hat from yesterday.

"Is it really you?" Toria's voice was a disbelieving whisper.

He reached for her hands. His were warm and strong. "It's me, my love." His voice was husky as he pulled her into his arms.

I didn't know what to do. Part of me wished I could fade away and let them have their privacy. But I didn't want to risk disappearing. I lingered in the background, experiencing every aching moment with Toria.

She smelled the crisp autumn scent that always clung to him. He buried his face in her neck. She felt his lips there. So did I. Warm and soft. A kiss. It had been so long since he'd kissed her. It sent tingles down her back.

She wanted more. Her lips found his. She didn't care about anything else. Just Alistair.

When they finally paused to catch their breath, she said, "I've never stopped looking for you."

"As I've searched for you."

He smiled at her and she felt like her heart would explode. She didn't know when she would see him again. This might be their only chance.

The words rushed out of her mouth. "I love you so much. I'm so sorry I left you. If only I had been stronger, I could have saved Sebastian. I could have saved us all this pain."

He caressed her cheek. "I love you, too. It wasn't your fault. I'm sorry I wasn't strong enough to end your torment before you did it yourself. I should have done something before your father banished me."

"No one should have to do that." She confessed, "I couldn't bring myself to kill you, even if it would have saved your soul."

He winced. "You're not damned."

"Maybe not the way people think, but it is hell not seeing you or touching you or talking to you."

"I know." His voice filled with understanding. "I'd do anything to remedy it."

"Would you?" Tears flooded her eyes. Alistair blurred. She blinked them away. She couldn't bear to lose sight of him. Not now. Not when their time together was so fleeting.

"We don't have much time," he murmured.

She glanced at Vivian and wrapped her arms around his neck. "We can't take Kat's and Evan's bodies." Her whisper was a fevered rush of words. "But we can take others'. We just need to find other relatives who are susceptible to ghosts."

"We can't steal their lives." His voice hitched on *steal* like that was the only thing holding him back. "It's a dark act."

"We've been so good and we've been so punished." She kissed him slowly, reminding him of all they missed out on. She pulled back to look into his hazel eyes. His thick black eyelashes couldn't hide the desire burning there. He wanted more time with her. "Think of it Alistair, we could finally be together."

This tiny moment that I had given them wasn't enough.

Toria touched the curl on his forehead. How she missed touching that curl.

He cradled her face in his palms. "I will find my way to you again."

"I will never give up on you," Toria promised.

He kissed her like she was the most precious thing in the world.

My lips were still on Evan's when Toria and Alistair left our bodies.

A few hours later, I was curled up against my headboard, playing with a throw pillow. Evan had taken the chair next to the bed and stared at my desk with an inscrutable expression on his face.

"Do you remember any of it?" I asked.

"A little." He refused to look me in the eye. Which gave me some idea of what he remembered.

My cheeks kindled and flamed. I remembered all of it. The first and the last time he kissed me. I mean, Alistair kissed Toria. His lips were warm and strong. His hands felt so right against my back. I shook my head. It was Toria and Alistair. Not Evan and me.

"They will find a way to be together even if they have to break the rules to do it." And I didn't blame them. The idea that they might possess relatives should have revolted me, but instead it made sense to me. I wondered if I would have felt that way before the spell or if the precious memory I'd lost had created some darkness in me.

His expression clouded over with concern. "Wouldn't you stop them?"

"How could I? They had been denied too much already." I got up and wandered around the room. "If only he could have killed her."

"Kat!"

"What? She was going to go insane and take her own life. At least that way, they could be together in death." The coldness in my logic didn't bother me.

"Look at Percy and Ellie—they can never see each other in death."

"But Sarah and Percy can."

"Because she didn't kill him."

"Then Alistair should have gotten someone to kill Toria." I took the next logical leap, but something inside me whimpered like it didn't like where my thoughts went.

"Could you really do that to someone you love? You'd be deciding to extinguish his life." For the first time, I heard fear in his voice. Fear at what I'd become because of that spell.

"I hope I never have to make that choice. But knowing what I do about the unbelievables, I would do what I had to do to save the person I love from an eternity of torment."

"You would, wouldn't you?"

His tone chafed my ears. I paced more quickly as I tried to explain my thoughts. "I'd weigh the eternity of consequences against the momentary pain in this life."

"You don't think there are consequences for killing what you love?" he asked.

I folded my arms around me, holding onto myself. "Maybe not if you do it by proxy. And if it let you see them as a ghost, wouldn't it be worth it?"

He leaned forward, linking his hands together and resting his chin on them. "I can't believe we're having this conversation."

Neither could I, but we needed to have it. "You're bonded to your amulet as much as I'm bonded to mine. If Joshua dies an unnatural death, we could lose our minds and kill ourselves. That's a possibility I've thought about. And I want you to know I would want you to have someone kill me, if that happened."

"Well, I wouldn't do it."

His words were an arrow shot through my back, aching and throbbing. "Really? You'd sentence me to eternity without what I loved most?"

"Kat, I couldn't end your life—not by proxy or by my own hand. I'd find a way to stop the legacy."

"Don't you think Alistair did everything he could?" The agony of what we were talking about shredded my voice.

"He didn't have the Kingsley dagger."

"Fine. So, you'd do all you could to save me." My voice tightened. "But what if you couldn't? Would you have someone kill me before I killed myself?"

"I don't want to talk about this." There was something dark and smoldering in his voice. A fire he would not be able to contain.

It was morbid and awful, and I hated that we had to have this conversation. But we did. "There are bad things we're going to face. And we need to be prepared for the worst."

"The worst being I need to have you killed?"

His eyes asked me to stop pushing, but I couldn't. "The worst being we fail Joshua and we lose our minds. I don't want that for you. I've felt what it did to Toria. I saw what happened to her." I remembered how broken Toria was in the courtyard. She let the shadows come for her. I never wanted that to happen to Evan.

"Would it be that easy to have me killed?" Pain beaded up in his voice like blood rising from a cut.

I stopped and faced him. "It would be the hardest thing I'd ever do. I don't want you to die, but I don't want you to go insane and kill yourself and ruin eternity, either. That's the worst fate."

"But don't you think having me killed would have consequences for you? Consequences you'd have to deal with for eternity?"

"I'd still do it, to save you from what Toria's going through."

"You'd risk eternity for me?"

I nodded. "Wouldn't you do the same for me?"

A sad smile flickered across his face. "When you put it like that, I think I would."

Chapter 38

The next two days flew by in a flurry of training. Vivian taught me spells for silence, binding, unlocking, invisibility, and a few more for healing at Jacqueline's request. She seemed convinced I'd get wounded. I appreciated her confidence in me.

When I wasn't in the chamber of mirrors, Jacqueline kept me in her conservatory for hours, grilling me on the properties of plants and herbs and how to use them for magic.

Evan continued his training with Percy's ghost. I envied him. He just had to learn to fight and wield the dagger. I had to learn all about magic.

Today, I stood at the stone worktable in the chamber of mirrors, preparing another healing spell. While I shredded birch bark into a bowl, Vivian sat on a stool watching me.

"When are we going to do some defensive spells?" I wanted to learn how to use magic to fight, not just to heal.

"Those take the most energy. I'm saving them for tomorrow." She sounded almost excited. "We'll start with shielding and a few basic attack spells."

"Shielding will be more than enough for tomorrow." Jacqueline weighed in while she sorted through her herbs.

"You underestimate our Kat." Vivian gave me a supportive smile and spoke to me. "In fact, with a few more days of training, you should be ready to leave here."

"Great." I needed to get back to my life at McTernan Academy.

237

Jacqueline frowned like she disagreed. "We need more mugwort for the next spell." She looked at me expectantly.

"You trust me alone in your conservatory?" I couldn't keep the shock out of my voice.

"Not when you put it like that." Jacqueline headed back upstairs to get the mugwort.

My thoughts turned to the one Langley I longed to see. "When will I meet my father?"

Vivian rested her elbows on the table and studied my face. "As soon as he gets here, we'll send word to you. You can come here through the locket's mirror. You'll get to see him."

That night I dreamt of the Isle of Acacia. Not the one I'd visited last summer, but the one that had existed hundreds of years ago. I saw Lorelei on the cliffs and raced to stop her from damning Ian and herself to an eternity of torment.

I stood in front of her with my palms stretched out to keep her away from the edge. "Don't do this," I pleaded, but she didn't seem to hear or see me.

Words spilled from her lips and splashed over me. Ancient words. She poured all her emotions into them. The words took on a life of their own. And then she leapt right through me like I was a ghost.

She didn't scream when she hit the water. I scanned the dark blue depths for her, but all I saw were waves and rocks below. She was gone. Ian was gone. And they would never meet again.

My heart leapt into my throat, filling my mouth with more emotion than I could handle.

Suddenly, I heard Jacqueline's voice. I didn't see her, but her angry whispers invaded my dream. "She can't see him like this."

"She needs to understand what he went through to see her." Vivian's voice was low, but resolute.

"Give me until morning," Jacqueline said.

"No."

I heard Vivian calling my name. It sounded far away at first, but her voice got closer and closer. More insistent. It pulled me out of my dream. Things went black, and then I was being shaken awake.

"Kat, get up," Vivian said.

"What's going on? What time is it?" I sat up in bed, but everything was blurry without my glasses. I groped for them on the nightstand.

Vivian handed them to me. "Your father's here. It's three in the morning."

I slid them on, tossed the covers aside, got up.

Jacqueline blocked my path. She was still formidable in her nightgown and robe. Her expression reminded me of a gargoyle, fiercely vigilant. "He had a rough journey. Let him rest and recover."

I'd waited almost eighteen years to see him. I wasn't waiting another moment. "No." I pushed past her.

Vivian led me to the room across from Evan's. I barely noticed the burgundy furnishings and chestnut paneled walls as my gaze went to the bed. My father lay there. The lamp on the nightstand illuminated his bruised and bloodied face. His right eye was swollen shut. Grime and dried blood were caked on his hands. His shirt and jeans were torn and filthy, like he'd gone through a warzone to get to us. One arm was wrapped in a bandage. His ankle was covered in an icepack.

Everything inside me tightened, preparing for the worst. "What happened to him?"

"He didn't have an easy time getting here. But he'll be okay. Jacqueline already gave him a healing," Vivian said.

"How did he look when he arrived?"

"Worse." The starkness in Jacqueline's voice hollowed out my heart.

I stared down at my father. *My father.* "I could do a healing spell too."

"Mine are the strongest. I'll get him better by tomorrow," Jacqueline said.

Unsure what to do, I just stood there until Vivian handed me a bowl of soapy water and wash cloth and said, "You can wash his hands and face."

I put the bowl on the nightstand, dunked the washcloth in the water, and wrung it out. Gently, I rubbed away the blood and dirt on his face. His dark hair was buzz cut to his head, making it easier to clean him up. His skin wasn't pale like mine, but tan with an olive undertone. Sun lines radiated out of the corner of his eyes. Permanent thinking lines creased his forehead. I couldn't tell what kind of nose he had. It was swollen and probably broken.

I wanted so badly for him to wake up and look at me, but he didn't. "Is he okay?"

"He will be, eventually." Jacqueline sounded brusque. "I gave him a sleeping potion. He won't awaken until morning. That's why we didn't need to disturb you."

I dipped the washcloth in the bowl a few times to rinse it and carefully wiped away the grime and dried blood that clung to his knuckles.

He was here. Right in front of me. I was holding my father's hand. I could feel the steady beat of his pulse. It made my own heart quicken in my chest.

I had never thought this was how I'd see him for the first time. Worry wrapped its fingers around my throat and squeezed, squeezed, squeezed.

"Could you step outside for a moment?" Vivian asked.

"Why?"

"We need to get him changed," Jacqueline said.

"Can I help?" I asked without thinking.

"He'd be mortified." Jacqueline shooed me out into the hallway and shut the door behind me.

I leaned against the wall and stared up at the ceiling.

He was here. My father. He had come to see me. A lifetime of emotions flooded through me. I trembled from trying to hold them all inside.

Seeing my father was all I'd ever wanted and it scared me to death. I wanted to be happy, but part of me held back. The part that had spent so long waiting for him. She was holding her breath, waiting to be disappointed and praying she wasn't.

Evan's door creaked open. He stepped out into the hallway with his hair messier than I'd ever seen it before. He was in a T-shirt and plaid pajama bottoms with his dagger attached to the waistband. "Kat?"

"It's me." I didn't recognize my own voice. It was so tight with fear and longing.

Evan closed the distance between us. "What's wrong?"

"My dad." My voice wobbled. "He's here."

"Is he okay?" His voice was a blanket draped over my shoulders—

comforting and warming.

I wrapped my arms around myself. "He looks like he had to fight an army to get here."

Evan rested his hands on my shoulders. "He'll be fine. Jacqueline and Vivian have brought us both back from death's door, remember?"

"I know...it's just...I've never seen a parent look so fragile before." Parents were supposed to be the strong ones.

Evan pulled me into his arms. I rested my head on his chest, listening to the steady rhythm of his heart, and hoped my father wouldn't break mine again.

Chapter 39

Vivian and Jacqueline offered to sit with my father so that I could rest in my own bed, but I refused to leave his side. Jacqueline tucked my father in like a little boy, leaving his arms above the comforter. Vivian brought me a blanket and pillow, and I settled in for the night.

For a while, I just stared at him. His right eye remained puffy, but his split lip had healed. A dark bruise blossomed across his angular jaw. His nose was mending nicely. While I waited for his eyes to open, I memorized every line on his face.

Now that his knuckles were no longer bloodied or bruised, they looked familiar. I placed my hand right beside his and realized that we had the same knuckles. My fingers were just like his. I never knew it, but I bet Mom noticed. It must have hurt her every single time she held my hand because it was as close as she could get to his hand.

And now, here he was.

I stuffed my pillow into the top corner of the chair and curled my legs under me, settling in to watch him sleep. I never thought I would get to do something so simple with my dad. Most kids took it for granted. I didn't.

I kept the lamp on the bedside table turned on. Partly, so if he woke up he would know where he was; mostly, because I wanted to see him. My eyes eventually started to get heavy. I figured I'd close them for a few minutes.

Daylight snuck through my eyelids, summoning me back from the world of dreams. When I opened my eyes, my father was lying on his side, staring at me.

"Ahh." I jerked and dropped my pillow.

A smile cut across his face and lit up his light gray-green eyes. They were much lighter than mine. His face was healed. Completely healed. And I was right, he was very handsome, especially now that his nose was back to normal.

I scrambled for the first words to say to my father. It felt like they should be something special. I'd had so many years to come up with an amazing opening line. But right now, all I could do was stare at him in awkward silence.

"Sorry I scared you. I just wanted to watch you sleep." His voice was deep with a slight rasp. The kind you'd expect from a gunslinger in a Western.

"It's okay. I did the same thing last night." I sat up and tried to stretch the kinks out of my neck. I heard a familiar pop and felt my shoulder shift. "How are you feeling?"

He propped himself up in bed and kept looking at me like I wasn't real. "Much better. I'm guessing I have Aunt Jacqueline to thank for that."

"She wouldn't let anyone else heal you." I couldn't stop the irritation from inflaming my voice.

"She is the best healer in the family."

I wasn't sure if he was defending her or simply explaining. Either way, I let it go. "What happened to you?"

"The trip here was more difficult than I expected."

Understatement of the century. "You looked like you fought your way here through a warzone."

"It felt that way too." He rubbed his hand over his head.

"Are you in trouble?" I lowered my voice, inviting him to confide in me.

"I'm a Langley with green eyes. I'm always getting into trouble—or getting out of it."

"Doesn't sound like a fun way to live."

"That's why I didn't want this for you." His eyes burned into mine.

Yet here I was, living the same life as he did. With the added responsibility of being the Langley heir. I bit my tongue to stop those words from escaping.

"What's wrong?"

"Nothing," I lied.

"Your mother's forehead wrinkled up the same way when she was upset about something."

"You haven't seen her in seventeen years."

"You never forget a woman like Valerie." Longing lodged in his words.

I rubbed my lips together and fidgeted with the blanket. I had so many questions. And I didn't know where to begin.

"Ask me," he said.

"I'm not sure I'm ready for the answers." I took a deep breath and dove in. "Did you love her?"

"Still do."

"What about me?"

"Always."

Relief rushed over me, but doubt overtook it. "Then how could you leave us?"

He reached for my hand. His was big and strong and wrapped around mine so easily. "Katarina, I wanted to have a life with you two. I wanted that more than anything."

"Then why didn't you?"

"Shannon and I researched it. We thought that if we kept you far from the Langleys and the ring, then it wouldn't choose you. We thought we'd found a loophole to the Langley legacy."

The lie Sarah had told her parents had come back to bite me in this lifetime. "But you didn't. It still chose me."

He pinched the bridge of his nose. "At the time, it was my only hope. I didn't want this life for you."

"But we could have been a family." My voice cracked under the strain of holding back a river of reactions.

He pushed aside his comforter and slid to the edge of the bed. Our knees brushed. "I wanted that more than you'll ever know. But I wasn't going to be selfish with you or your mother. I'd have had to keep you both here at Dumbarton. Valerie would have hated it."

"She would have done it for you."

Dad gave me a sad half-smile. "Eventually, she would have hated me for taking her away from her work and her world. She would have hated the life we would have given you."

"You don't know that. No matter what, we'd have been together." Anguish cut through my words.

He rubbed the back of his neck. "Sometimes being together isn't enough."

"It would have been for us." He had no idea how lonely Mom and I had been without him. What we'd have given up to have him with us. "It wasn't your decision. It was ours. And you made it for us."

"I'm sorry." He took both my hands in his. "I'm sorry for all the birthdays and holidays that I missed."

I heard the pain in his voice, but it didn't make up for all the pain I'd felt. "I wished you were there. Every birthday. You were my birthday wish, from three to fifteen. Then I stopped wishing."

He winced. "I hate that I missed out on so much of your life."

"Me, too." I didn't know what to say next. The star sapphire in my ring glinted at me. I held my hand up. "Why did you send the ring to me?"

"After Shannon died, the ring appeared on my hand. I thought it had picked me, but it hadn't. Shannon's last spell was to send it to me. She was trying to stop it from picking you. But she only delayed it."

Inside me, a Ferris wheel of emotions was spinning round and round. I couldn't sit here holding his hand like everything was okay. I tugged my hands out of his grasp and got up. "If you didn't want me to have the ring, why did you give it to me?"

"I didn't have a choice, Kat. It was clear that the ring wanted you. It would have found you."

"But why didn't you bring it to me yourself? Why did you mail it? Why didn't you explain to me what it meant?"

He started to speak, and then stopped—as if he was trying to figure out which question to answer first. "Surely Vivian and Jacqueline have told you that it's not safe to be together. And I figured that you probably hated me for leaving. I guessed that if I just sent it to you with the note that it was yours and I loved you, you wouldn't be eager to wear the ring.

As long as you didn't put it on or use it, you wouldn't be a target."

He'd been right. Because it was a gift from him, I'd put the ring in a drawer and ignored it for months. "Why didn't you tell me not to wear it?"

"The ring wouldn't let me warn you. It wanted you."

"Why didn't you send someone else to warn me then?"

"I couldn't risk exposing you. Everything I did was to keep you hidden from the ring and the Dark One." He made it sound like the situation was bigger than he was.

"What about after I started wearing the ring? Why didn't a Langley come to help me?"

"Toria and Lorelei were sent to watch over you because your powers are rooted in the past."

Ghosts were sent to protect me. It almost made sense.

He scratched his cheek. "I wish we could have done better for you. The moment you started using the ring, you were on the Dark One's radar."

I moved faster, trying to shed some of my frustration through my feet. I bumped into a side table and stubbed my toe. I muttered something that would have made my mother scold me.

My father repressed a smile. He lifted his pointer finger and flicked it up. The overhead fixture flooded the room with light. Vivian had mentioned he could move things with his mind. He flicked his wrist and water poured from a pitcher into a glass on the desk. Then he levitated it across the room to him and took a long sip.

"Showing off?" I leaned against the dresser, watching him.

"Making sure I don't have to hear such language again." He winked at me.

We were getting off topic. Then again, this was my first conversation with my father. Everything was on topic because we had decades to catch up on. "What could Shannon do?"

A shadow crossed his features. "She was like me. Her powers were tied to the present. She could project her thoughts and communicate over great distances."

"I'm sorry you lost her." I pressed my palms against the wooden dresser, needing to hold onto something solid.

"It should have been me. The ring should have picked me." He sounded gutted by the loss of her.

"She blamed herself, you know."

"Have you seen her ghost?"

He sounded so hopeful, I regretted having to explain. "Vivian and I found some letters that Shannon wrote to you. I read them."

"Shannon wouldn't let anyone help her. Because she was the last heir with an amulet, she thought she had to do it all on her own." His eyes lost focus like he was back in those moments with his sister.

"We're fixing that."

"How?" His expression teetered somewhere between a flash of hope and a bolt of fear.

I filled him in on how I'd recovered the Radcliffe necklace and the Kingsley dagger. That when I was stronger, I was going to find the Mallory bracelet.

His eyes widened. "You're doing it." He got out of bed and stood there looking at me.

"What?"

"Fulfilling the prophecy. Changing everything." There was something a little awestruck in his voice.

"I'm just doing what I can to help."

"I can't believe it. You're the one they wrote about. The one who can go to the past and fix things."

"I'm trying." My cheeks flamed.

"I'm so proud of you."

I never thought I would hear those words from my father. Something inside me broke. That dam I'd maintained for seventeen years collapsed. Tears burned my eyes. I couldn't stop them. He opened his arms up and I walked into them. He smelled like woods and safety. Like a dad should.

Chapter 40

The cheerful curtains and pink tablecloth in the breakfast room were a complete contrast to my inner turmoil. It was my first family breakfast with my dad and I couldn't stop staring at him. I missed Evan's request to pass the salt until he nudged me. Then I nearly knocked over my orange juice in my rush to get it to him.

"He won't disappear if you look away," Evan whispered.

I knew that, I did. I tried to relax, but the anxiety inside me got worse with each minute. Evan and I were supposed to head back to school as soon as I finished my training. How could I leave my dad now?

"Are you excited to learn some defensive magic today?" Vivian took a bite of her toast.

"Maybe Jacqueline is right about just doing shielding today." I tried to drag out my training. And my time with my dad.

Vivian shot Jacqueline a you've-shaken-her-confidence look.

Jacqueline stopped stirring her tea and clanged her spoon on the saucer. "Please. She never listens to me. She just doesn't want to finish her training and leave Max."

Heat crept up my neck. Was I that transparent?

"I'm not going anywhere," my father said.

I wanted to believe him, but I couldn't. "I don't want to rush my training."

"What?" Evan did a double take, probably because he was the one who kept asking me to be patient about getting back to school.

"Are you afraid to leave because you think your father will be gone before you can get back here?" Vivian picked her words carefully.

I just nodded.

"Kat, getting here wasn't easy. I'm in no rush to get back out there." He must have seen the doubt on my face, because he added, "Besides, I want to help train you. Defensive spells are one of my specialties."

"Really?"

"With his telekinesis, he can throw spells." Jacqueline sounded proud.

"I promise I won't leave without saying goodbye," Dad said.

That should have been enough to calm the fluttering in my stomach, but it wasn't.

"You need to focus, Kat." My father said it like I hadn't been focusing the past six times he had broken through my shield.

We'd been in the chamber of mirrors for three hours, working on shielding. I had no idea it would be this hard to visualize a flexible see-through bubble around me and maintain it while he fired spells at me.

Sweat drenched my back. My face was a dripping mess. "I'm trying." I gritted my teeth and tried to remain standing despite the burning ache in my muscles.

Vivian sat on the bench with a worried expression on her face. She hadn't said anything, but I could tell she didn't like the way the training was going.

He moved his hands in intricate patterns, drawing his energy from the mirror. It reminded me of tai chi on speed. A burst of blue light flew from his fingertips and slammed into my shield. The vibration went through my teeth and settled into my bones. The shield warped, but withstood it.

"See?" Before I could catch my breath, he threw two more spells at me in a blinding flash of red and purple. They obliterated my shield and slammed into me with the force of a deer.

I flew backwards and landed on my behind. I tried to get up, but I couldn't move. Not one muscle was working. Anywhere. One of those bursts of light must have been a paralysis spell.

Then I saw things. Things that should never be in the chamber of mirrors. Pastor Fitzgerald's ghost stalked toward me. Giant shadows writhed and overtook the light. I saw Evan dead on the floor. It had to be some sort of hallucination spell. *This isn't real*, I screamed inside my head, but my heart refused to hear me. It doubled and tripled in speed. Fear sweat burst across my upper lip and brow.

All I saw was the darkness coming for me. Panic took over. It reached inside the ring and words I didn't know flew through my mind. Suddenly, the purple light exploded from my chest and I could move again.

I scurried backwards, trying to escape the darkness. I tried a clarity spell for the hallucinations, but they continued. I didn't know what that second spell was, so I didn't know how to stop it.

Pastor Fitzgerald and the shadows reached for me. I threw my hands up and screamed.

Suddenly, Pastor Fitzgerald and the shadows were gone. Vivian was holding me. Her palm rested on my forehead, spilling soothing emotions over me.

"What was that?" My teeth chattered.

"A fear spell." My father's expression was dark with disappointment.

"Max, those are the hardest to counteract. We never use them this early in the training," Vivian chided him. "Let's take a break."

I looked up at him, trying to understand. "Why are you being so hard on me?"

"Because our enemies will be and I want you to survive them," he said. "You have to be stronger than Shannon."

I took a deep breath, got up, and brushed myself off. "Okay, let's go again."

No matter how many questions I asked my father, a lifetime of questions remained. I wanted to know everything. I asked him questions on the way to and from the chamber of mirrors, during breaks, over lunch. Whenever I could squeeze in time with him.

His favorite book? The *Tao Te Ching*. His favorite color? Indigo blue.

How old was he when he learned to swim? Four. What countries had he visited? I lost track of them as he ticked off all the places in Asia.

He peppered me with questions about school, hobbies, and my childhood. We tried to condense a lifetime of getting to know each other into a few days.

He never asked about Mom. Whenever I asked about anything that had to do with her and him, he'd say, "Ask your mom."

When we were on a break in the chamber of mirrors, he used that response again and I had to tell him, "She doesn't talk about you."

"Oh." Something in his eyes shut down.

"It hurts too much." I took a swig of water and sat on the stone bench. "She never got over you."

He just stood there beside me, not saying anything.

I let the silence linger as long as I could before I asked, "Why haven't you asked about her?"

"I gave up the right to know what she was doing when I left her."

"I wish you would tell her about the Langley legacy and why you left us. She needs to know the whole truth."

"She knows we couldn't be together."

"What about now?" It was the question I'd wondered about since he'd arrived. Now that I was the heir and his absence couldn't possibly protect me, now would he want to be a family? Or was that something that would never happen?

"It's dangerous. I don't want to pull your mother into this."

"She's already involved."

"She can't possibly want to see me after everything that happened." His voice sounded cluttered with things he wouldn't tell me.

"Why don't you let her decide that?" I asked softly.

He shook his head.

"The Dark One knows you're here. There's no harm in talking to her."

The corners of his eyes tightened. So did his lips. Like he was fighting himself. "It's not a good idea."

"Neither is me being the heir or risking my life to fight the Dark One, but I'm doing it."

"You don't really have a choice."

"I could run. I could give up. Those are options."

"That's not who you are," he said.

"Is this who you are?"

He rubbed his hand across his eyes. "It's who I've become."

"Why did you come back?"

"For you."

"But not for Mom?" He didn't want to be a family. The realization sent my heart freefalling.

"It's complicated. Your mom and I have a history that we can't undo. We hurt each other. We hurt you. We aren't good for each other, but I want to be here for you."

I guess that had to be enough. I'd pack up that stupid dream of having a mom and dad who were together. A family. It was something a little girl would want. And I wasn't a little girl anymore.

Chapter 41

I stood in front of the worktable in the chamber of mirrors with Vivian, Jacqueline, and my dad all watching me. On the table were hundreds of tiny jars and bottles of oils, herbs, and other spell ingredients. Bowls, knives, spoons, and all sorts of tools were lined up there too. Magic emanated from the Langley mirror, ebbing around me and waiting to be summoned. I rocked on my heels, suddenly anxious about performing a spell in front of everyone.

"It feels like a test."

"It is," Jacqueline said.

Vivian gave her a quelling look. "It is not. It's a milestone."

Before we left Dumbarton, I had to do a cloaking spell for Evan's dagger. He needed to always have it with him, but walking around Georgetown University, let alone D.C., with a knife visibly attached to his belt wasn't an option.

"Remember cloaking requires something to disappear to others. To not be sensed by them." Vivian's hint was accompanied by a reassuring smile.

"And I can build off the invisibility spell you taught me?" I asked.

"Exactly. There will be times you won't have a spell book to consult. You have to rely on what you know," Vivian said.

Jacqueline nudged a tray filled with tiny bottles of oils toward me. "Which ones do you think would work?" Her voice was one-quarter question, three-quarters challenge.

Evan shifted beside me. His arm brushed mine. "You've got this."

I wasn't the same girl who'd reluctantly cast my first spell on the Isle of Acacia. I was the Langley heir who was fulfilling the prophecy and changing things. I could handle this, too. I straightened my spine. "Rue for protection, red sandalwood to grant a wish, and patchouli to mask it from all who should not see it."

Vivian gave me a quick nod and her auburn curls bounced against her shoulders. "Excellent start."

Jacqueline reached for another bottle and stopped with her hand in midair. "What else?"

I stared at the bottles of oil. "Lavender to calm and myrrh to muddle the senses."

"And?" Jacqueline asked.

"Could I add juniper to divert the senses?"

"Good choice," Vivian said. "But use the berries, not the oil."

Jacqueline and my dad exchanged a look. She gave him a slight nod.

He picked up a bottle and passed it to me. "A bit of mercury to force people away from it."

I didn't take it. "Isn't that deadly?"

"Not after Jacqueline's worked with it." He put it in front of me. "Just two drops. It's potent stuff. Poisons are great deterrents."

"All done?" Jacqueline asked in a way that told me I wasn't.

"No?" I hated how my answer came out like a question. I scanned the bottles and jars, hoping something would jump out at me. "Maybe the owl feather for camouflage."

Jacqueline nodded. "And?"

It was like she had the exact spell in her head and didn't want me to deviate by a single ingredient. I refused to blindly guess. "That's it."

"What about raven's nail?" my dad asked.

Jacqueline flashed him a smile that transformed her face. "I was just about to suggest that," she reached for a jar that was at the back of another tray, "for invisibility."

"And a few drops of my blood." I hated this part of the spells. But over the past week, I'd started to get better at it.

"Are you sure you're up for this?" Evan asked.

"You should see what I can do with a shield now. This is easy in comparison."

"All right." He smiled and I felt like everything was okay.

The great aunts positioned us to do the spell.

Evan and I stood on the Langley mirror. I swore I didn't need the mirror to power this spell, but they insisted. Each spell had a price, usually in energy or emotion taken from the caster. The mirror could help lessen the cost on my body.

With a few moves of his pointer finger, my dad levitated the table with all the ingredients for the spell and set it down beside Evan and me. I poured the herbs and the raven's nail into a mortar and ground them with the pestle until they became a fine powder.

I used a pin to prick my finger, squeezing it until three drops of blood fell into the powdered ingredients. After I stirred everything together, my blood activated the magic in the herbs and made the mixture sparkle.

I dipped the owl's feather into the mixture and spread the dust over Evan's dagger. The air shimmered around him, glittering gold at me. As I said the incantation in Scottish Gaelic, I felt the power stirring from the mirror and rushing through me until my body thrummed with magic.

My voice deepened as I spoke the words to cloak the dagger, making it both invisible and untouchable to everyone outside our four families—Langleys, Kingsleys, Mallorys, and Radcliffes.

To seal the spell, I mixed four drops of the lavender and myrrh oils with two drops of the quicksilver. I dipped the feather into the mixture and drew a rune symbol over the dagger.

As I stepped back, the glow around the dagger and Evan made his eyes greener. I couldn't look away. For a moment, everything else disappeared. I swear I could hear his heart beat echoing in my ears. I blinked and everything went back to normal.

"Did it work?" I asked.

Vivian gave me a proud smile. "Excellent work."

Jacqueline nodded.

"How do you feel?" my father asked.

"A bit tired, but less than a spell would normally affect me."

"That's because of the mirror." Jacqueline couldn't help using her I-told-you-so tone.

"Thank you." Evan reached over and squeezed my hand.

"You can go back to school now," Jacqueline said.

Right. School. Senior year. I had to go back to classes and tests and papers. I had to leave my father.

"Tonight?" Evan asked.

"Tonight," I agreed.

Epilogue

I barely had time to settle back into my classes before Morgan was begging for a night out. Our last one had been just three weeks ago, but everything was different now. Morgan and Seth, of course, knew nothing about what had happened to Evan and me while we were at Dumbarton. Not that she hadn't asked. She did. But I'd sidestepped her questions.

I think Morgan felt the shift in things. That's why we were back at the club, recreating our last night out before I'd gone to Dumbarton. The last night that there had been no secrets between us.

The music pounded against my body. Strobe lights flashed across the crowded dance floor. I glimpsed Seth standing by the bar. I couldn't believe I had kissed him. Now it seemed like an act of sheer insanity.

"Are you going to kiss Seth again?" Morgan teased.

"Once was enough," I shouted over the music.

She cocked her head to the side. "Was it? You seemed to really enjoy it."

"It was a great kiss. But...it was just a moment."

"A moment you'd like to relive?"

"If I could be the girl from that night again? Maybe."

She gave me a weird look. "It was three weeks ago. You're still the same girl."

But I wasn't. I'd almost died twice. I'd found my father. I'd formed an unbreakable bond with Evan.

Nothing was like it had been that night.

Seth weaved his way through the crowd, heading in our direction. He was closing in when I felt a pull. A gentle tugging at my soul. Someone else was here. Someone more important. I didn't need to see him to know it was Evan. Ever since we left Dumbarton, I'd known when he was nearby. He felt it too. It was weird and comforting.

I turned and Evan was standing near the entrance. Our eyes met and I moved toward him.

When I got there, he looked past my shoulder. "I think Seth was going to hit on you."

"Then he was going to be disappointed."

"Does he know that?" He raised an eyebrow.

"Would he care?"

"He might." Evan's eyes were intense. He looked away, scanning the crowd. "So, are you planning to kiss anyone else tonight?"

"I probably should, considering how much we have hanging over our heads." I promised myself more fun before I died.

"We're going to change things. It's what we do." He touched my hand so lightly that most people wouldn't notice, but because it was him, a tingle raced to my fingertips.

"What if we can't? What if right now is all we have?"

"Then we have it together." His gaze locked on mine. I couldn't look away. The air thickened. It felt like centuries of promises lingered between us. A history neither of us remembered and neither of us could escape.

He took my hand and pulled me out on the dance floor. Morgan and Seth joined us and we danced like there was only tonight.

The Kingsley Dagger
Design by

Marina A. Raye

Acknowledgements

Mom, there are thousands of things to thank you for. Thanks for reading my newsletters and blog posts and believing in my books. You've always been there and I couldn't do what I do without your endless support and love! Thanks for being the best wing-woman and helping sell books! And for laughing with me about the skinny-dipping deer during late night rides. Dad, thanks for listening to me talk about my writing and promo activities and always lending your support and wisdom.

To Anthony Dvarskas, thanks for dreaming up this world with me and letting me explore it further. It's been almost three decades of knowing you and I can't imagine what my life would be like without you in it! You always come through with a nugget of knowledge that keeps me going in the worst of times. To Brett Helgren, for holding my hand and encouraging me when my courage was failing. You help me over so many writing hurdles by listening and making me laugh. To Audra, for the dinners and lunches where you cheered me up and onward. To Aunt Robin, for always helping spread the word and loving my books. To Emerson Langley, for being the quirkiest dog who makes me laugh when I need to and play when I should.

To Beckett Publishing Group, for seeing something special in my books and sharing them with the world! To Jessica Jernigan, thank you for your steady, guiding hand in making this series all I dreamed it could be. To Paramita Bhattachargee, for bringing Kat to life again with another awesome cover design. To Nick DeSimone, for making the interior as pretty as you did. To Rik Hall, for a great job designing the ebook.

To Tim Grahl, for teaching me everything I didn't know about launching a bestseller. Seriously, you made this book launch so much more fun than any of the other ones! To Giselle at Xpresso Book Tours, for a terrific cover reveal and blog tour. You were always so responsive and kind—I can't thank you enough! To Sage at Sage Book Tours, for helping find early reviewers for the ARC and being a delight to work with! To Young Adult Books Central, for a fantastic giveaway and spreading the word about my book.

To Paige Shelton, for always find the time to read my books and saying such awesome things about them! To Stephanie Robinson, it was a pleasure being at B&N with you. Thanks for reading my story and sharing your thoughts with your readers. To K.R. Conway, for finding the time to read my book and sharing your marketing knowledge at the NESCBWI conference.

To Margie Lawson, your five-day immersion master class helped me take my writing to the next level and make this my best work yet! Hugs to the Rockin' Rhetorical Radicals for being my writing buddies and helping me grow so much from our master class.

To Jacqueline McDowell, for answering my archaeology questions and helping me craft believable scenarios for Kat's mother's work. To The Cheeseheads—This book wouldn't be here without your support. Thanks for cheering me on and spreading the word about my books! Special thanks to Kelly Miller, Audra M., Ariane Sevillano, Abby Brown, Mikki Heyden Parchim, Pamela Bayer, Anthony Dvarskas, and Robin Colangelo—for being early reviewers! I couldn't ask for a better group of friends or readers. A heartfelt thank you to all the early reviewers on NetGalley who posted reviews about the book! Carrie, JM, K. Lyn, Kathryn, Andrea, Sue, Mayumi, Jill, Audrey, Jenny, Vanessa, and the rest of my amazing blog buddies—writing can be a lonely activity, but not when I have all of you in my blog realm.

And to my readers—thank you for coming back to Kat and The Unbelievables. I know how precious your time is, so when you spend it reading my books, I'm truly grateful. It's so amazing to talk to you about my characters and see how much they matter to you too.

Reader Discussion Questions

1) Given the star-crossed nature of the Langley-Kingsley relationships (Sarah and Percy, Toria and Alistair), what might Evan and Kat's future hold?

2) Kat's father has been absent her entire life. How has that impacted the character and how does that play out when she finally meets him?

3) How did Shannon's death impact the Langley family? Discuss how Max, Vivian, and Jacqueline's behavior (including their treatment of Kat) may be affected by what happened to Shannon.

4) We know that Pastor Fitzgerald joined with the Dark One. Do you think Lydia also did? How might that impact the upcoming battle with the Dark One?

5) Compare the Radcliffe coat of arms and Langley coat of arms, specifically the unicorn, stag, griffon, and dragon representing the four families. Make sure to consider how their placement differs in each coat of arms.

6) Do you think Toria and Alistair's punishment in the afterlife fit their crimes? Can you understand their decision to try to possess relatives?

7) The Langleys powers are connected to the past, present, or future. Discuss how this connection influences how each family member perceives fate and their ability to change the future. (Shannon, Jacqueline, and Max have powers that are connected to the present. Vivian and Toria have powers connected to the future. Kat's powers are connected to the past.)

8) The time travel involves a body snatcher element. Does possessing forms in the era that they time-travel to make things easier or harder on Kat and Evan?

9) Would you cast spells if you knew that each spell cost you something? Would you give up your most precious memory to help someone else like Kat did for Toria? Why or why not?

AN INTERVIEW WITH
K.C. TANSLEY, AUTHOR OF
The Girl Who Saved Ghosts

THERE'S BEEN A PUSH FOR GREATER DIVERSITY IN BOOKS. GIVEN THAT EVAN'S PARENTS ARE CHINESE AND ENGLISH AND MORGAN IS LATINA, DID THAT CALL FOR DIVERSITY INFLUENCE YOUR CHARACTER CREATION IN THIS SERIES?

Since this was the first book I ever wrote, it went through many changes in terms of point of view, tense, setting, and even characters. Ultimately, for my characters, I drew from my experiences in college. Georgetown University has a diverse student body, and I wanted to have characters that reflected the world I lived in.

So my inspiration for the characters drew on my own background and my friends' backgrounds. Kat's the descendant of Russian immigrants on her mom's side, just like I am. My best friend in college is from Texas with Mexican and Native American roots and she is a jumping off point for Morgan. Evan was inspired by a friend who is of Vietnamese and Irish descent. Seth is Irish and Argentine and was inspired by a few friends.

In Book 2, we travel back to Connecticut to the Langley family estate, Dumbarton. What inspired you to bring the characters back to Connecticut?

Connecticut is where I was born and raised. It's also where I currently live. When I was creating the series, I always saw it set in Connecticut. As the books continue, you will find out why. In a way, setting the series in Connecticut kept me close to home when I was living in New York. Dumbarton was a place I visited in D.C.—Dumbarton Oaks—and I wanted to keep alive my ties to that city after I graduated, so I gave the Langley estate that name.

In this book, Kat and Evan time travel to 1831 Vienna, how did you decide on that time period and location?

Long before I wrote book 2, I knew the family heirlooms would be a central point for each book, so I had to know what happened to the heirlooms. Or at least in what order they were lost. In Book 1, the Radcliffes rubies are the last heirloom lost in 1886. Kat has the Langley heirloom—star sapphire ring. Since the heirlooms are amulets that make each family powerful, I needed the heirlooms to be lost at different times, so the families would slowly become weakened. I decided on the early 1800s for the Kingsley dagger to disappear. The time period came into focus as I researched Vienna more.

I went to Austria in 2009 for a week and fell in love with the art, culture, history, and cuisine. In Book 1, Kat and Evan time-travel to 1886 Connecticut. This time, I wanted them to go somewhere more historic that they could really geek out over. Vienna during the Austro-Hungarian Empire was it. Of course, I had to do research on what Vienna in 1831 would be like. I had a lot of fun discovering that!

Are there any authors or books that inspired you in writing *The Girl Who Saved Ghosts*?

I was reading Cassandra Clare's Mortal Instruments series during editorial revisions and was influenced by the amount of visuals and the smoothness of her storytelling. I saw each book unfold in my mind as I read it and I strove to deliver that same experience to my readers. Richelle Mead's pacing from the Vampire Academy series also impacted my writing.

Reading the Amanda Quick historic romances during the 1990s influenced my desire to write family sagas with historic estates and family heirlooms.

As a kid, I loved Edgar Allen Poe stories, which probably contributes to the creepy, supernatural stuff in my stories. And Emily Bronte's *Wuthering Heights* gave me a taste for the haunting love story that plays out between the Langleys and the Kingsleys over the centuries.

What's next for Kat and Evan?

In the next book, Kat and Evan learn more about their abilities and time-travel in search of the Mallory bracelet. They face new obstacles with the unbelievables and their bond is tested.

CAST OF CHARACTERS
The Girl Who Saved Ghosts

KAT PRESTON LANGLEY

A seventeen-year-old prep school student who talks to ghosts and helps them with their reckonings (last wishes). She is the Langley heir, which means she must protect the Radcliffes from supernatural threats and can cast spells. Her life is in danger because her enemies are threatened by her ability to travel to the past and change it, upsetting the balance between good and evil.

EVAN KINGSLEY

A college student who is a teacher's assistant for Kat's professor. He and Kat bonded after they time-traveled and broke a curse together over the summer. His family has a historic tie to the Langleys. Despite how infuriating Kat is, he finds himself wanting to help her.

VIVIAN AND JACQUELINE LANGLEY

Kat's great aunts, who live at the ancestral home, Dumbarton. They are skilled in magic and know more about the family's history. They train Kat to use her magic and time-traveling abilities. Jacqueline is a healer and Vivian can see the future.

TORIA LANGLEY

Kat's headstrong ancestor is a ghost that tries to protect Kat in the present day. Toria is also a piece of Kat's soul that broke away in the reincarnation process and remained behind. She was the Langley heir in the 1880s.

PERCY KINGSLEY

He was the Kingsley heir in 1831 and worked side by side with Sarah Harding, the Langley heir. He was protecting Ellie Harding when he died and lost the Kingsley dagger. The mystery surrounding his death will draw Kat and Evan back in time to 1831.

ELLIE HARDING

Her ghost begs Kat to help prove her innocent of Percy's murder in the present day. In 1831, she was the younger sister of Sarah Harding and Percy was charged with protecting her.

SARAH HARDING

The Langley heir in 1831. She risked her life to save the Radcliffe heir. She was Percy's ally and they shared a bond that went beyond friendship.

Photo by: Brett D. Helgren

K.C. TANSLEY lives with her warrior lapdog, Emerson, and two quirky golden retrievers on a hill somewhere in Connecticut. She tends to believe in the unbelievables—spells, ghosts, time travel—and writes about them.

Never one to say no to a road trip, she's climbed the Great Wall twice, hopped on the Sound of Music tour in Salzburg, and danced the night away in the dunes of Cape Hatteras. She loves the ocean and hates the sun, which makes for interesting beach days. *The Girl Who Ignored Ghosts* is her award-winning and bestselling first novel in The Unbelievables series.

As Kourtney Heintz, she also writes award-winning cross-genre fiction for adults. You can find out more about her books and her at: **http://kourtneyheintz.com/**

Want Inside Scoops?

Sign up for author updates and I'll immediately send you my unpublished short story, **And Then There Were Three**, and give you the inside scoop on my books—new releases, sale days, free book deals, giveaways, and behind the scenes info you can't find anywhere else!

http://kourtneyheintz.com/contact

(Note: I won't share your email address and you can unsubscribe at any time)

Thank you so much for reading my novel! I'd love to hear what you thought of this book. No matter how short or how long, readers' reviews make a huge difference. Hopefully more readers will take a chance on my book when they see that others already have. Thanks!